# Inspired by True Events

# CITIZEN WARRIOR SERIES-BOOK 3

# CROSSING

by J. Thomas Rompel

# Acknowledgements

Many thanks to my good friend John Jannetto and Tia. To my son Tommy and daughter Trisha who have always been and continue to be an inspiration to me. To my lovely wife Linda and her continued love and encouragement. To all the men and women in our military and law enforcement who have given of themselves so we can enjoy our God given freedom. And to all the Citizen Warriors who are out there just waiting to be called if needed! Keep up the good fight!

*"The patriot's blood is the seed of Freedom's tree."*

*Thomas Campbell*

## Tuesday, 1:38 PM
## Tia Elena Restaurant
## Tucson, Arizona

"Let's get out of here," Congressman Hector Granada said to his niece, looking into his empty beer glass.

"Ok, let me run to the bathroom and then we'll go," FBI Special Agent Sylvia Granada said, glancing at her phone checking for messages. She picked up her purse... and opened it, pushing her plate away and throwing her phone inside. Reaching over to the back of her chair, her uncle knocked a glass of water over, splashing it onto the open purse.

"Dammit, my phone's in there," she said, grabbing the purse from the small pool of water formed around it on the thin, well-worn, white table cloth.

"Let me help you," said their waiter, walking up to their table with a white towel in his hand.

"Go ahead to the bathroom... I'll make sure your phone's ok. We'll dry it off; it'll be fine," Hector Granada said, pointing in the general direction of the bathroom.

"Ok, just make sure my phone's ok," Sylvia said over her shoulder, walking fast towards the bathrooms. Sylvia stood looking and then turned, not being able to hold it any longer.

"Here, let me have the towel. I'll get it—go away," Hector said to the waiter. Haphazardly, he wiped the purse. Looking in the bathroom's direction, he opened Sylvia's purse and pulled out

6

her iPhone. In her rush to go to the bathroom and the upset of the spilled water, she'd failed to turn the screen off. Looking up again, then back at the screen, he went to the address section and scrolled down until he stopped at Rebecca Harper's name. Awkwardly, he laid Sylvia's phone on the table with Rebecca's name, address and phone number displayed and snapped a picture with his phone. Looking up, he saw Sylvia making her way back to the table just as he put the phone back in her purse.

"Here, good as new," said Hector, handing her the purse. Sylvia opened it up checking her phone to make sure it was working.

"Thank you," said Sylvia, pulling her phone out.

"Maybe I've time for another cerveza," said Hector, holding up his empty glass.

"No, I think you've had enough, Uncle. That's weird. The screen's still on… it should have turned off after a minute. I hope the water didn't mess it up or I'll be in big trouble. It's a department-issued phone," said Sylvia, peering at the lit screen on her phone.

"If it did, it'll dry out. Put it in a bowl of rice when you get home," said Hector, glancing at Sylvia and then the phone, which finally turned off. Pushing his chair back, Hector stood and placed his hands onto the table for support.

"Here, let me help you," said Sylvia, putting her left arm around his right arm.

Amidst the stares and murmured whispering, she stumbled, trying to support her overweight uncle, Hector. More than once while heading to the door, he bumped the corners of tables, interrupting people's meals and knocking a man's glass of beer over. At five feet, seven inches, and 295 pounds, he was a lumbering sight. Whispers of recognition from people sitting at the tables reached their ears. Sylvia couldn't get him out of there soon enough. A waiter stepped forward to help. Once through the door, the congressman stopped and raised his right hand to shield his eyes from the sunlight. Swaying, he looked towards the parking lot to their right.

"Where's my car? Let go of me, I can do it," he retorted in a slurred voice, pulling away from her and lurching forward.

"You took an Uber to get here. I'll give you a ride. Where are you staying?" Sylvia asked, holding onto him to keep him from falling. Even with the help of the waiter, the weight and bulk of him pushed her back, forcing her to land on the bench just outside the entrance. Half standing upright, he looked down at her and smiled. His eyes moved from her face to her breasts and then back to her face and then back to her breasts. She turned to the left, hoping to stop him from looking at her like that. Turning, her uncle ran his tongue back and forth on his lower lip.

"I… I took an Uber to get here? I… I'm staying at the Westin La Paloma. In the foothills. You going to take me there?"

"Yes," she said, lifting herself off the bench and grabbing his arm, pointing to the parking lot. With Sylvia on his right and the waiter on his left, the three of them moved towards Sylvia's car.

"Come on, Congressman, let's get you to her car," the waiter said, relieving Sylvia's support of her uncle.

"Who the f... fuck are you? Who the fucks is he?" the congressman said, looking first at the waiter and then Sylvia.

"He's helping us, Uncle. Come on, don't be difficult, he's a nice man."

After the waiter helped the congressman into the front passenger seat, Sylvia reached over to grab the seat belt and buckled her uncle in. As she did so, he put his right hand on the back of her neck, awkwardly pulling her close to him to kiss her. She winced at the smell of his breath, mixed with the Mexican food and beer, and turned away. She breathed deep, fighting a wave of nausea.

"You're so pretty."

Sylvia slipped her left hand and arm under his arm, raising her elbow up as she pulled away and walked around the car to get into the driver's seat. Sitting straight up, she started the car and backed out of their parking spot.

"Thank you, Tío . I think maybe you've had too much to drink," she said, looking straight ahead, pulling out of the parking lot and turning right. More than once in her life she'd been around him when he was in this condition. She hated it. Putting his hand on her neck was something new. Speeding up halfway down the block, she felt his left hand on her neck again as he began rubbing it. "Stop, Tío," she said, pushing away his arm. "You shouldn't be doing that, I'm your niece." Continuing to look straight ahead, she squirmed in her seat, took a deep breath and put her right hand over her mouth. The taste of the enchiladas she had for lunch wanted to make a second appearance. The sting of bile burned the back of her throat.

"Did what's-her-name say anything to you about the legal pad?"

"You mean Agent Harper? No, she hasn't said a thing," Sylvia said, wondering whether to press him further about her discovery of his name, a reference to Stinger missiles and a known Syrian woman terrorist's name written on a yellow legal pad she'd found in Rebecca Harper's desk. The notes also mentioned they had shipped the Stingers from Benghazi, Libya, to Guaymas, Mexico. She started biting a nail on her left hand, something she hadn't done since grade school after she'd got caught by a teacher cheating on a test. The teacher told Sylvia she wanted her to meet with her and her mother the next day. Sylvia promised she'd tell her parents what happened that night, but didn't. Because of this, the teacher called her mother the next day asking her to come to school at the end of class to sit down with her and Sylvia. After the meeting, Sylvia's mother was livid and told Sylvia's father when he came home from work. He took a belt to her and through raining tears she apologized, promising never to do it again.

Unconsciously, Sylvia moved her left hand, touching her behind and then back to the steering wheel.

"Tío, what's going on with your name being on that legal pad in my boss's office? Tell me. Between you and me."

"I, I told you, probably because I'm on the Congressional International Arms Committee. CIAC. We talk about that sort of thing all the time. You shouldn't have been snooping around her desk. Do you think she knows that you looked inside the drawer and read her notes?"

"I don't think so. I don't know… I shouldn't have but I did," Sylvia said, not believing what her uncle was telling her.

"Do you think anybody else knows about what's on her legal pad?" Hector asked.

"I don't know. Last week, she called me into her office and asked me again if I knew anything about your involvement in an illegal shipment of Stinger missiles and this woman Assal. I checked her out… She's number three on Interpol's most wanted list." Sylvia paused. She didn't enjoy having this conversation with him in his drunken state, but couldn't contain her curiosity. "Her name was right next to yours with the word 'girlfriend,' followed by a question mark. What's going on?"

"It's nothing—I'm sure it has to do with the committee work I do. As… Assal… oh, I think there might have been a woman I met at a cocktail party by that name. I… I really don't remember though. Is this agent… wha… what's her name again?"

"Rebecca Harper, Special Agent Rebecca Harper or, now, Supervisor Harper."

"Ok, this Agent Ha… Harper. Do you think she's doing anything with the information?" Hector asked, looking at Sylvia with heavy eyes.

"I don't know. So far she hasn't."

"Wh… wh… Why do you say that?"

11

"We have a system that logs all open investigations. I was in it this morning on another case and looked for anything about this. There's nothing in the system mentioning you or anything that's on the legal pad. Maybe she doesn't feel she has enough to go on. I don't have a clue. There's a standard protocol everyone follows before launching an investigation. I don't know what the deal is. So, as far as I know, she's not doing anything with the information on the legal pad. But… last month, I overheard part of a conversation she had with our former boss, Ben Nottingham. It was loud, even with the door closed. She was pretty pissed off about something that had to do with this. Other than that, nothing more."

"What did she say to this guy?"

"Basically, what I just told you."

"Since you're her partner, don't you think she'd mention something to you?"

"Well… I'm not her partner anymore. She got a promotion and now she's the new Tucson Station chief. I'm not sure who'll be my new partner. Besides, because you're my uncle, I don't think she'd say anything to me. Tío, I'm concerned about it. But if you say it's nothing, then I believe you."

"I'm sure it had to do with being on the committee, that's all. Really, not sure who this Syrian woman is. Tell me about Rebecca Harper. Is she married? Does she have a boyfriend? Children?"

"She's not married and, as far as I know, she doesn't have a boyfriend. She's got a nine-year-old. A daughter she adopted from

China. Kimyung. But I shouldn't be talking to you about Agent Harper. Why are you asking?"

"Ju… just curious," Hector said, shifting in his seat and dropping his head.

The entire conversation was uncomfortable for Sylvia and she stopped pressing him any further, especially in his drunken state. It scared her, the thought of what he might be up to and what could happen if she got caught covering for him. *Jesus, what if Rebecca discovers I snooped in her desk and thinks, somehow, I'm involved in what my uncle's up to? Oh God, I could end up in prison.*

She looked over at her uncle, who'd fallen asleep like he usually did after drinking. Pulling into the Westin La Paloma, she reached over to stirring him awake.

"Stop shaking me," Hector said, pushing her hand away and looking around as the car came to a halt under the covered entrance. A doorman walked to Sylvia's side of the car and another opened the passenger door.

"Greetings, sir. Do you have luggage?" the passenger side doorman asked Granada.

"No, I'm already checked in. Do you want to come in for a dri… drink?" Granada said to Sylvia.

"No, Tío. I've got work to do. When are you leaving and heading up to Prescott?"

"Tomorrow morning, and then I'm go… going back to Washington. Have a reception party there on Thursday night.

Want to come with me?" he asked, smiling and reaching over to put his pudgy hand on her right knee.

"Tío, don't. Stop it, you can't be doing that. I've got to go," she said, moving her knee left while pushing him off with her right hand. She glanced over at the doorman with a pleading look and he hurried over to help get her uncle out of the car.

Pulling away, her thoughts went back to the consequences of being found out for snooping in Rebecca Harper's desk and her uncle coming on to her. Driving down the road that lead out of the hotel grounds, Sylvia wiped a tear from the corner of her eye. She felt flushed and pulled onto the shoulder, skidding to a stop. Yanking the door open, crying, she ran to the other side of the car, took a deep breath, belched, leaned over and vomited. *God, please help me.*

## Tuesday, 3:54 PM
## Tucson FBI Field Office

Rebecca had finished her report on the recovery of the Stingers missiles in the Nogales incident. She knew the two Islamic terrorists she'd killed while saving the lives of Carter Thompson and Doug Redman were connected to the Madkahl Mosque in Tucson. But, with no direct evidence to prove it, she'd come to a standstill in the investigation.

Under the previous White House administration, terrorists on American soil got a pass, but with the present administration that wouldn't happen… that is, as long as she had rock solid proof. No mention of her saving the life of Carter Thompson and Doug Redman was in the report.

Sitting back in her chair, her thoughts drifted to different scenarios of how things could've gone, like if Carter, Doug and the others hadn't stopped them. Travel in the country would've stopped, with airplanes grounded and the economy grinding to a halt.

Being promoted to Supervisor of the Tucson Field Office was a surprise to her. After a month, she'd found herself pleased with having accepted the position. Throughout her career, Rebecca avoided taking on a leadership role because of the office politics involved. She'd decided a long time ago not to have any part of it. To her surprise, she'd found it suited her well and she embraced it. Now, she had control of what cases to pursue and which not to. Her silence regarding Carter and Doug's group activities, which on two occasions resulted in many felonies, would continue… at least for now. Stopping dangerous people when her own government wouldn't was all the justification she needed to look the other way. She felt good about it, knowing that sometimes breaking the law to protect the people and country you love is the right thing to do.

Hearing a knock on her office door, Rebecca looked up and then down at the computer screen and hit the save button on the file.

"Come in," Rebecca said, watching Agent Sylvia Granada approach her desk.

"Excuse me, do you have a moment to talk?" Sylvia interlaced her fingers, then put her hands behind her back like she didn't know what to do with them.

"Sure, sit down," Rebecca said, gesturing to a chair in front of her desk. Sylvia gestured back with her head, and Rebecca fought back a smile. *What's with the hands?* "What's up?"

"I, well, I'm trying to figure out… I," Sylvia started, just as Rebecca's phone rang in her purse.

Checking it under her desk, Rebecca saw it was Dax calling.

"I'm sorry Sylvia, I've got to take this call. Can we talk later?" Rebecca asked, looking at her and then nodding in the door's direction.

"Sure, it's ok," Sylvia said, biting her lower lip as she got up and walked to the door.

"Just a sec," Rebecca said, waiting for the door to close. "Hi, Dax. How are you doing?"

"I'm good. I was just calling to see how you're doing. And how's the new job? Can you talk?"

"Sure... I'm good. You know, it's weird... I like being a supervisor, except for having to deal with the BS out of Washington. It's challenging but rewarding at the same time. It's nice to be running this office old school style. I've got my agents doing some actual investigative work instead of politically correct assignments to bolster their careers."

"Have you been able to wrap up the incident that involved you and my guys last month?" Dax asked.

"I was just doing that now. Your guys? Can't imagine what you're referring to... It was just me and the two terrorists who pointed their AK's at me. Hope they're enjoying the seventy-two virgins," Rebecca said with an innocent laugh.

"That's good to hear, Rebecca. Hopefully, I won't have to activate them again, but if I do, it's good to know they're off the radar. That's part of why I was calling... You put my mind at ease. I can't say enough about the risks they've taken to protect our country and citizens."

"They're an incredible, unselfish group of guys, Dax. Our country needs more like them. When are you coming down here again?"

"Not sure, but shouldn't be too long. Listen, I'll be back in touch with you about the congressman. Right after you guys recovered the Stingers in Nogales, Granada made another trip over to Syria. I had one of my ground assets keep an eye on him. He spent some time with his Syrian girlfriend. Such a fool...

thinks she's in love with him. Proof that you don't have to have brains to be a politician. I'll keep you posted on what I find out."

"Sounds good, Dax. Talk soon," Rebecca said. She looked at her watch and realized it was time to pick up her daughter from her piano lessons.

"Hey, Dax. I've got to run. Got to pick up Kimyung from school."

"Ok. Hey, how's she's doing?"

"She's doing great… straight A's."

"Outstanding! She's a smart little girl. Listen, I know you've got to run. Talk soon. Love you, kiddo!"

"I love you too, Dax. Thanks for helping me get my head on straight about your guys and the supervisor job. Talk soon for sure."

# Wednesday, 5:03 AM
# Westin La Paloma Resort, Room #3345
# Tucson, Arizona

*You have the right to remain silent. Anything you say can and will be used against you in a court of law. "The cuffs are too tight." You have a right to, you have a right to, you have... you, you, you...* It wasn't so much the confusion of the nightmare as much as it was the pure dread of it that woke Hector. Stuck in the gray zone between dreaming and the conscious world, the feeling they'd caught him hung on him like an anvil. Life as he knew it had just ended. *No more living off the expense of the taxpayers, no more escorts, no more limo rides, no more cocktail parties... no more Assal.*

Trembling and sweating, he opened his eyes... *No... that was a dream, not real.* The congressman looked over at the clock on the nightstand and then around the darkened room, taking a deep breath. *Thank God that was a dream. Fuck, that was real. Rebecca Harper... She knows too much. Why does she have my name and Assal's on a legal pad? How the fuck did she find out? Oh my God... that dream could become real. She's got to be stopped.*

Grabbing his phone off the nightstand, he scrolled through the directory and hit the green call button.

"You have reached Senator Saul Ritz's office. Please leave a detailed message." Halfway into the recording, Granada realized he'd called the congressman's office and not his cell phone. Hanging up, he scrolled again, this time making sure he had the right number.

"Granada, you fat bastard, how've you've been? How's that little Syrian slut of yours doing? You going to have a baby with her? Hey, if you tire of her, let me know… I've got something for her."

Ritz was a loud and pompous New Yorker and the chairman of the CIAC. He'd been a senator for thirty-eight years, and if you wanted something done in Washington, D.C., he was the one to talk to. He's one of the most powerful men inside the beltway and knows where all the bodies are buried.. He annoyed Hector Granada but, because of who he was and his connections, Granada tolerated it… He was a means to an end, especially for making money. Ritz was also the only other person who knew about his affair with Assal and never avoided giving Granada a hard time about it. Well, at least up until now, he'd thought Ritz was the only one that knew about his affair with Assal.

"You're a funny man. Speaking of Assal and our business with her… I've… Maybe we've a problem. I'm going to be back in D.C. tomorrow. You available to get a drink? I'd rather not talk about it over the phone," Granada said, feeling a streak of jealousy at the thought of Assal pleasing another man, especially someone like Saul Ritz.

"What do you mean 'we might have a problem?' You got a turd in your pocket? That little thing you got going over there with her and south of the border is on you. But yeah, I've time for a drink. Usual place? Say eight o'clock?"

"Yeah, that's good. See you then," Granada said.

Even after hanging up the phone, his feeling of dread from the dream wouldn't go away. Something had to be done about

Rebecca Harper, and soon. Is there an investigation going on? *Saul Ritz should be able to find out... He's golfing buddies with the director of the FBI, who's also on his payroll, and he and Ritz hate the new president. If there is an investigation, maybe he can get it buried.*

Granada looked again at the nightstand clock. 5:28 AM. He laid back down, trying to go back to sleep. Thirty minutes later, after tossing and turning, he got up, made some instant coffee and turned on CNN. "The Mexican government has agreed to step up efforts to halt the flow of drugs heading north into the United States. Meanwhile..." Granada turned the news off and called room service.

"Room service. What would you like to order?" the woman's voice said on the other end.

"Send up a pot of coffee and three bloody Mary's, double shots in each one," Granada said and hung up the phone without waiting for an answer. *That Harper bitch better not fuck with me.*

# Wednesday, 6:00 AM
# Carter Thompson's House

Carter reached for the snooze button and turned over putting his arm around Kim. She stirred and pressed against him. They eased into their caress, feeling the warmth of their bodies. Carter dozed off again and ten minutes later reached over to snooze his phone a second time. He laid back with her resting against him.

"Good morning, fiancé," she said.

"Good morning to you, my fiancée. Did you sleep well?" Carter said.

"I did, how about you?"

"Like a rock."

"Yeah, you were hard as a rock last night," Kim said, reaching up to bite his left shoulder.

"And did you expect anything less?"

"Hey, what time is it?" she asked.

"Six-ten. Why, you got to be somewhere?"

"Not until nine. I'm supposed to meet Liz for coffee and afterward she's going with me to help pick out my dress."

"Dress? What are you getting a new dress for? You've plenty of old ones." Carter winced as Kim punched him in the shoulder.

"You funny man, but that's ok cause I love you good, love you long time," Kim said with the two of them laughing. "Hey, why don't I see if she and Doug are available for dinner this week?"

"That sounds great," Carter said, pleased to know that Kim and Liz had become friends. Would they have, under normal circumstances? He'd wondered sometimes. Not unlike the friendship of relatedness between military wives that forms when their husbands are off at war.

"Honey, is it ok if I ask you a question?" Kim said.

"Sure... What is it?"

"I know you don't know for sure but... do you think you, Doug and the team... I mean, do you think you'll be needed again? I worry about it."

"I don't know. Only time will tell. The truth is, honey, part of me wishes never again, but then there's a part of me that longs for it. It feels good doing something for our country and living on the edge in the process... I've never felt so alive. It's almost like a craving for more... like wanting to play that great football game I played in high school all over again. You know, glory days. The only difference is that this is here, now, and it's for keeps. It's not a practice drill. You know, I'm not a religious guy, but sometimes... I feel like I've been called to do this... you know... My time to get in the game. I feel good about it," Carter said.

Though Kim didn't know what Carter, Doug and the others did when they were gone, she knew it involved danger and it frightened her. She'd been at the hospital and comforted Carter when Mick had passed.

"Are you ok with that?" Carter asked, sitting up and resting on his left elbow to look into her eyes. "I mean, I want to be honest with you. I want you to understand who you're marrying. I'm not the same guy you met before all of this started."

"No, I'm not entirely ok with it… I appreciate whatever it is all of you guys do. I understand it saves people's lives and helps the country. I just worry… I want nothing to happen to you… ever. Mick died. I… I know it wasn't a hunting accident. I won't press you about what happened, but I don't believe he died in vain… I don't want to lose you. I plan on growing old with you… Do you hear me?" Kim asked, wiping a tear from the corner of her right eye.

"I hear you, honey. It makes a difference to me that you understand how important this is to me. It's kind of weird… I've done lots of things in life, but it isn't until now… later in life. You know, it'd be alright with me if we never had to go out again. Listen, I don't want anything to happen to me either, or any of the other guys. I love them. They're like brothers. And yes, I want to and will grow old with you, Kim. I love you."

"I love you, too. I like that Liz and I've become good friends. She's an exceptional woman. I admire how she's always taken care of the kids and everything while Doug's deployed somewhere halfway around the world. She's strong. I admire and like her very much. I'll see if they're available for dinner."

"I'm good with that. Besides, it'd be nice to hang out with Doug other than in training or… Hey, we better get moving. I've got a meeting at eight-thirty this morning," Carter said, looking over at the clock.

## Thursday, 7:22 PM
## Jade Lounge
## Washington, D.C.

Pushing through the crowded area, Congressman Hector Granada made his way to the bar. Finding no empty spots, he used his bulk to push his way through the men and women enmeshed in conversation. Hector looked at his watch, then back in the bartender's direction, working his end of the bar. He turned, scanning the entrance, then glanced back at the bartender, who was moving at a speed only Superman was capable of. Enviously, he watched him, imagining that the bartender had nothing to worry about. All that guy had to do was draw and pour beer, mix drinks and top them off with cherries, olives or lemon twists. His thoughts drifted back to Rebecca Harper and the yellow legal pad. *Why the fuck is my name and Assal's name written on a legal pad in her office? How does she know about the Stinger missiles? I mean, if she knew anything, I'm sure Saul would know. Oh, fuck.* Granada then thought about his days living in Prescott and life as a local politician…. a much simpler time then.

"What can I get you," the bartender asked, putting a white napkin and a small bowl of nuts down on the twelve square inches of real estate in front of Granada.

"I'll take a Corona with lime in a chilled glass. Make it two," Granada said. *Fuck that bitch… I've got to stop her.*

25

"Coming right up," the man hollered back over the bar buzz.

"Hey, you fat son of a bitch, what the fuck you got yourself in an uproar about?" asked Congressman Saul Ritz, putting a heavy hand on Granada's shoulder.

"Hey. Jesus, man… I'm afraid we might have a problem," Granada said, eying Saul Ritz with his slicked back, thin, jet-black dyed hair, which started at the middle of the top of his head. He was thin, not tall and an unimpressive-looking man. The only thing people seemed to remember about him was his eyeglasses, always sitting at the end of his long-pointed nose. Even though he's a lawyer and graduate from Harvard, he didn't come across as particularly bright… slick, yes… good bullshitter, yes, but bright? No. The thing about Saul Ritz that drew Hector to him like a moth to a lamppost was that Saul's a rainmaker. He's the ranking member of the CIAC and one of the most powerful people in Washington. Hector always felt uncomfortable and unsure of himself around Saul Ritz and knew he was racist. Hector didn't have a college degree and grew up in Arizona, never really traveling much until after he became a congressman. Saul Ritz was as smooth as they came. Hector was outclassed and he didn't like it.

"Excuse me, bartender, I'll have a martini with three green olives. What the fuck do you mean we might have a problem? Who the fuck is 'we?'"

"I'm serious," Granada said, downing the first beer, putting it down and draining half of the second one.

"Two more," Hector hollered to the bartender.

26

"Cancel the two beers. Bring my amigo a margarita," Saul Ritz hollered.

Hector looked down, clenching his fists.

"Come on, speak up. What fucking problem are you talking about?" Saul Ritz said, again putting his right hand on Hector's shoulder.

"Remember that shipment of Stingers we sent to Benghazi? You know, the ones the CIA wouldn't transport for us a few years ago? Remember?" Hector whispered, looking around to assure himself no one was eavesdropping on their conversation.

"Stingers, Benghazi, Stingers... Oh yeah, a few years ago. Kinda, sort of, maybe I remember. I'd forgot all about those fucking things. What about them?" Saul said, raising his voice an octave.

"Well, they may have... they may have made their way into Mexico."

"What the fuck are you talking about? 'May have made their way into Mexico?' Did they or didn't they?"

"They did," Hector said, nodding his head and looking down.

"Are you shitting me? How the fuck did that happen?" Saul Ritz said with alarm.

"I had them sent over to our contact across the line... you know... Juan Ortiz."

"Juan Ortiz? Why? What the fuck for? When did that happen?"

"Recently, Ortiz needed some, supposedly so he could keep our pipeline going. You know, the cut we get from the drugs and the young women he smuggles into the country. He's worried this new president we've got is going to secure the border and force the Mexican government to come after him. I guess he wanted them to defend him against the Mexican military if needed."

"Ok, so how many did you have sent to him? Two, three, five?" Saul asked, grabbing his martini and taking a healthy swig of it.

"How many?" Hector echoed sheepishly, weighing whether to be straight with the senator or lie about it. He knew it was going to be a problem either way. *Son of a bitch… this is fucked up. I'll give it to him straight and take my lumps. Oh, Jesus, what did I do?*

"Yes, how the fuck many? Like over five?" Saul Ritz straightened his posture, looking at Hector like a man in a boat that just discovered a leak.

"Yeah."

"Yeah, what? Come on, for fuck's sake…. how many?"

"Thirty-eight."

"Oh my fucking God, what the fuck did you do? Are you telling me Juan Ortiz has 38 Stingers? Jesus fucking Christ. I know of the one that hit our helicopter, but what the fuck?" Saul said, picking up his martini and taking a large gulp of it.

"No," Hector mumbled.

"No? Well, then where are they?"

"Some are back in the country. I know the FBI got their hands on twenty-eight of them but the rest, I'm not sure," Hector said, picking up his margarita and drinking three-quarters of it. He thought it prudent not to mention the loss of the original shipment of missiles to Juan Ortiz.

"Two more Coronas and another martini," Hector yelled.

In two minutes, the veteran bartender had two Coronas in front of Hector and a martini for Saul Ritz.

"Oh my fucking God. How did you get them over here?" Saul Ritz asked, looking around, shaking his head.

"You know the person we dealt with when we had them shipped to Benghazi from Qatar?"

"Your little whore? Oh, no. Don't tell me, Hector. You got played. You know that she's one of the top three on Interpol and Homeland Security's lists? I'd heard you made two trips back over there. Fuck… why do the FBI have some of them?"

Hector came clean with Saul, explaining about the first shipment going to Juan Ortiz and the unknown persons raiding Ortiz's drop houses in San Miguel, taking most of them and destroying the rest. After that, he told him about the second shipment arriving and how Juan Ortiz sold twenty-eight to some Islamic terrorists out of Tucson. He then mentioned to Saul that an FBI agent intercepted them and how she killed the two terrorists who were in Nogales to pick them up. Saul Ritz sat quietly, looking at him, then put both hands on the bar.

"Ok, I'll take care of it. I'll fix it so nobody will trace the missiles to our committee. No one will know. And besides, if it does, we'll just lie our way out of it," Saul Ritz said, downing the last of his second martini.

"Well, there's still a problem I need help with," Hector said, downing another Corona.

"What problem? I just told you I can fix it so nobody will know. What the fuck are you talking about?"

"Somebody knows, or at least knows my name, the Stingers and Assal."

"Who knows your name and all the rest?" Saul Ritz asked.

Hector explained to him about his niece Sylvia Granada being a new agent with the FBI and getting assigned to the Tucson Field Office. How she was in her boss's office and discovered his name, Assal and Stingers written on a legal pad in Rebecca Harper's desk drawer. He continued explaining that it didn't appear Rebecca Harper had done anything more with the information and that he wanted to make sure she'd stay silent.

"I don't know why she hasn't followed up on the information, but it appears she hasn't. Either way, I need to make sure she says nothing, permanently if need be," Hector said, nursing his beer.

"No good killing an FBI agent. Does she have any children?"

"Yes, my niece told me she has a daughter, adopted from China. A young girl, nine years old. Why are you asking?" Hector said, leaning closer to him over the noise of the crowd.

"Motherly instinct is to protect their young. They'll do anything. What if we were to arrange for her daughter to disappear for a couple of days? You know, just long enough to ensure this agent gets the message not to fuck with you. Do you think your buddy Juan Ortiz might be of some help to us?"

"I don't have a problem with that. How would we do it?" Hector said, looking around the room.

"I've got someone—I'll have him contact you. His name is Victor Livingston. He's done some work for us before. Very good at what he does. Former special forces guy. I'm thinking we have Victor snatch the kid and, if you can arrange it, we'll hand her over to your amigo Juan Ortiz for safekeeping down in Mexico. Shouldn't take more than a few days for that agent to get the message, and then we'll get her back to her mother. Guarantee, she'll get the message," Saul said.

"Why Mexico? Why not just hide her somewhere in Arizona?"

"The Feds will launch a massive manhunt looking for her. Too many cameras all over the place... not like the old days. Tucson is right there near the border. We can get her across quick and then we won't have to worry about law enforcement finding her. After that, you'll give a message to this Special Agent Rebecca Harper to make her little legal pad go away. Are you up for that? Hey, get me another martini," Saul said to the bartender as he was serving a drink to a patron three stools down.

"I guess, but what if she's already passed the information off to someone else in the bureau?"

"Not to worry, I've got a few on the seventh floor in my pocket. Hey, there's the law of the land for the little guys and then a second set of laws for us. I'm not worried about it, but first we've got to muzzle that agent. Besides, if it comes up, I'll arrange a golf game with the Attorney General. Hopefully, her legal pad with your name and everything else hasn't left her desk. Besides, I think it'd be a good thing to teach this agent a lesson about fucking with a congressman. She needs to learn that when you do, you're going to get burned. Her job is to enforce a set of laws that aren't for us," Saul Ritz said, laughing.

"I don't know. Kidnapping? Shit, I could go to prison for that," Hector said, shaking his head and loosening his tie.

"Listen, Congressman Hector Granada… the reality is that selling Stinger missiles to a Mexican cartel and Islamic terrorists would put you away probably longer than getting arrested for kidnapping. Think about it. I'm just trying to help you out here," Saul Ritz said.

"You… you make a good point and you're right… I don't think I've much of a choice. Fuck it, let's do it. Problem solved. Have your buddy get a hold of me," Hector said.

"He's not my buddy. In the meantime, why don't you get a hold of Juan Ortiz and let him know what we're up to. We don't want her hurt or anything, you know. Just keep her for a short while. After you've talked to him and made arrangements, let me know. I'll have Victor get in touch with you. We should do this right away. I don't want any of this crap coming back to me and our committee. We've elections next year," Saul Ritz said as Hector, holding on to the bar countertop, steadied himself.

"Ok, Saul. I'll get in touch with him. Or rather, I'll get in touch with his cousin Mario Quintana. He's his right-hand man and go-between for me."

"I don't care who the fuck you talk to down there, just get it set up," Saul Ritz said. Hector nodded and the two of them clinked glasses.

# Thursday, 8:17 PM
# Hermosillo, Mexico
# Cake and Ice Cream

"Swing hard, mija," Mario said to Marianna, his ten-year-old daughter. The lights in the backyard strung overhead brightly illuminated the red, yellow and green swinging donkey piñata. With a blindfold on her eyes, Mario's wife eased the girl close to the piñata and stepped out of the way. "Ok, mija, swing." As the little girl swung the bat, Mario pulled on the rope, moving the donkey just beyond the reach of the stick. With the second swing, he lowered it just as the three-foot stick hit it with a dull hollow thud, stopping and bouncing the donkey in the opposite direction. He raised it up slightly.

"Swing again, mija."

The small girl took a breath, raised the stick over her head and swung down. Though not strong, the impact of the stick hit behind the donkey's neck, putting a hole in the crepe paper, making it bounce and jiggle from side to side.

"My turn, my turn," yelled a stocky boy, who reached in and grabbed a hold of the stick. Marianna tried to hold on to it but couldn't against the boy's strength.

"Let go! My turn!" the boy yelled, yanking it out of her hands and throwing her to the ground. Mario ran to his daughter.

"Ok, mija, you did really good. It's ok to let him have a try," Mario said, looking at the boy, then at the boy's father, Juan

Ortiz, standing behind him. Helping his daughter up, he brushed the dirt off her knees.

"Come on, papa, I want another turn. Juan can wait. Come on, papa, let me hit it again."

With her blindfold pushed back up to her forehead, Marianna glared at the boy. Mario wanted to let her keep going but knew better.

"That's ok, honey, maybe Juan Jr. will miss and then you can swing at it again," Mario said, knowing better. Twelve other children chaotically started pleading for the stick, not understanding why Juan Jr. was always first in almost everything. All the parents knew what was coming next. Juan Sr. stepped forward, took the blindfold off Mario's daughter and put it on his son, leaving it so the boy could look up underneath the bottom.

Mario went back to holding the rope attached to the piñata, raising it slightly higher than the boy's head.

"Ok go, son! Beat the crap out of that donkey," Juan Ortiz hollered.

Mario, watching the boy look up and knowing he could see the piñata, slightly jiggled the donkey. Juan Jr. swung the stick and the sound of the impact ran through the silent crowd. Two more hits broke the piñata open, spilling candy and little toys onto the ground.

"That's it, mijo. Way to beat the crap out of that thing," Juan Ortiz said as the children rushed in, throwing themselves on the ground and grabbing the candy and toys. Juan Jr. yanked off his blindfold and threw the stick to the side, hitting one of the mothers in the shin. Juan Jr. pushed a little girl out of the way, grabbing the candy in the area she'd been.

Mario looked at the father of the young girl that had just been pushed. It was easy to see Juan Ortiz's son pushing his daughter incensed the father. The father and Mario made eye contact. Mario looked at him, then at Juan Ortiz and shook his head. The father heeded the warning and walked over to his tearful daughter, picking her up. Mario knew... everybody knew... you don't object, you don't protest... you just go along with whatever Juan Ortiz and his son want to do. Mario scanned the crowd, seeing Captain Sanchez standing in the back. *I wonder what he really thinks about his boss.* He knew the captain was in the same situation as he and everybody else. Nobody went against Juan Ortiz or anyone in his family.

Mario's wife Adela walked over to him, shaking her head and looking down. He knew she'd always expected him to stand up to Juan Ortiz and talk with him about being disrespectful to him and his family. Mario tried on multiple occasions to impress upon her how dangerous Juan Ortiz was, but she'd always push back. She'd told him many times that because her uncle was a U.S. congressman, he could arrange for them to move to the United States and escape the life they'd been living since Juan's nephew, Reggie, was killed. She'd doubted Mario's explanation that there was no escaping the reach of Juan Ortiz. It didn't matter where they went. If he turned his back on him, it would mean torture and death for the entire family. She continued to be unreasonable about the issue and didn't understand the threat.

Just as Sylvia started to say something, Mario's phone rang.

"Mario, I need a favor from you," Hector Granada said.

"Favor? What kind of favor?" Mario asked.

"We've got a bit of a problem up here and I need you and my niece to look after a package for me."

"What do you mean 'look after a package?' What kind of package and what kind of problem?"

"I don't want to go into details, but it's important for our future business together. I can get it delivered to you in Hermosillo. I just need you to look after it for a couple of days."

"Like I said, what kind of package are you talking about?"

"It's… it's going to be a young girl… Asian. I need you and Adela to look after her. Just a couple of days," Hector said.

"Jesus, what the fuck are you talking about? When are you thinking of delivering her?        I got to talk with Juan. You know how he is."

"Soon. I'll make it worth your while. Besides, you and Juan owe me for arranging for the Iman at the mosque to buy those Stingers. Don't tell me he didn't make a ton of money on that deal."

"I think maybe it's better I don't mention to Juan you think he owes you. Hey, what happened with those Stingers? I heard that after we brought them through the tunnel, the two men picking them up were killed and your government has them."

"Yeah, something like that… That's part of why I'm calling. Look, are you going to help me out or not? It's important."

"I guess I can. When are you bringing her down here?"

"I'm not—someone else will deliver her. I need you to make sure she's in safekeeping while she's down there. I want nothing happening to her. Do you understand?"

"Comprende, but like I said, I've got to let Juan know what we're doing."

"Fine, do whatever you've got to do. I'll be in touch," Hector said.

Mario hit the "end" button and looked over at Juan Ortiz, then his wife and daughter, and sighed.

"Time for cake and ice cream?" his wife called out.

# Saturday, 10:33 AM
# Congressional Headquarters, Fourth District
# Prescott, Arizona

Congressman Granada appeared rarely at his campaign headquarters in Prescott. Like all the men and women in congress, he enjoyed the privileged and lavish lifestyle, along with its perks at the expense of the taxpayer. But an election was coming up and it was time for him to press the flesh with the locals. At this point in his career, he detested doing so, but knew it was part of the game. He'd rather be in Washington, D.C. He enjoyed the life of a politician, and couldn't pass up the extra deals on the side to make money.

For the last hour, outside the campaign headquarters, a crowd of local supporters had gathered, expecting him to come out and do a speech. Talking about himself and lying to his constituents about what he was going to do for them was something he enjoyed. Hector, like most congressmen and women, viewed themselves above the voters. At the cocktail parties in Washington, many times the conversations would gravitate to how stupid and gullible their voters were. Politicians were always promising the moon and the stars and delivering nothing. It was the big joke amongst elected officials that the morons kept voting them back in.

"Excuse me, sir. I've got everything all set for your eleven o'clock speech. They can hardly wait to hear from you," the enthusiastic twenty-two-year-old staff member said.

"Ok, thank you, dear. You look very nice today. You have beautiful eyes. How long have you been working for us?"

Granada asked, putting his right hand on the young woman's shoulder, rubbing and massaging it gently.

"I've been here two months, sir," the woman said, taking a step back.

"Call me Hector. What's your name?"

"Veronica."

"Beautiful name. I've a special project I'm working on that's a bit hush-hush… maybe you could help me with it. Can you meet me here later tonight, say around ten? Everyone should be gone by then. I'll be in my office."

"Thank you, sir, but I've other plans I've already committed to."

"Ok, well, some other time then," Hector said, turning and looking through the front window at the growing crowd of people gathering. A small group of people, some with red hats on, were waving signs in the back of the crowd. One read "Do Your Job and Secure The Border Now!" Another one read "Make America Great Again!" Shouting began between some of his supporters and the people with the signs.

The young woman turned, making her way outside to help the other staff and volunteers calm the growing crowd. Hector's phone rang.

"Hector Granada?"

"Yes, who's this? How'd you get my number?"

"A mutual acquaintance asked me to call you… said you had a job for me," the voice on the other end said.

"A job? Who's our mutual friend?" Hector asked, bewildered by the caller on the other end and distracted by the growing voices outside.

"Saul Ritz."

"Saul Ritz? Victor… Ahh, yes, I was expecting your call. How are you doing? I mean, I guess we need to talk. I can't go into it right now. I'm not in a place where I can talk," Hector Granada said, nervously looking around to make sure he wasn't being overheard.

"We shouldn't talk on the phone. We need to meet. I'm in Tucson. Where are you?"

"I'm up in Prescott, but on Monday I'm heading to Phoenix to catch a flight back to D.C. Would you be able to meet me there? My flight is at 12:45."

"I can do that. There's a restaurant, just northeast of Phoenix in Fountain Hills Drive by the name of NY Deli. How about we meet at nine?"

"Nine will work. How will I find you?"

"Don't worry, I'll find you. Oh, and make sure you bring everything."

"Ok. Bring everything? I'm not sure I understand what you mean."

"Did Saul call you?"

"I'm not sure. I've been busy this morning."

"Call Saul and make sure you bring everything or get someone else," Victor said.

"Ok, I'll call him," Hector said as the sound of the crowd grew louder and police sirens were heard. *What the fuck is he talking about? Bring everything?* Looking up Saul's number, he hit the green phone icon.

## Saturday, 10:54 AM
## Hector Granada's Congressional
## Headquarters, Fourth District
## Prescott, Arizona

"Saul Ritz, here. Who am I talking to?"

"Saul, it's me, Hector. I just hung up the phone with Victor and he said to bring everything. Bring what?"

"Sorry, I got busy and meant to call you. I didn't think Victor would be so quick in getting a hold of you. But hey, what can I say? He's an efficient kind of guy. One hundred and fifty thousand. Bring it in cash—twenties, fifties and hundreds. Equal amount of each. Make sure it's in a suitcase with wheels. Victor hates duffle bags."

"One hundred and fifty thousand in cash? What the fuck, Saul?"

"What do you mean, 'what the fuck Saul?' Do you think guys like him work for free? Hey, you put yourself and the rest of us in a dangerous position. Do you want this thing to blow up and you go to jail? Because I can promise you I'm not going with you. Do you understand what you did and because of it you could drag the rest of the committee down with you? Did you think of that? No, you didn't! Get this shit fixed, Hector, because I can tell you, myself and the rest will not go to jail because you sold some fucking Stinger missiles to a Mexican cartel and Islamic terrorists. Are you fucking shitting me? No. You goddamn fix this shit and fix it now. And don't tell me you don't have the money. I don't know how much you made off the Stinger deal or whatever else

43

you're involved in, but I know this… you didn't include me in the profits. Did you?"

Senator Saul Ritz not only unmercifully berated Hector Granada, he flat out frightened him. Over the years, there'd been a trail of bodies left in his wake, all suicides. All forty-three of them. Many of them took their life by shooting themselves in the back of the head... Imagine that. Even a guy like Hector Granada, not known to be very smart, could figure that one out. Then there was the infamous Ritz Foundation with its connection to the Russians and their purchase of some shares in a uranium mine in the U.S. On more than one occasion, Hector had accompanied the senator and others in a Gulf Stream jet down to a small island in the Bahamas, where girls and boys under the age of sixteen were the main course on the menu. He knew the senator had pictures of him with naked young girls and boys.

If Saul Ritz said get one hundred and fifty-thousand in cash, then that's what he'd do. From Hector's point of view, he had no other way out. He had to make sure Rebecca Harper didn't further investigate his involvement with the cartel and terrorists.

"Fine, I'll get it done," Hector said, holding the phone away from his ear and squinting.

"Make sure you do," Saul Ritz said and hung up.

"Congressman, they're waiting for you," one of the volunteers said to Hector.

"What?"

"They're waiting for you to speak. They're so excited to have a great man like you, who represents our core values. I'm so proud to know and help you with the campaign."

Hector stood there for a moment, gathering himself, then put the phone in his jacket, looked outside and took a deep breath.

"Ok, let's go," Hector said with a feigned smile to the young man.

## Saturday, 6:53 PM
## Jacobs Restaurant, Catalina Foothills
## Tucson, Arizona

"Right this way, Mr. Thompson, Suzy will take you to your booth," the hostess said to Carter and Kim, motioning with his right hand toward the young woman. Walking to the booth, Carter couldn't help but notice that the young woman reminded him of someone else. The hair, the figure and the pretty face. The horrifying events of that Black Friday when another young woman, just like her, working at a phone kiosk caught a round from an AK-47 to her forehead, blowing the back of her skull out. Racing through Carter's mind, the scene unfolded… remembering being in the bookstore that day… *being drawn to the sound of gunfire… explosions.* For reasons unknown to him, the young woman at the mall that day drew his attention. She was busy helping a middle aged man, woman and two teenagers at the phone kiosk. *The excited, young teenage girl holding a purple rhinestone studded phone to show her father. The young woman at the kiosk turning to the sound of gunfire… her head snapping back, followed by a ball of red mist exploding from the back of her skull.*

"Carter… Carter, sit down honey," Kim said, grabbing his right arm. Carter, lost in his thoughts, didn't notice the young woman motioning with her right hand in the booth's direction for him to have a seat.

"Oh, sorry," Carter said, sliding in next to Kim, still fixated on that day and the memory of it. It'd changed his life forever.

He'd never taken another man's life before. On that day, he became brothers in arms with Doug Redman.

"Honey, are you ok?"

"I'm fine. They should be here anytime now. We're early. Are you hungry? I am," Carter said, taking a deep breath and shifting his attention to the present.

"I am, I'm starving. What do you think you're going to have?"

"Steak, ribeye most likely."

"So predictable," Kim said, smiling.

"Well, it is a steak place," Carter said, watching the same young woman seating another party at a table. Blinking and shaking his head, he turned away from her. His mind drifted to the lunch he and Doug had after what'd happened at the mall and Doug wanting to buy him a steak. The long conversation they had and Doug's asking about his background because of his skills. *Déjà vu?*

"Carter, Kim, how are you doing?"

He looked up, seeing his friend, retired Colonel Doug Redman and his wife Liz. Carter got up, giving both a hug. Behind him, Kim, now out of the booth, did the same.

The four sat down and eased into conversation. Kim and Liz, sitting across from each other, were chatting between themselves with Carter and Doug doing the same. Other than getting together for a meal a few days after the mall incident, the two men had only been together while either training, on a mission or at a funeral. Both shared the same point of view on danger to the country because of the unsecured border and the consequences that came with that. Their friendship, forged in life and death conflicts, was one of mutual respect and honor.

Spending time with Doug without a rush of adrenaline was out of the ordinary for Carter, having been so used to it. He looked across the table at Doug, thinking about how many times in the short while they'd known each other they'd stared down death in the face. And here they were, at dinner with their wives. These two men were not used to small talk, but they were weaving through it.

"I'm going to the powder room. We'll let you two boys talk for a bit," Liz said, looking at Kim.

It was understood without either of the women or two men saying anything that leaving a few moments alone for Carter and Doug was a good idea. Sitting back down, after letting their wives out of the booth, both men watched the two beautiful and classy women walk through an upscale crowded restaurant.

"How's Garrett doing, and Mic's wife?" Doug asked.

"Garrett's ok and Mic's wife is healing… I guess we all are in our own ways," Carter said, leaning back as a busboy poured water in all four glasses.

"I know, it never gets easier. Are you and Garrett up for going to the canyon and throwing some lead down range next weekend?" Doug asked.

"I am, for sure. How's Rocco, Conway and Mike doing?" Carter said.

"They're good. Mike took a contract job in Afghanistan running security for one of the head honchos at Dynatherm. It was just for two weeks. He should be back tomorrow or the next day. So, this weekend would be the two of you, Rocco, Conway and me."

"That sounds good. I'll give Garrett a call in the morning. If he can, I'm sure he'd want to join us. How's Dax doing? Have you talked with him lately? Thank God he was there to help us with some resources last time. I'd sure like to buy lunch, dinner or whatever for that FBI agent. If not for her we wouldn't be sitting here talking right now. But… I understand it's better that we don't and never will sit down and just have a cup of coffee or something. Great gal. The country could use a lot more like her," Carter said, looking at Doug.

"To tell you the truth… I'm kind of happy I haven't heard from Dax… As much as I like the man, when he calls it's because something bad happened. Either there's a danger for the country or someone is in trouble. If our government would do their job, secure the border and protect our citizens, people like us wouldn't be needed. Not likely to happen though. I've a feeling at some point Dax will call again."

"I read the president threatened Mexico with tariffs if they don't help stop the flow of illegals into our country. Nice to have a president with some balls, demanding they help stop the flow of drugs and human trafficking into our country. Someone I know, who leans left of center, called the president unpredictable the other day. This guy acknowledged that was a good thing for negotiating. I…" Carter was about to continue his sentence when he felt a warm, soft hand on his right shoulder and the familiar scent of the woman he loved.

"We're back," Kim said, as Carter and Doug got up to let their wives back into the booth.

As soon as they sat back down, the waiter came up to the table to take their orders for dinner. After dinner, the four continued to chat, with Liz sipping on a decaf coffee. Thirty minutes later found the foursome making their way out of the restaurant. Outside, Carter and Doug handed their claim checks to two parking attendants, who sprinted off in the direction of the valet parking area.

"This was fun. It was good getting away, sitting and having a meal together. I'll be there next weekend for sure, and hopefully Garrett will join us. See you then," Carter said.

As good friends do, they hugged, said their goodbyes and were off for the night.

## Monday, 9:03 AM
## NY Deli
## Fountain Hills, Arizona

Sitting in a booth facing the entrance, Hector looked at his watch for the sixth time in the last two minutes and gripped the handle of the rolling suitcase pressed against his left knee. He thought about past events and what could happen if he were implicated in his involvement with the Stingers. He also knew if that happened, he'd be a dead man. There was no way with the history of Senator Saul Ritz and his cohorts that he'd ever be allowed to talk with law enforcement, let alone testify in a congressional hearing or criminal trial. Saul Ritz and his associates knew, if given the opportunity, Hector Granada would do anything, including expose the whole committee, to save his own hide. He looked again towards the front door of the deli.

"Hector." A man's voice from behind startled him.

Hector watched as a thin, muscular, middle aged man, five feet, ten inches tall, dark-skinned, good looking, with a receding hairline and a deep movie star voice, slid into the seat across from him. The man's eyes glanced at the suitcase and then back at him.

"So, tell me what you need done and by when you need it done."

"You're Victor… right?" Hector said.

"The one and only. Like I said, what do you need done and by when do you need it done?" Victor said, holding his eyes on Hector.

"Ok, nice to… ok, I need, I mean… oh shit. I've done nothing like this before. I don't want anybody hurt. I just need to send a message, you know, a little persuasion."

"Ok, I'm listening. Saul said you needed my help. Take a deep breath, relax. My work is all-encompassing. So, like I said, what do you need done and by when?" Victor asked, looking straight into Hector's eyes.

"I…."

"Excuse me, gentlemen. Have you looked at the menu? Coffee?" the gum chewing waitress asked.

Hector, catching himself mid-sentence, stopped and looked up at her and then back at Victor.

"Coffee, just coffee," he said.

"Same as my friend," Victor said, leaning back in the booth.

"Ok, nothing else? Breakfast of some sort?"

"No, I'm good. Just coffee," Victor said.

The waitress looked at Victor and then at Hector, raised her eyebrows and smacked her gum.

"Do you have bagels?" Hector asked. The waitress looked at Victor, shaking her head smiling, and then looked at Hector.

"Honey, this is a New York style deli. Yes, we have bagels. It's what we're known for," she said, looking back to Victor, who was holding back a smile.

"Oh yeah, that's right. Ok, how about a bagel, cream cheese and some strawberry jelly? Lots of it," Hector said.

"Got it, two coffees, a bagel with cream cheese and strawberry jelly... lots of it. Coming up."

She turned left and walked away.

"So, you were saying, Hector?"

"I... I need you to kidna... I mean grab a young... oh fuck..." Hector took a deep breath. *Fuck it.* He looked around.

"Ok, this shit... It's between just you and me, right? I mean, you aren't the police or..."

"Hey, do you think Saul would still be around, doing what he does, if he didn't have resources like me to help him now and then? No, I'm not a cop. And this is staying between you and me. So, tell me... what is—"

"I... I need you to kidnap a young girl for me, take her somewhere and turn her over to someone else," Hector blurted out, not letting Victor finish his sentence.

"Ok. Let me make sure I understand you. You want me to snatch a little girl and take her somewhere, then turn her over to somebody else?" Victor asked, leaning forward in his seat and cocking his head to Hector's left.

"Right. Yes, that's what I need you to do."

"Ok… How old is this little girl, who is she, where do I snatch her from, where do you want me to take her and who am I supposed to give her to?" Victor said.

"She's… she's eight, maybe nine… nine. I'm not sure the ideal place to grab her, I'll leave that up to you."

"Ok, fair enough on where to grab her. I'll figure that out. Ahh… so, like I said… who is she and where am I taking her and who am I giving her to? Since you're not sure on the location, I need to know who her parents are and where they live so I can do surveillance on them for a few days. You know, pick up their daily patterns, which are going to include their interactions with their daughter. The mother is the key, but not always. I assume you know who the mother and father are, right?"

"She doesn't have a father. She's an adopted Asian girl. Only has her mother. Her mother is single and I don't think she has a boyfriend or anything like that."

"Ok, and where do I find the mother? Where she works is the best place. Neighborhoods can have busybodies who might notice a strange vehicle or person walking around. Do you know what she does for a living and where she works?"

"In Tucson. The mother and daughter live in Tucson. Yes, I know where she works," Hector said, hesitating.

"Ok, and where in Tucson does this mother work and what's her name?" Victor said, looking at Hector with growing annoyance.

"Here you go, gentlemen. Two coffees and a bagel with cream cheese and extra strawberry jam, lots of it," the waitress interrupted, allowing Hector to gather himself.       "Ok, anything else?" she asked, watching both of them shake their heads, not saying a word.

Without taking his eyes off of Hector, Victor raised the coffee cup to his lips, took a sip and put it back on the saucer.

"Listen, Hector. I've been doing this work for a long time. Stop holding back on me—it's annoying. Just tell me what I need to know. I get it. This is scary stuff for you. I'm not here to judge; I'm just here to do a job. So, who the fuck is the mother and where does she work? Come on, stop beating around the bush."

Hector, spreading the cream cheese and strawberry jam on one half of the bagel, stopped, looked at Victor, then back down at the bagel, and finished smearing the cream cheese and jam around. He took a bite and put the bagel back down on the plate. He breathed in through his nose, raising his shoulders up, and exhaled. Victor's abrupt straight-talk and his ability to cut to the chase startled him, but the strength and confidence was calming. It was a quality he lacked but admired in people. Victor kept his gaze on him.

"Ok, her name is Rebecca Harper, and her daughter's name is Kimyung. Rebecca Harper is an FBI agent, in charge of the Tucson Field Office."

Victor raised his eyebrows, smiling, and took a big sip from the coffee cup, then put it down on the saucer and continued to look at Hector.

"Ok, once I snatch the kid, where do I take her?" Victor said, leaning forward.

Hector, relieved by Victor's calm reaction, took another bite of his bagel, wiped the right corner of his mouth with his fingers, licked them and took a sip of coffee.

"I need you to take her to Hermosillo. Someone will be there, waiting."

"Hermosillo? As in the capitol of the state of Sonora, Mexico? That Hermosillo?"

"Yes."

"Ok, so let me make sure I understand the assignment. You want me to kidnap a young Asian girl, whose adopted mother is an FBI agent, excuse me, the FBI Station Supervisor of the Tucson office, and then take the kid across the line down to Hermosillo. Do I have that right?"

"Ye… yes," Hector said with a mouthful of bagel.

"Ok, and who do I deliver this kid to?"

"My niece's husband, Mario Quintana."

"Ok… so, tell me about this Mario Quintana. Besides being your niece's husband, what else can you tell me about this guy? You know, his appearance, height and weight, the kind of vehicle he drives and anything else you think I should know."

"He's around your height and maybe a little heavier. He drives a black Cadillac Escalade and has a job," Hector said.

"Ok, he's got a job. Good. What kind of job?"

"He works for… He's like an assistant for a guy," Hector said, wishing he had mentioned nothing about Mario having a job.

"Ok now, don't start being vague with me again. What kind of job?"

"He works for a guy named Juan Ortiz. Runs some of his business affairs, from what I know."

"Juan Ortiz. The same Juan Ortiz who's the head of the Magdalena Cartel in Hermosillo? That same Juan Ortiz?" Victor said, leaning back, cocking his head to his right again and raising his eyebrows.

"Sí, I mean yes, the same Juan Ortiz."

"I see. You know, when I spoke with Saul, he didn't give me all the details. How much you got in that suitcase?" Victor said, looking down at the case.

"One hundred fifty thousand."

"Double it," Victor said, looking straight faced at Hector.

"Double it? Come on! Saul said you'd do it for one-fifty. Give me a break," Hector said, his left hand reaching down for the bagel.

"Saul said I'd do it for one-fifty? Why don't you let him do it for you? If you want me to, it's three hundred or I get up now and leave. This conversation never happened and you'll never see me again. Choose... Which is it?"

Hector looked down at the suitcase and back at Victor.

"Come on, man, I..."

"Last chance. Choose," Victor said, getting up from the table and throwing a twenty dollar bill down. Raising his eyebrows, he looked at Hector and then at the suitcase.

"Come on, you can't just leave me here. I don't know anyone else," Hector said, pushing the suitcase towards Victor.

"First, I've never kidnapped a kid before and she's an FBI agent's daughter. Then, a trip into Mexico and a Mexican cartel? I'd have to be batshit crazy to do it for what you got in there. Besides, this entire business of kidnapping a young girl bothers me. Three hundred or nothing... good luck," Victor turned, heading in the direction of the entrance.

"No, wait. Come back. Ok, I agree to your terms," Hector said, taking a deep breath and wiping his perspiring brow with his napkin.

Victor stopped mid-stride and turned around.

"Come on, sit down, let's talk about when you can do it. Come on. Look, the girl will be safe. Mario's family will have her for a couple of days and then she'll be returned safe and sound to her mother. I promise no harm will come to her. It's not that sort of thing… really," Hector said. *There goes my money from the Stinger deal.*

"Are you boys all done?" the waitress said, walking up to the table just as Victor sat back down.

"I'll have more coffee," Victor said, not taking his eyes off of Hector.

"Me too," Hector said, resolved to commit to the price and happy Victor sat back down.

"When do you need the balance?" Hector asked, lowering his voice.

"What's the girl's name?"

"Kim… Kimyung."

"Ok, Thursday."

"Thursday what?"

"The money. Bring me the money on Thursday. And nothing happens to that girl… you understand?"

Hector knew he was in no position to stall Victor. He also knew Victor picked up on his fear and just took advantage of him. *Victor, or maybe prison.*

"I understand. Ok, Thursday I'll have the balance for you. You drive a hard bargain, amigo. The one-fifty in the case should get you started… right?"

"Consider me started," Victor said, reaching over to pull the suitcase next to his right leg.

"Ok, how about I meet you in Tucson on Thursday and give you the rest?"

"That'll work. It'll give me a few days to figure this all out. No later than then. When I do a job, once I start, I go until it's done. You understand? No turning back and absolutely no refunds."

"I understand."

"Good, I'll be in touch. See you on Thursday in Tucson. I'll text you and we'll figure out where."

"Ok," Hector said, putting his hand out to shake Victor's. Victor got up, pulled the handle out on the rolling suitcase and looked down at Hector.

"Put your hand down. This meeting never happened."

"You're right. I've a plane to catch," Hector said, finishing his bagel.

## Monday, 11:18 AM
## Sky Harbor International Airport
## American Airlines Terminal Gate 14

Hector, because of his meeting with Victor, arrived at Sky Harbor two hours earlier than he planned. Gate 14 was coming up on his left. Walking more than a hundred feet for the congressman was an effort, and he struggled to make his way to the gate. A throng of people moving in the opposite direction didn't make it easier. Breathing heavily, he angled off to the right, to a row of empty seats across from his gate. Overhead, the speakers announced boarding for the next flight. He sat down and leaned against the seat like a marathoner who'd just crossed the finish line. Wiping his brow with the back of his hand, he looked at his watch. With two hours to kill, now was as good a time as any to call Mario. Mario's wife Adela was his niece and the older sister of Sylvia Granada. Hector pulled up Mario's phone number and hit the green call button.

"Hola. ¿Qué pasa, Mario? ¿Cómo estás?"

"I'm good, Hector, and you?"

"I'm good. Hey, how's our friend Juan doing?" Hector said.

"He's doing fine. Why, what's up?"

"You said you had to talk to him about me bringing the girl to you."

"Right. I did," Mario said. "I'll call him right now and call you back and let you know what he says. Assuming I can reach him right away. But if not, I should be able to call you no later than tomorrow."

"Ok," Hector said and hit the end button. *Jesus Christ, what the fuck did I get myself into?* He knew even if he had to pay Juan Ortiz some money, Juan would hold it over his head. He hated giving Juan the power to manipulate him. It was the one thing Hector didn't want to have happen in dealing with the head of the Magdalena Cartel.

He looked at his watch again. Down the concourse he remembered passing a lounge and got up and started walking to it. Halfway there, his phone rang. It was Mario.

"That was quick. You talked with Juan?"

"I did. He's ok with the ten thousand to me, but he wants fifty thousand for himself."

"Motherfucker, you tell that... Ok, fine," Hector caught himself mid-sentence.

"He wants to know who's bringing her to Hermosillo? You?"

"Not me! Are you kidding? A gringo by the name of Victor will bring her."

"Ok, let me know a day or so ahead of time. I won't say anything to Adela until then."

"Talk soon." By the time Hector finished the call, he was at the entrance to the lounge. Looking around, he made his way to the bar.

"What will it be?" the bartender said.

"Corona with lime, two of them."

# Tuesday, 7:30 AM
# Victor Livingston
# Tucson, Arizona

He knew it was going to be a long day, but they always were when he was setting up for a job. One thing he knew for sure was that starting the day off with a substantial breakfast was a necessity for him.

"Good morning. Is anyone else joining you?" the hostess at the restaurant asked as Victor walked in.

"No, just one," Victor said. Out of habit, he scanned the restaurant. It's not that he expected any threats; it was more of an involuntary reaction anytime he walked into an area with a lot of people.

"Ok, would you like to sit inside or out on our patio?"

"Either is fine with me."

"Of course, it shouldn't be too long. Five to ten minutes. What's your name?"

"Victor."

"Ok, you're welcome to have a seat over there and we have complimentary coffee if you'd like," the hostess said, handing Victor the square plastic device that would vibrate and light up when his table was ready.

"Thanks," Victor said, making his way to the half empty row of seats. Sitting down, he reached over and picked up a copy of the Arizona Daily Star (aka Arizona Red Star) that was laying on the table in front of the seats. "Mexico Sends 1,000 Troops to Their Southern Border," read the headline. Victor read how the Mexican military had stopped and detained people trying to cross into Mexico from Guatemala. Reading a couple of paragraphs told him enough about the rest of the article. Turning the page, he saw an article about some creature that was preying on people's pets in a place called Oro Valley. Another article spouted the joy of the writer that there were no Republicans running for the upcoming Tucson mayoral election and how all three Democratic candidates were in favor of Tucson becoming a Sanctuary City. The plastic square vibrated and lit up.

"Victor?"

Victor got up, tossed the paper onto the coffee table and followed a young, attractive woman with tattoos down both of her arms and neck to a booth. In less than two minutes, another young woman approached him, asking for his order. While waiting, he pulled out a small five-inch by eight-inch lined yellow writing pad and began making a numbered list of tasks for this part of the assignment. Number one on the list was to set up surveillance of the FBI field office. He'd grabbed a recent picture of Rebecca Harper from the announcement of her recent promotion on the FBI website. As with most government pictures, it looked like it was dated and she too young to be a station chief.

After eating and paying his bill, he made his way outside to his rental car. Once inside the car with the door closed, he turned the car on, pulled up Google Maps on his phone and entered the address. In less than twenty minutes, after following the GPS directions, he arrived at the Tucson field office for the FBI. He drove down Commerce Park Loop, past the guard gate and on to North Bonita Avenue, turning right a block down to West Alameda Street. After making two more righthand turns, he arrived at the end of a short cul-de-sac. Just to the east was a four-foot block wall with two feet of steel fencing on top, which extended around the entire perimeter of the FBI offices.

It didn't take long for him to determine the best spot to draw the least attention, for him to watch the comings and goings of the personnel in the building. One hundred yards away from the office building was the parking lot of Pima Community College. It would provide him with an alternate viewing location. He never stayed in just one spot. Having two or more locations prevented people from wondering why a guy in a car was parked in one spot all day, and also provided him additional coverage for access and egress of the area. He pulled his car in facing the entrance to the FBI office, pulled out his ten power Zeiss stabilization binoculars and sat back. From that distance of one hundred, seventy five yards, the guard's glasses, mustache, bald head and gold earring in his left ear couldn't be missed.

## Tuesday, 9:49 AM
## Rebecca Harper's Office
## Tucson, Arizona

Drumming her fingers on the desk, Rebecca leaned back in her chair, looking at her watch. She needed to be at Kimyung's school at ten-thirty10:30 for a conference with her teacher and was hoping the conference call with her boss out of Washington, D.C. would wrap up in the next minute. Illegal aliens had been gaming the United States system by claiming asylum. The results were pulling U.S. Immigration and Border Patrol officers off their normal duties. Because of this, it reduced the ability of the Border Patrol to work down on the line, leaving gaps along the border. It also gave free rein to drug and human traffickers to come across unimpeded. Besides this, the western boundary of the Tucson Sector, the Tohono O'odham Nation Reservation, had 53 miles of southern border with Mexico, giving the traffickers unencumbered passage through the reservation. They could travel north to I-8 and, once there, it'd be just a quick ride to the sanctuary state of California. If they don't want to head west, then they could head east on I-10 and fan out into the interior of the country.

Amongst the drug and human trafficking are women and children. Many younger women cannot pay for their passage into the U.S., so sex becomes their ticket in. Many go on birth control pills prior to their journey. Rape trees along Arizona's southern border are common, with the bras and panties of victims hanging from tree limbs like ornaments on a Christmas tree. They believe that, once into the U.S., the sexual assaults and sexual favors will stop, but they don't. Once in the U.S., most of these women and children end up living a life of sex slavery.

The meeting was called because of the recent murder of an Arkansas state senator and a former Oklahoma state senator. The list of suspects involved in the child sex trafficking included a number of Washington politicians. It was believed the two men were murdered because they'd uncovered suspected sexual abuses of minors involving members of Congress. They'd also exposed the mishandling and abuse inside of Child Protective Services in different states. The bureau had learned of a local Satanic cult using children for sexual rituals. Included in this was the drawing of blood from the children. Members of the cult would then inject themselves with a mixture of the blood and low doses of adrenaline, believing it would produce a euphoric sexual high. Because of this coming to light, Washington had assigned an additional twenty agents to the Tucson Field Office under Rebecca's command.

Eleven minutes later, Rebecca made her way to the parking lot and her car. It was ten after ten and she'd have to hurry to be on time to meet the teacher. Pulling out of the parking lot, she made her way to North Bonita Street and turned left to Congress Street. Two blocks behind her was a black Hyundai Sonata.

# Juan Ortiz's Compound
# Hermosillo, Mexico

"Mario, what's up?" Juan Ortiz said, sitting on the back patio overlooking the grounds and the pool area of his hacienda.

"Hola, Juan. I'm good. How about you? Listen, I wanted to make sure something is ok with you. My wife's uncle, Hector Granada, called me asking to help him with something…"

"What's that fat pig congressman want you to help him with?" Juan Ortiz said, interrupting Mario mid-sentence.

"I was getting to that. He asked me if Adela and I would look after a young Asian girl for him. She's from the other side. I told him I needed to check with you first," Mario said.

"A young Asian girl? How old of a girl and why is he wanting you to look after her? Is he having sex with her? Did he get her pregnant? I know how politicians in the United States can be. Everyone knows about the former president from years ago, and others made lots of trips to an island in the Caribbean. I think they called the private 737 the Lolita Express. Hey, is she pretty?" Juan said with a sick laugh.

"She's only ten. I think he's having her," Mario said, waving off answering Juan's other questions. He'd heard talk of Juan having young girls and boys kidnapped and brought to his compound for his sexual fantasies. Whoever the girl was, he didn't want to get caught up in that or be part in harming a young child.

"Ten? I like that. Are her parents bringing her to you or someone else?"

"Someone else, someone who works for Granada."

"Ok, you tell Senior Fat Boy Congressman Granada we'll be glad to look after her, but it'll cost him twenty five thousand. If he doesn't like it, he can find someone else to look after her."

"Ok, I'll let him know. He's paying me ten thousand," Mario said.

"Ten thousand to you, huh? Ok, I change my mind. Tell Granada it's fifty thousand to me. That's what he gets for not thinking of me first. He must have some big problem on his hand. What's the story here? Is he having her kidnapped, or something else?" Juan asked.

"I don't know, I didn't ask. I'll let him know what the deal is."

"Perfecto. They can deliver the money to you along with the girl. I'll let Captain Sanchez know what's going on and have him come to your place and pick up my money. How soon is she supposed to be there?"

"Soon, maybe the next few days."

"Good," Juan said, hanging up. He looked at his cigar, seeing it'd gone out, and grabbed a lighter off the table and lit it. After four steady draws, he put the lighter back on the table, leaned backed and looked up, blowing out a large smoke ring. *Young Asian girl, beautiful and sexy…*

## 2:33 PM
## Mario Quintana's House
## Hermosillo, Mexico

Mario hated being the guy in the middle, the go-between for Juan and whoever he's doing a deal with. But he didn't mind the money. Taking in a deep breath, he thought about his conversation with Juan. He wasn't surprised by Juan's demand for the fifty thousand, but wasn't comfortable with the conversation about girl. The thought of children being sexually assaulted repulsed him.

Mario would do his best to protect her, but if Juan wanted the girl, then Juan would have her. He was powerless to do anything to stop his cousin. After having his way with her, he'd turn her over to one of his captains to sell her into one of the child sex-trafficking rings in the United States. Mario pulled up his wife's number and hit the send button.

"Hello, honey. What's up?" Adela said.

"I'm good. Listen, something's come up. Your uncle called me and asked if we could look after a young, ten-year-old Asian girl for him. Something about her family being involved with trouble, so she needs a place for a few days to be safe."

"What? What are you talking about? My uncle called and wants us to look after a young girl so she can be safe? From who? Which country, Mexico or the U.S.?" Adela said in a raised tone.

"As far as I know, she's a U.S. citizen. Hey, it's your uncle. He sounded a little stressed about it. I told him I'd talk with you first. He doesn't want you to mention anything to your sister Sylvia about this."

"How long are we going to look after her?"

"I think just for a few days. He's going to pay us ten thousand dollars. What do you say? I think it'd be good to help him out and we can always use the money."

"Does Juan know about what you're doing?"

"Yes, he does… It's not a problem. Well, I should say, not a problem as long as your uncle pays him fifty thousand dollars."

"Wait a minute, we're the ones looking after her and Juan gets fifty thousand and we get ten? I hate this life you've gotten us into, Mario."

"I know, honey. It sucks and I feel terrible about it, but that's the way it is… We've had this conversation before. Captain Sanchez will come by when the girl and the money arrive."

"I don't understand, why is the captain coming by?"

"To collect the money and take it to Juan."

"I've heard tales of Juan having young girls and boys at his hacienda and having sex with them. Is the girl staying with us or going to Juan's?" Adela asked, brushing her hair out of the way.

"No, the girl is to stay with us, just for a few days. No big deal… relax."

"I don't like this, Mario. I don't like this one bit."

# Aqua Prieta, Mexico Federal Police Headquarters
# Captain Sanchez's Office
# 2:53 P.M.

"Honey, I should be home by dinnertime. We've got to run down to Nacozari de García. May be home by six. I'll call you when I'm on my way," Captain Sanchez said to his wife of twenty three years. He'd always kept his professional life, including his work for Juan Ortiz, separate from their marriage. It's well known in Mexico amongst the population that to be a Federale is to be working for one of the cartels. His wife knew this and accepted it.

Nestled in the northern end of the Sierra Madre Occidental Mountains was the small town of Nacozari de García. It sits sixty-six miles southwest of Aqua Prieta. The town is a staging point for Juan Ortiz's drug shipments coming up from the rich growing region of Bacoachi. The captain and his men would be there to make sure that the twenty-five tons of marijuana made it onto the awaiting semi-tractor trailers for shipment to Naco, Sonora, on the U.S.-Mexico border.

Captain Sanchez would take twelve of his men and use them as an armed escort for the shipment into Naco. He'd ride along in the convoy. It was something Juan Ortiz demanded. After fifteen minutes on the road heading south to Nacozari de García, the captain's phone rang.

"Hola, Juan. ¿Qué pasa?" Captain Sanchez said, hearing his boss's voice. The captain and Juan Ortiz went back to their days as kids on the streets of Aqua Prieta. He didn't like him then, and through the years of watching Juan rise through a trail of blood to the top of the Magdalena Cartel, he grew to despise him. Many times, he'd thought about killing him.

"I have a job for you. In the next few days, a young Asian girl is going to arrive at my cousin Mario's house along with fifty thousand dollars. I want you to go there and get the money and the girl and bring them to me," Juan said in a low voice.

"Ok, how old is the girl?"

"What difference does it make? You bring her and the money to me. I'll call you when she gets there. Make sure nobody touches her. ¿Comprende?"

"Ok, I understand. Just let me know when. I'll take good care of her and the money. Not to worry," Captain Sanchez said. *God, how I want to kill you.*

"Make sure you do," Juan Ortiz said, ending the call.

The captain also knew of Juan's ways and his sexual fetishes. He'd delivered young women, girls and boys to him in the past. Each time turned his stomach. Each time he'd sworn to himself he'd kill him one day. The killing of the American seniors pushed him to have those thoughts again. Juan's demand for the young girl steeled his resolve. The only question was if he were to kill Juan Ortiz, who would take his place as the head of the Magdalena Cartel?

# Wednesday, 7:55 AM
# Coyote Run School Parking Lot

"You have a great day and study hard. I love you," Rebecca Harper said to Kimyung as the girl opened the passenger door to Rebecca's government issued car. Despite the traditional view of FBI cars always being black Fords, Rebecca's was an impound vehicle. They used cars they seized during criminal activity, which provided the agency with a large fleet of undercover vehicles for agents to pick from. In Rebecca's case, she'd chosen a late model, mid-size Jeep SUV. Kimyung's favorite color was pink, so Rebecca had picked red, the closest thing to pink she could find.

She watched her daughter jump out of the car, running with her Little Kitty pink backpack bouncing. Two of her friends joined her as they ran through the front door, held open by a teacher. Rebecca preferred a private charter school to the public ones in the area. The school district in Tucson, District One, was one of the poorest performing school districts in the country. She felt it was a disgrace and laughed when the "Red for Ed" movement arose, stating the additional money was for the children. She knew the money wasn't for the kids; it was to increase the teachers' pay and benefits. *Not bad, working nine months and getting paid for twelve.*

She sat there until Kimyung was out of sight. Rebecca worried about her. Rebecca had adopted Kimyung when she was six months old from China. She'd surprised herself at how quickly and easily she'd adapted to motherhood. Since then her daughter was her number one focus in life. Kimyung was shy until she got to know someone, and then the vibrant Kimyung made her presence known.

"Harper. What's up?" Rebecca said, answering her phone making her way out of the parking lot and turning left onto the street.

"We've a meeting on Saturday at JEH (J. Edgar Hoover Building.) I need you there," said Ben Nottingham, Rebecca's former Tucson supervisor and now her regional supervisor.

"Fuck, what time? I had something planned with my daughter. Do I really need to be there? Last time it was nothing more than BS about the new procurement procedures," Rebecca said.

"Yes, it's mandatory. We've got an alert on something happening just south of you. Word is the cartels want to kidnap one or two of our Border Patrol (BP)officers. Our new president has convinced the Mexican president to step up and secure the border on their end. It's having a serious impact on all the cartels. They're not happy and word has it they want to grab some of our officers to send a message. It's a serious threat. You've got to be here on Saturday. Plus, the boss wants to talk with you about the incident last month with the Stinger missiles. He wants to know how you came to find out about it and why you killed two young middle eastern men. The IRC (Islamic Relations Consortium) found out about it and is raising a stink."

"Two young middle eastern men hellbent on attacking America are terrorists. Please, don't give me any sugar-coated PC bullshit. Call them what they were… Islamic terrorists," Rebecca said, pursing her lips, shaking her head. *Grow a pair, you little wimp!*

"Alleged Islamic terrorists, you mean?" Nottingham sniped.

"Alleged? Yeah, you're right, Nottingham. How stupid and racist of me to think two young, middle eastern, fighting age men caught with thirty-eight Stinger missiles were planning on harming America. My bad. We wouldn't want to get people thinking our own government wasn't protecting our country. Nothing to see here… right?"

"Calm down, Agent Harper. You need not get so riled up. Anyway, you'll be here on Saturday, right?"

"You know, you and the agency's political correctness is going to get Americans hurt and killed… In fact, it already has," Rebecca said, taking a deep breath in and reaching for a pack of cigarettes in the center console that wasn't there. Even though she'd stopped smoking, when she became upset or angry, the impulse to smoke was as strong as ever. "Yes, I'll be there. I'll catch a flight out on Friday. What time is the meeting on Saturday? If it's early enough, maybe I can catch a late flight back to Tucson."

"It's at one o'clock, and will probably run all afternoon. How do you like being in charge of the Tucson field office?" Nottingham asked.

"One o'clock. Ok, got it. New job, yeah, it's fine. I like it. You know how it is," Rebecca said.

"I do. More my speed being back here in D.C."

"Makes sense. Listen, gotta run. Anything else?" Rebecca asked, not wanting to have any kind of conversation with Ben Nottingham other than ones about work. As far as she was concerned, he was a career climbing, back-stabbing bureaucrat fuck that had no business being in law enforcement. Everything he did was for his own personal gain and nothing to do with honoring his oath to protect the citizens of this country. She knew agents like Ben Nottingham were typical of the corruption at the top of the bureau. She took a deep breath.

"No, that's it for now. See you Saturday."

Rebecca didn't respond other than to hit the end button on her phone.

*Fuck, I hate going back to that cesspool. Two more years and I'm done.*

Driving back to the Tucson office, she thought about the rest of the day, Thursday and Friday. Despite always having a lot on her plate at work, above and beyond anything else, Kimyung was her number one priority. She found joy in taking on the role of a mother at this late stage in life. To her surprise, it seemed to come naturally. Rebecca adjusted quickly to the amount of work involved and, like with everything else, embraced it with focus and intensity.

Fifteen minutes later, Rebecca was at the gate leading into the parking lot of the Tucson field office.

"Hello Agent Harper. How's our new boss doing today?" said the guard standing by the doorway of the security shack.

"Hi Bobby, I'm doing good. Hey, stop calling me 'boss.' I liked it better when you just called me Rebecca. Nothing's changed… I'm still Rebecca," she said, smiling at the seventy-plus-year-old security guard. He'd been there before they transferred her to Tucson and probably would still be there when she retired, despite his age. He always had a smile for everybody.

"Ok, you got it, Rebecca."

With the gate lifting, she smiled and drove forward. The black Hyundai Sonata that had been following her turned right off of North Commerce Loop onto North Bonita Street.

# West Fresno Street
# Tucson, Arizona

For surveillance work, Victor preferred to use smaller mid-size cars, rather than a large SUV. Nosey neighbors seemed to be tolerant or not even notice a strange mid-size car parked in their area, versus a big SUV... especially a black one. But, then again, it depended on the neighborhood. Working class neighborhoods tended not to have anyone home during the day and, if they did, it was because they worked a night shift and spent most of the day sleeping. And then there were neighborhoods where people just didn't care or even notice an out-of-place vehicle being parked for hours on end.

Pulling up at the end of West Fresno Street, Victor turned right and backed his rental car up a dirt alleyway behind a row of houses. Now, facing the FBI field office at a forty-five-degree angle, he looked to his right towards the houses. A tall row of oleander bushes obscured his view of them, assuring him that they couldn't see him either. Raising the Leica laser rangefinder to his eyes, he activated it and read the distance of the guard shack and then the front entrance to the building. On the screen, the numbers read one-hundred-eighty-two yards from his position to the entrance of the FBI office and one-hundred and thirteen yards from the guard shack and gate. Close enough for detailed observations through his binoculars and far enough away not to be noticed.

Victor liked to have three to five days of surveillance on a subject. Here, three days would be sufficient because of the target, Rebecca's daughter Kimyung. After yesterday's and this morning's surveillance of Rebecca and her daughter's movements, the only question for Victor was when and where he'd take her. At the school or their house? With the Arizona sun glaring off the hood, he decided on the "where."

It was looking like Friday was most likely going to be the "when." He just needed to make one phone call to an asset.

"How's Albuquerque treating you?"

"Same old, same old," Hal said.

"Listen, I'm in Tucson. I've got a quick and easy job for you. Can you be here by Friday morning?"

"I can be. Maybe. What's the deal?"

"A snatch and grab, and then a drop off two miles away. After that, you're out of here."

"Who are we talking about?"

"A kid."

"A kid? What the fuck, man? Snatching an adult is one thing, but taking a kid is different. Guarantee if we get caught, it's twenty years minimum. Minimum!"

"We won't get caught. Believe me," Victor said, hoping Hal wouldn't ask who the kid belonged to.

"What's with the kid? Who do they belong to?"

"Damn, I didn't think you'd ask… Do you really need to know?" Victor said, drumming his fingers on the steering wheel.

"No, I don't. It's just—I've never been involved with any kid stuff. Going to cost you."

"It always does. How much?"

"Well, I've got my drive over there, a room and then…"

"How much?"

Victor enjoyed using Hal. Great driver and good at disappearing after they completed a job. He also had ice in his veins and never lost his cool. They'd been friends for a long time and he'd heard Hal's preamble about money so much, he'd resorted to cutting him off to get to the bottom line.

"Fifteen grand."

"Damn, you're getting pricey. Ok. When can you be here?" Victor asked, knowing Hal was right about the sentencing guidelines. Nine-year-old kid… mother is an FBI agent, going into Mexico, maybe dealing with the Mexican cartel. *The congressman must be in one hell of a bind… What was I thinking? I should have charged that fat pig a lot more. Just another dirty politician sucking off the tit of the taxpayer.*

## Thursday, 6:15 AM
## Walmart Parking Lot, 1st and Wetmore
## Tucson, Arizona

Except for a few cars here and there, there was nothing but an occasional shopping cart scattered in the big lot. Victor, leaning against the hood of his rental, watched the car approach him. He dropped his hand, feeling the Glock 21 inside his waistband holster. Taking a last drag on his cigarette, Victor flicked it to the right, pushing himself off the hood into an upright standing position. He continued to watch the car rolling up, stopping four feet to his left.

"Hey, you son of a bitch. You're just as ugly as ever," Hal Ringo said, opening the door and lifting his six-foot, three-inch frame out of the black 2008 Ford Crown Victoria Police Interceptor, with a black push guard in the front, black rims and black sided tires.

"I'm surprised you didn't hit your fucking head getting out of that cruiser. Excellent choice for what we'll be doing. How the hell have you been?" Victor asked as the two men shook hands. Victor enjoyed working with the unassuming looking Hal. Besides being a crack driver, he was also a wiz at defeating any security system on the planet. A computer geek by trade, the late thirty-something Hal had one of those brains that spoke code. Victor knew he was always calm under any conditions. He'd never seen him get rattled during any of the jobs he'd used him for. Over the years, they'd become good friends.

"I figured you'd like it. I've done a few modifications to it. It's got an inducted air intake system and a Magnaflow exhaust system," Hal said with a grin, nodding towards the modified four hundred-fifty horsepower beast. "Plus, it got a..."

"Stop... I get it. It runs like a bat out of hell. It's got the look we need for this job. Ok, why don't you leave your black screamer here, and we'll go set up?"

"Sounds good to me, boss."

Victor watched Hal maneuver his car into a parking space.

"Hey, I'm hungry. Do you think we've time for breakfast?" Hal said, adjusting his glasses and pushing his hair out of his face.

"We do. Heading there now," Victor said pulling onto the street and making a left. We've got about an hour to kill. No worries."

# Thursday, 7:31 AM
# Rebecca Harper's House

"Kimyung, are you ready?" Rebecca said, calling from the kitchen to her daughter's room.

"Coming, Mother. I'm trying to figure out which color ribbon to tie my pony tail back with. Be right there," Kimyung said back to Rebecca.

Rebecca smiled, picturing her daughter in front of the mirror holding up the different colored ribbons. She rinsed off the last plate, put it into the dishwasher, closed it and made her way to the hallway to Kimyung's room.

"Coming honey," Rebecca said, knowing if she didn't help her, they'd be late getting her to school by eight o'clock. By the time she got there, Kimyung had picked out a pink ribbon to go with her pink dress. Rebecca stood in the doorway, watching as the girl arranged her jet black hair through the ribbon with her thin little fingers. She smiled, walking over and giving her a hug and a kiss on the top of her head. From early on, Rebecca only intervened to help her daughter when needed. She was not one to fuss over her. She wanted Kimyung to learn how to solve problems early in life. Already at nine, she was self-reliant, articulate and strong willed... just like her mother. Rebecca turned her daughter around, holding her at arm's length and pulled her in for another hug.

"I love you," Rebecca said, feeling her daughter return the affection.

"I love you too, Mommy."

"Ok, grab your backpack and let's get moving. Got a full day of learning ahead of you and I've a full day of work ahead of me."

The two made their way down the hallway to the garage door. They lived in a modest three-bedroom home in the Sam Hughes district, near the University of Arizona. Rebecca had bought it within six months of being reassigned to the Tucson office eight years prior. She'd requested the transfer to Tucson to get away from the liberals, taxes, and craziness of California. With the ever-increasing taxation, illegals pouring in and the drug usage, coupled with people crapping in the streets, she was grateful to have fled. Rebecca traveled there for a case two months prior and was stunned seeing the trash and makeshift shelters lining the nicest of streets. So much for socialism.

In the car, she looked over, making sure Kimyung was buckled in. Rebecca maneuvered back down the driveway and onto the quiet street, making her way to Campbell Avenue by turning right at the stop sign.

"Listen honey, I've got to go back to Washington D.C. for a couple of days tomorrow and I'll either be back Saturday evening or Sunday at the latest. Maria will stay with you and will come early tomorrow morning before I leave and drive you to school. I've got to catch a flight at six. Ok?" Rebecca looked over at Kimyung, holding a book she'd been reading the night before and looking outside at the scenery going by.

"Oh, yoo-hoo. Did you hear what I just said, sweetie?"

"Yes, Mommy. You said Maria will come by tomorrow morning to take me to school because you have a flight to catch at six in the morning and she'll be staying with me. You also said where you are going... to Washington, D.C., and you'd try to be back Saturday or Sunday at the latest," Kimyung said, still looking out the window.

"That's right. Read back correct." Rebecca continued to not be surprised by the brilliance of her sweet little daughter. Kimyung had been tested and showed she had a very high IQ and a very good understanding of her environment and the world. *Sometimes I wonder if my kid has some alien intelligence... or something.*

Pulling into the school drop-off area, Rebecca watched Kimyung avoid the cracks on the sidewalk separating the two playgrounds. With her backpack bouncing and a book in hand, she arrived at the entrance to the school. Reaching the doorway, she turned and waved to Rebecca. A block and a half away, a black Hyundai Sonata maneuvered itself between two parked cars facing the front of the school and the playground.

Rebecca looked at her watch, pleased she'd gotten her daughter to school a few minutes early. She pulled back onto the street, turning left, and began her drive to the FBI Tucson field office. As she drove, she went over in her mind the things she had to do for the day, including getting ready for her flight in the morning. *Fuck... never enough time. Oh shit, I forgot to remind Kimyung to let her teacher know that Maria would drop her off tomorrow. I'll call later.*

# Friday, 7:58 AM
# Maxwell Street, Running Coyote School

"Ok, so that's the little girl? Who's the woman who dropped her off?"

"I don't know, not her mother. Maybe a nanny? Fuck if I know. Doesn't matter. We'll proceed as planned," Victor said, watching Kimyung skipping up the sidewalk to the school entrance. He'd left his car two miles away on a side street just a block away from 22nd Street. A straight run to the west down 22nd Street would have him to I-10 in less than five minutes. Once on I-10 it was a five-minute run to the turnoff to I-19 and a thirty-eight-minute run to the original border crossing going into downtown Nogales, Sonora, Mexico.

"I can't believe they don't have a fence around the playground. Un-fucking-believable. I thought grade schools were supposed to have super security? Fuck, she's coming this way," Hal said, watching the woman who dropped the girl off through his binoculars heading in their direction.

"Chill and put your binoculars down. No worries. Yeah, that's what I thought about playgrounds too," Victor said, bringing his binoculars down to his lap and looking down so the woman in the passing car wouldn't see his face.

"So, what happens next?"

"We'll just sit tight for now. Two days in a row, they broke for recess at ten-thirty for twenty minutes. It looks like the younger kids are on the playground on the other side of the

89

sidewalk. Our target and her friends hang out on this side of the playground by those trees. That's a good thing for us. Did you bring what I told you to?"

"Got it right here, boss," Hal said, pointing to the fanny pack wrapped around his waist.

After two hours and twenty-five minutes, Victor opened the big Ford Crown Victor's right front door and stepped onto the sidewalk. He began walking towards the school, watching Hal drive off to the north side of the school. Stopping at the corner across from the school, Victor turned right and kept walking. Crossing the alley behind the school, halfway down the block, the recess bell rang. He proceeded to the end of the block, turned left, crossing over, and headed toward the trees on Kimyung's corner of the playground. One hundred feet away from the trees and the playground, an explosion reverberated off the buildings on the street. The noisy chatter of the    children on the playground stopped.

Victor reached the trees, watching the monitor on his side of the playground turn and run in the explosion's direction. All the children began running behind the monitor, with Kimyung and her friends beginning to take steps in that direction.

"Kimyung," Victor called out, striding onto the playground towards her.

She stopped, turned and looked at him, cocking her head as he took three long steps before grabbing her arm. She tried to pull away, kicking at him, but it was too late. Victor stuck her in the arm with the syringe.

"Hel...," Kimyung tried to call out as her words drifted into silence.

Turning while catching her, he lifted the lifeless girl up in his arms and ran back to the sidewalk, heading back toward the alley. Within five steps, Hal pulled up, leaning over opening the rear door. Victor stepped inside with Kimyung and reached over, pulling the door closed. Gently, he put her on the floor between the front and back seat. He leaned back, feeling the acceleration of the car turning left, heading away from the school.

# 10:37 AM
# Multi-Purpose Room

After the initial reaction of the children and the playground monitors running in the explosion's direction, order was restored. The monitors moved the children back into the school and to the multi-purpose room. All doors were secured and they put the school on lockdown. It would remain in this condition until law enforcement declared it "all clear."

The multi-purpose room buzzed with the sound of children milling around.

"Don't run, Michael. This isn't the playground," said Mrs. Ryan, one of the third-grade teachers assigned as a monitor that day. She scanned the kids milling around, attempting to take a head count of her class, but giving up because of the chaos in the room.

"I wonder what that was all about. Scary. Sounded like a gunshot. At least the kids are safe and having fun," said Ms. Compton, the twenty-two-year-old first year teacher standing to Mrs. Ryan's left. Ms. Compton taught second grade and was constantly asking the senior Mrs. Ryan questions. To the annoyance of Mrs. Ryan, the young teacher wanted her opinion on the smallest of things. Mrs. Ryan felt Ms. Compton, a millennial, personified her generation: scattered work ethic, spacey, always on her cell phone, poor command of the English language, naïve about the world around her, insecure and liberal. She'd asked Mrs. Ryan what she thought about the twelve different genders and their social impact. At the time, Mrs. Ryan looked at her, smiled shaking her head and turned away without saying a word.

"I don't know what it was. I'm sure they'll tell us later. Hey, it's time to round them up and get them back into the classroom so we can do a head count," Mrs. Ryan said, looking straight ahead to Ms. Compton.

"Head count? Oh, you mean attendance," Ms. Compton said, looking like she'd just won the lottery with her revelation of understanding the term 'head count.'

"Yes, Ms. Compton, taking attendance is what I meant by 'doing a head count.' Pretty cool, huh? You learned a new term," Mrs. Ryan said, taking a step forward, sighing and shaking her head. Raising her left arm, she looked at her watch, catching the attention of another seasoned teacher across the room.

"Ok, kids. Let's go. Time to go back to class," Mrs. Ryan said, clapping her hands and projecting her voice over the chattering noise of the children. Behind her, Ms. Compton clapped her hands, mimicking her instructions. Mrs. Ryan smiled, taking another step forward to the protesting of some children who wanted just a few more minutes of play.

"Come on, let's go," she said to a boy in her class. He purposely dragged his feet, looking down with a grin on his face.

Twenty-two minutes after the bell for recess, Mrs. Ryan was directing the children into their seats.

"Let's go, everybody. Get into your seats. Come on," she said, clapping her hands twice. She was an "old school" teacher who didn't put up with any guff from her students or their parents. Every year, Mrs. Ryan's fourth grade class tested in the top ten percent in the state.

"Ok, quiet. We're going to do attendance."

"But we already did that this morning. Why do we have to do it again?" asked the boy who'd been dragging his feet, and was now sitting in the third row of desks.

"I know we have, Johnny, but because of the interruption at recess, we're doing a second one," Mrs. Ryan said, scanning the room. Three seats were empty. *Was it two kids absent this morning or three?*

"Michael Cohen."

"Here."

"Shane Michaels."

"Here."

"Raphael Sanchez."

"Here."

"Kimyung Harper," she said looking around the room.

"Kimyung… Kimyung was here this morning, right?"

"Yes, Mrs. Ryan, she was. I thought she came in with us after the loud noise. We were playing together at recess by the trees until that big bang… I thought I saw her come in," Mary Downs said, looking around the room.

"Did any of you see Kimyung in the multi-purpose room?" she said, scanning the class, hoping for an answer. She knew Kimyung to be a very bright and disciplined child. Mrs. Ryan listened as a few children said they'd seen her and others said they hadn't seen her in the multi-purpose room. Mrs. Ryan was aware of Kimyung's past circumstances. *I wonder if the explosion triggered something in her and she's hiding.*

"Ok, let's get through attendance," Mrs. Ryan said, continuing to call out names. Except for Kimyung, all the children in the classroom were accounted for Mrs. Ryan made her way back to her desk and sat down, then grabbed the phone and dialed the number to the office.

"This is Mrs. Ryan. We have one student who was here this morning but isn't in the classroom now. Some kids thought they saw her in the multi-purpose room and some said she wasn't there. Her name is Kimyung Harper."

"Ok, I'll have someone check the multi-purpose room, hallways and bathrooms. We're still in lockdown, so if she's here in the school, we'll find her. If not, we'll try to reach her parents in case they picked her up. We'll let you know," said the unemotional voice on the other end of the phone.

"She's single—I mean, Kimyung's mother is a single parent. You should be able to reach her, no problem. If you don't reach her right away, call the alternate number. I think her nanny's name is Maria. You should have her number."

"I'm sure we'll reach her mother, but if we don't on the first attempt, we're required to wait thirty minutes and try again. You know, we've got to attempt three calls before we call the alternate number. We'll get on it right away."

"Ok, but if you don't reach her mother right away, why don't you just call the nanny?"

"We can't; you know the rules. We've got to make three attempts to one or both of the parents in the course of an hour before we can go to the alternate number. You know the drill, Mrs. Ryan. First, we call the parents, then the alternate, and if we can't reach them, we call Child Protective Services who'll send someone out to the child's house. If they don't find her, then we contact the police. I don't make the rules," the voice said, like she was reading back an order at a fast-food restaurant.

"Yes, I know the drill; it makes little sense. Look, her mother's out of town and that's why someone else is looking after the girl. Why not call the alternate now just to eliminate possibilities?"

"Can't do it... like I said I..."

"I know, I know... You don't make the rules. Ok, I'll wait to hear from you." Mrs. Ryan said, interrupting the woman's repeating of the followed protocol. Looking down at her desk, she picked up a pencil and began tapping it on the desk. *This doesn't make any sense.*

Kimyung was not only the brightest and smartest child in the class, she was also the most responsible and wouldn't hide out in a bathroom or anywhere else. Mrs. Ryan had spoken with her mother frequently and knew she was an FBI agent. She knew her mother or the nanny wouldn't pick her up without letting someone know. She looked out the window and then at the door.

"Ok, everybody, open your arithmetic books to page forty-seven," she said, forcing her mind to focus on the task at hand. *I don't like this. This isn't right. Damn protocols.*

# 12:05 PM
# Highway 15 - Fifteen Kilometers South of the Line
# Sonora, Mexico

Heading south, Victor looked to his right, passing the Mexican Immigration Office. By Mexican law, it's mandatory for any foreign visitor to get a tourist visa before traveling in the country. Passing the fifteen-kilometer mark without one put him in the country illegally, a fact he was aware of.

Reward versus risk was the filter Victor operated on, never on emotions. He'd weighed the odds of getting pulled over by Mexican law enforcement and asked to show his visa. Usually, greeting the officer politely and offering a little mordida, or bite/bribe, would eliminate the need for having a visa. The trick was to have enough money to satisfy the arresting officer. If it didn't work, the consequences were real, as compared to the same situation in the United States. Mexico doesn't play catch and release with someone entering their country illegally. First, he'd be taken to the nearest local jail and then transferred to a prison. Along the way, Mexico's finest would steal money, watches, cell phones or anything else of value. Getting caught without a visa wouldn't be the biggest problem he'd encounter. There was also the unconscious nine-year-old girl, covered by a blanket on the floor in the back. Besides getting caught without a visa, he'd be charged with kidnapping if he couldn't provide proof of legal guardianship for Kimyung.

The result of being charged with kidnapping would land Victor in a Mexican prison for a very long time. Kimyung would end up sold to one of the cartels, who'd smuggle her back into the U.S. to be sold into a sex-trafficking ring after being passed around for their own pleasure.

Now, on the reward side of things, it was very simple. If he didn't get a tourist visa, then nobody would ever know he'd entered Mexico. And if nobody knew he was in Mexico, then they wouldn't be able to tie him to the kidnapping. When he traveled back across the line, U.S. Customs wouldn't track if he'd entered Mexico legally or not. Their only concern would be with their border and who was coming in. Using a forged passport and phony name gave him further insulation from the threat of being discovered. And because of this… the reward and the risk for Victor made sense. As long as he didn't run afoul of the law in Mexico.

Ten miles further down the road, he pulled his phone out of his righthand pants pocket and looked up the number. He kept it to his ear, listening to it ring. A voice answered after the fifth ring.

"Who's this?" Hector Granada said.

"I'm twenty-five miles across the line with the package. Who's my contact in Hermosillo? What's their number?" Victor said.

"You did it? I mean, it's done, you've got the girl?"

"Yes, I've got her. Who's the contact and number?"

"Did you have any trouble? I mean, is she ok? Do you think anybody knows you've got her?"

"Yes, she's fine. Now stop with all the fucking questions and tell me what I need to know."

"Ok, the number for you to call is 630…"

"Don't tell me—text it to me along with a name," Victor said, shaking his head. Merging onto the four-lane divided highway, he sped up to ninety miles per hour.

"Ok," Hector said.

"Good, I'll contact you when I'm back across," Victor said, hitting the end button. Five minutes later, Victor received Hector's text. He punched in the numbers and hit the green button, calling Mario Quintana.

"I'm a friend of Hector's and I've a package for you. I'm about two-and-a-half hours away from Hermosillo. Is there a place where we could meet north of Hermosillo?" Victor asked Mario. Knowing Hermosillo was a town of one million people, he didn't want to navigate his way through busy street traffic to Mario's location. The sooner he could turn around and head back to the U.S., the better.

"Yes, about forty miles before Hermosillo, you'll come to a turnoff heading east to the small town of Carbo Municipality. There's a Pemex station just before the turnoff. It'll be on your right. I'll meet you on the north side of the parking lot," Mario said.

"Ok, what are you driving?"

"I'll be in the gold Cadillac Escalade. What are you driving?"

"I'll find you. Come alone. See you soon."

Victor arrived forty-six minutes early and set up five hundred yards north of the Pemex station on the east side of the road. With binoculars, it would be easy for him to pick up most details.

"Where's my mom? What's going on? Where am I? Where's my teacher? I'm thirsty," Kimyung said in a shallow, weak voice.

"It's ok. Your mother's not here. It'll be ok. Your teacher sent you on a quick trip. You'll be back home before you know it," Victor said, lowering his binoculars and looking down at Kimyung, stirring under the blanket on the floor.

"I can't move my arms or legs. I'm scared. Who are you? Where's my mommy? I want to go home. Help me," Kimyung said, crying.

"It's ok, you'll be fine. We're on a brief field trip. You'll be home soon. Go back to sleep."

"No, I don't want to sleep. I'm thirsty. I want to go home. Who are you? Take me home," Kimyung said, continuing to cry. She started kicking her legs against the back of Victor's seat. "Are you a bad man?"

"No, I'm not. I won't hurt you. Here, sit up a bit and I'll give you some water."

Victor, careful not to look over the seat to avoid Kimyung from seeing his face, reached over and grabbed her duct taped hands to pull her upright. He unscrewed the lid on the extra water bottle he'd brought. With his right hand, he held her head up and, with his other hand, reached down putting the bottle up to her lips. He listened to her taking little sips. After thirty seconds, he moved the bottle away from her lips.

"How are you feeling? Your name is Kimyung, right?"

"Yes, but I want my mother. I want to go home. You're a bad man. Let me go. I want to go home."

"You can't go home yet. It'll just be a little while," Victor said, turning his attention back to the Pemex. Looking at his side-view mirror, he watched approaching traffic. Not that he was expecting to see the gold Escalade yet—he was more concerned about this being a setup with the cartel or Federales. So far, he'd seen only semi-truck rigs, cars and pickups coming and going from the Pemex, with no one stopping on the north side of it. He continued focusing his attention on his side-view mirror and the Pemex, ignoring the sounds of the whimpering behind him. Over the years, he'd been involved in many snatch and grabs, but never with a child. Turning his head back to the right, he couldn't help but feel bad for the girl. *Have I stooped to a new low? You got to be shitting me, Victor.* He shook his head, putting his attention back on the Pemex where he saw a northbound gold Cadillac Escalade turning into.

It veered left, into the oversized parking lot, making its way to the north side of the lot. He looked at his watch. He'd wait for another fifteen minutes. Raising his binoculars up, he continued to scan the area and then focused on the Escalade with a man behind the wheel. His phone rang.

"I'm here at the Pemex, on the north side. How soon do you think you'll be here?" Mario said.

"Shouldn't be too long," Victor said, watching the man in the Escalade holding a phone up to his ear, verifying he was the one. From Victor's position, it looked like he was alone. He knew someone could be laying down in the back seat or rear compartment of the Escalade. Risk versus reward. The risk was Mario could have someone else with guns in the vehicle. If all went well, then the reward was to turn around and get back across the border before dark. The bonus reward would be escaping the sounds of Kimyung's pain and suffering. He shifted in his seat, clearing his throat.

"Kimyung, are you ok?"

"No, I want to go home. I want my mommy. Please mister, I'll be good, let me go home. I don't like being on the floor. It hurts. I have to go to the bathroom."

Victor listened to the nonstop pleading from the child.

"I have to go to the bathroom now or I'm going to wet my pants. Please let me go to the bathroom. It hurts."

Victor thought about taking her to the bathroom over at the Pemex, but decided against it. The more time he was there, the more exposed he was to something happening beyond his control. Over the years, he always maintained control of an operation, avoiding letting the circumstances dictate his actions. On more than one occasion, he'd abandoned an operation when circumstances or events escalated beyond his control. Now a little ten-year-old girl was dictating his next move. Remembering a dirt road leading off to the mountains in the east, five miles back, he started the engine and turned around.

"Sit tight. I'm going to find a place where you can go to the bathroom."

# 4:15 PM
# Dulles International Airport
# Washington, D.C.

The jolt of the landing, along with the reverse thrusters being deployed, pulled Rebecca out of her sleep. She looked around the crowded cabin and then at her watch. 1:15 PM. She made a mental note about the three-hour time difference. It felt good to stretch with two torso twists. Her right hand shifted to her Sig pistol that'd dug into her side while she'd slept. Yawning, she shook her arms, getting some circulation going. Customary on flights, the airlines had a mandate to put any armed federal law enforcement officers in an aisle seat. Rebecca stretched her legs, happy to have the aisle seat. Ten minutes later, the plane lurched to a stop at the walkway. People standing up along with the sound and reverberation of the overhead bin doors being opened filled Rebecca's ears.

Pulling her phone out of her jacket, she thought about calling Maria. The school day in Tucson wouldn't be over for another two hours, but Rebecca couldn't resist the urge to call. Looking down the aisle and with the noise level high inside the airplane, she decided against it. She knew that unless something had happened, Maria would have nothing to tell her about Kimyung. People began moving forward with the sound of the cabin door opening. She eased the phone back into her pocket. Besides, she'd rather hear her sweet little girl's voice than talk with Maria. *I'll call her in a couple of hours.*

It felt good to stand up. She reached into the opened overhead, grabbing her carry-on luggage. Carefully guiding it to the airplane's floor in front of her feet she pulled up on the carry handle with her left hand. Reaching over, Rebecca grabbed the magazine she'd been reading, unzipped her bag and put it in. As she did so, the sweater she was wearing rode up, exposing the pistol on her side.

"Mommy, Mommy, that woman has a gun. She has a gun," a short little girl standing in the aisle screeched, grabbing her mother's right leg.

Pulling her sweater back down, she smiled at the girl and then the mother.

"It's ok, honey. I'm law enforcement," Rebecca said, looking at the two of them and the other people around. She pulled out her wallet and held it up, displaying her FBI badge for everyone to see. She knew in these times some people suffer from an irrational fear of firearms, causing them to overreact at the sight of a firearm. *Hoplophobia.* The mother calmed her child, removing the grip the girl had on her leg.

"I'm sorry for my daughter making a scene. She's a police officer. It's ok, honey," the mother said with her arm around her daughter.

"I understand. It scared her. What's your name?" Rebecca asked, bending over to eye level with the girl.

"Melody."

"That's a pretty name. How old are you?"

"I'm eight," the girl said, starting to relax and looking up at her mother and then back at Rebecca. Her mother nodded her head in approval.

"What grade in school are you?"

"Second grade."

"I have a daughter just like you, but she's nine years old and in fourth grade. Her name is Kimyung. Your pretty black hair makes me think about her," Rebecca said, feeling people milling around behind her.

"I'm so glad to know we were well guarded while traveling. I appreciate what you and all law enforcement do for our country. Be safe out there," the mother said to Rebecca.

"Thank you very much. It means a lot to me and others to know we have the publics support. Have a good day," Rebecca said, waving to the girl and grabbing the handle on her luggage as she began pushing it down the narrow aisle. She smiled, thinking about Kimyung and what she was doing. *I sure miss her.* She stepped off the breezeway and headed down the concourse. Walking past a Starbucks, then a Wendy's, she thought about all the different ways you could feed your belly. At the end of the long concourse, she turned right at the sign pointing to ground transportation. After riding up an escalator and through the big revolving door, she stepped out into the crisp, cool spring air of Washington, D.C. She winced, hearing the cacophony of people talking and walking, horns honking and buses coming and going, along with hundreds of other vehicles. The smell of exhaust and cigarette smoke met her nose. Stopping at the curb at the crosswalk, she looked at her watch. She made her way to a taxi stand. As protocol dictated, she was required to call her supervisor and let him know she'd arrived. *Time to check in with my fearless leader.* Smiling, she hit the send button, but nothing happened. *What the fuck?* Rebecca tried it two more times before remembering she'd failed to take her phone off of airplane mode. She pressed her settings, revealing the airplane icon.

"Where would you like to go, ma'am?"

She paused with her finger about to press the airplane icon, looking at the cab driver hollering out the passenger door window. *Fuck Nottingham. I'll call him when I get to my room. He can wait. I'm going to call my daughter first.*

"Grand Hyatt near JEH," she said, pulling her carry on behind her and smiling, knowing Nottingham had probably already tried to reach her. Once seated, she turned off airplane mode. Instantly, messages telling her she had multiple voicemails and texts lit up the phone.

# 12:37 PM
# Twelve Miles North of the Pemex Station

Victor pulled over to the right after driving five minutes on the dirt road leading east to the distant mountains. He waited to open the door until the cloud of dust trailing behind drifted past.

"I've got to go to the bathroom. Please let me go to the bathroom," Kimyung said, crying.

"Ok, ok," Victor said, opening his door looking back in the direction they came from and then the other way down the road. Both sides of the road gave way to stands of mesquite and Palo Verde trees with greasewood and prickly pear cactus filling in the spaces in between. Seeing no sign of anyone on the road in either direction, he opened the left rear door, reached in and lifted Kimyung off the floor and out onto the road.

"It's ok. Go ahead, over there. Do you have to go number one or two?"

"Number one."

"Ok, go. Wait a second," Victor said, grabbing some tissue from the front seat and handing it to her. He pointed to the drainage ditch running parallel to the road.

"I can't."

"Why can't you?"

"Because," she said, whimpering and squirming back and forth holding her taped hands up to him.

"Oh, ok. I'll take the tape off as long as you promise not to run away. Promise?" Victor said, looking the girl in the eyes.

"Ok, please, I've got to pee."

Victor pulled a knife out from his left pocket, flicked his wrist, opening the blade, and lifted the girl's hands up carefully with the blade between her wrists. With one quick motion, he sliced through the tape, moving the blade away from her. She pulled her arms apart and ran to the ditch with the tape still stuck on her wrists. Stopping, she lifted under her skirt to take her panties off and stopped.

"Don't look," she hollered at Victor.

Victor reached into the car through his open door, grabbing the pack of cigarettes on the seat. Holding the pack in his right hand he tapped the open end against his left hand and grabbed one, putting it to his mouth. Reaching into his pocket, he pulled out his thirty-four-year-old Zippo, giving it a flick. He'd loved the sound of the metallic clink of the top of the lighter exposing the business part. With his right hand he flicked the top open, hit the striker on the flint and took a drag through his cigarette from the open flame. With one hand, he closed the worn lighter and put it back in his pocket. The smell of burnt lighter fluid reached his nostrils. He took a deep drag on the lit cigarette, inhaling the acrid smoke deep into his lungs, and leaned against the car. Exhaling, he blew two large smoke rings.

"Are you done?" Victor called to the girl without turning around.

"No, don't look."

"Don't worry, I won't. Just do what you need to do. Don't worry, I won't look."

Victor looked around at the stark beauty and ruggedness of the surrounding desert. After three more draws on his smoke, he called out to Kimyung.

"Ok, are you done?" Victor said, waiting for a reply.

"Hey, are you done? I'm going to turn around. Are you done?" Victor turned to his left, where Kimyung had been. *Son of a bitch.*

"Kimyung, hey! Where are you? Kimyung?" he hollered. He ran across the drainage ditch and through the edge of the tree line.

"KIMYUNG. Fuck," he mumbled to himself. She was his package and, in all his years, he'd never lost one. He squatted down to see if he could see a pair of little legs moving around. One hundred yards off, he glimpsed something pink and moving. He quietly jogged in that direction. Kimyung, seeing him coming, ran between a mesquite tree and creosote bush, scraping her arm on a branch, ripping her sleeve and scratching her left shoulder. She grabbed her arm slowing her down enough for Victor to come around from the opposite direction grabbing her other arm.

"Let me go! My mother is going to beat you up. You're a bad man," Kimyung said, trying to pull her thin little arms away from his grip.

"It's too dangerous out here for you. You'll be seeing your mother soon. Come on, let's go back to the car. I'll see if I've a band-aid for your arm."

"No, I don't want to go, leave me alone," she screamed, resisting him as much as possible.

After Victor dragged her ten feet, with her digging her heels into the dirt, he picked her up and threw her over his left shoulder. Picking up his pace, he walked back to the car with her pounding on his back all the way.

"I hate to do this to you, kid, but it's for your own good," Victor said, grabbing the duct tape sitting on the right front seat and taping her wrists.

"That's too tight," Kimyung said.

"It's fine. Ok, now don't move. I'm going to get a band-aid for your arm," he said, keeping his eye on her as he opened the hatchback and reached into the emergency first aid kit he carried with him. Kimyung, no longer crying, looked down at the ground, kicking at little pebbles in the dirt. After cleaning up the scrape and putting the bandage on her arm, he stepped back.

"Ok, your arm's only got a little scape. It'll be fine. Come on, we've got to go. You can ride up front with me," he said, opening the right front door for her. He reached in, putting the seat belt on her.

"Are you thirsty?"

"Yes."

Victor grabbed the water bottle, screwed the top off and handed it to her. Kimyung grabbed it with both of her taped hands and held it up to her mouth.

"Why don't you hang on to it? Here's the lid. Screw it back on when you're done."

Looking down the road to the east, in the far distance, a vehicle of some sorts was heading in their direction. He didn't want to deal with anyone. Besides, he knew he was in Magdalena cartel territory. It wasn't a good idea to be this far down a secluded road in the Mexican state of Sonora. He moved around to the driver's door, keeping his eyes on the approaching vehicle speeding towards them. It appeared to be a pickup truck with people standing inside the bed. He pulled the driver's door closed, not waiting to put on his seat belt, started the car, turned his wheels hard left and began turning around. The narrow dirt road wasn't wide enough for Victor to negotiate the turn without having to stop, reverse and then proceed. As soon as he'd stopped and put the car into reverse, red and blue lights lit up on top of the approaching truck. *Fuck. Federales.*

"Listen, say nothing. Let me do all the talking," Victor said, knowing he didn't have time to drug her again and hide her. He backed up, put the car in drive and pushed the gas pedal to the floor. The muffled sound of a M-60 machine gun followed three seconds down the road, with rounds hitting just to the left of them. He slammed on the brakes, sliding to a stop. *Keep your cool.*

A cloud of light orange dust raced forward, over his car, as the tan camouflaged pickup slid to a stop behind them. In the rearview mirror, he could see a man in uniform standing behind the M-60 mounted in the bed, pointed at them. Two more uniformed men with HK91 rifles came from behind, moving down both sides of the truck with their rifles up to their shoulders. The driver stayed behind the wheel while the uniformed man in the passenger seat opened the door, got out and sauntered towards the right side of the car. By the time the man in the cab got out of the pickup, the other two with rifles were flanking both sides of the car with barrels pointed at him. Victor lowered the driver and front passenger door windows.

"Hola, amigo. ¿Qué pasa? What are you doing out here?" said the man who'd walked over from the cab, and was now leaning into the open window, resting his left forearm on the door frame, not taking his eyes off of Victor.

"She had to go to the bathroom," Victor said, pointing back to Kimyung. Victor knew by their uniforms that they were Mexican Federales. It was obvious the man leaning on the passenger door was in charge. Looking at the bars on his shoulders, Victor knew he was an officer.

"Uh huh," the man said, looking at Kimyung.

"Señor, why does this little girl have tape around her wrists? What are you doing with her? What's your name?" the officer said, looking at her.

"Kimyung," she said, shifting in her seat. "Are you a policeman?"

"I am. What are you doing with this man? Has he been hurting you?"

"I don't know why I'm with him. I was at school this morning and now I'm here. I miss my mommy. Can you help me?" Kimyung said, reaching up with her taped wrists wiping away the tears streaking down her dirt covered face.

The man stepped back, opening the passenger door, undid her seat belt and helped her out of the car. He held her wrists up and carefully removed the duct tape.

She stepped forward and wrapped her arms around him, shaking. "I want to go home."

"It's ok. Don't worry. Where do you live?"

"Tucson. My mommy works for the FBI, and she's going to arrest and punish this mean man."

Victor, hearing the words coming through the window, pressed his right elbow against his Glock, sitting in its holster. He eyed the officer and the two men behind him on the right and left who'd lowered their rifles. He knew he had the speed and skill and had nothing to lose at this point. On one prior occasion, he had gotten himself into a compromised position like this. He made it out, leaving five dead bodies in his wake. He was prepared to do the same now. *With luck, I'm going to get out of here and deliver my package.*

"Keep your hands on the wheel, señor. I'll be back," the man said, turning and motioning Kimyung to the back of the truck. The officer nodded his head at his two men and they raised their rifles back up on their shoulders, trained on Victor.

Victor watched them in the rearview mirror. There was now more distance than he'd wanted; plus, he wanted to minimize the risk of the girl getting caught in the gunfire. If he was told to get out of the car, he'd shoot the Federale closest to him, then the man behind the M-60, the rifleman to his left, the driver and the officer. He decided on the officer last because he only had a handgun, which was in a secured holster. If he wasn't told to get out of the car, he'd open the door, dropping to the ground. He'd shoot the closet man, the machine gunner, then, laying on the ground, he'd shoot the young man on the other side of the car in the ankle, do the same with the officer, get up moving to finish the driver, and leave the officer and the other rifleman for last. He knew it was a lot of "ifs," but what the hell. For Victor, it was a "what the fuck" kind of moment... At least he had a shot at getting out of there alive and with his package.

Now out of view of the men, he raised his right hand up under his shirt, wrapping his fingers around the pistol grip. The officer stepped away from the passenger door and was talking on a cell phone. After a minute, the officer made his way back to the front passenger door window. Victor secured his hand and fingers on the grip of the Glock 21.

"Señor, you're free to go. The girl stays with us," the officer said, standing back three paces and bending down to look at Victor.

"I'm free to go? What about the girl?"

"I just said. She'll stay with us... We'll take care of her. Don't worry about it, señor. If you don't like this arrangement, my men can leave you here, slumped over the steering wheel with a bullet in your head. Huh? What do you think about that, gringo?"

Victor moved his right hand down to the seat, not wanting to give any hint he was armed. He looked in the side-view mirror and the rearview mirror. Both of the young Federales had their rifles up and trained at his head. He looked back at the officer.

"How about a little mordida? You let me go with the girl? What do you say?" Victor said, looking back at the officer.

"No, señor. I think it's best you move along," the officer said in a more threatening tone.

"Ok. What are you going to do with the girl?"

"Don't worry about it. We'll take good care of her," the captain said.

"I'm leaving, but there's something in the trunk for you to pass on to a guy named Mario Quintana. He works for Juan Ortiz. I don't want something happening to the girl because I didn't pass this along. I need to get it out of the trunk," Victor said, eyeing the captain.

"What is it?"

"Money," Victor said, hoping the name of the cartel head would get the officer's attention.

"Give my man the key to the trunk and stay where you're at. He'll get it," said the officer, nodding his head to his man on Victor's side of the car. After retrieving a blue athletic bag, the young Federale returned the keys to Victor.

"So, I was thinking. Why…"

"Stop talking, Gringo. I suggest you leave now or stay with a bullet in your head."

One of Victor's favorite songs by Kenny Rogers drummed through his head. *You got to know when to hold them, know when to fold them…* Victor knew it was time to get out of Dodge and get out now. He relaxed, taking in a deep breath, and started the car.

"Adiós, amigo," Victor said, looking at the officer, putting it into gear.

# Inbound to the Wilford Hotel
# Washington, D.C.

"Maria, what's going on? Where's Kimyung?" Rebecca said, gripping the phone, her throat going dry. After turning on her phone, she'd listened to the twelve messages left by the school and Maria.

"She's... I don't know, they called Child Protective Services," Maria said.

"What do you mean they called CPS? Why haven't they called the police? When did they notice she was missing? Did they search all over the school?" Rebecca listened as Maria explained the incident during recess and that it wasn't until after that that Kimyung's teacher discovered her missing.

"I asked them the same question about calling the police. I guess it's their protocol. And yes, they searched the school and the grounds multiple times... I'm sorry," Maria said. Rebecca looked at her watch.

"I'm going to call the school. We will not wait for them to call the police. I want you to call the police, tell them what happened and identify who I am... give them my number. I'll follow up. Oh God, Maria, I'm scared... Where's my little girl?" Rebecca said, wiping the tears streaming down her face. She breathed deep, pushing back an urge to vomit.

"I'll call you back, Maire. Call the cops, call them now," She said, hitting the end button then scrolling through the phone directory for the number to Kimyung's school.

"This is Rebecca Harper, Kimyung's mother. I want to speak with Mrs. Ryan."

"Hi Ms. Harper, I'm afraid we can't interrupt Mrs. Ryan. She's teaching right now. Let me get our school principal, Mr. Abernathy, on the line for you," the woman said sounding like she was passing a hot potato to someone. Rebecca, wiping her tears, gathered herself, gritted her teeth. *Oh God, please help.* She looked up, seeing the cab driver looking at her in the rearview mirror. He glanced away. Another wave of nausea swept over her. *Breathe, Harper. Stay calm. Just get the facts and what's being done about it.* She forced a deep breath.

"This is Mr. Abernathy. Is this Ms. Harper?" Rebecca heard him say, as if this was a normal call.

"Yes, this is FBI Special Agent Harper, Kimyung's Harper's mother. I just learned my daughter's missing. Have you located her?" she said in a stern and authoritative voice.

"No, we haven't. I'm so sorry. We've been trying to reach you."

"I just got off an airplane. I'm in Washington, D.C. Have you called the police?"

"No, we haven't heard from CPS yet and we have to wait before we call in the police. It's the district's policy. Are you sure she's not with a friend or at a relative's house? That's usually the case. Was she upset; do you think she may have run away? I mean, we've had it happen in the past."

Rebecca clenched her teeth, wanting to scream.

"No, Kimyung wouldn't leave school and NO, there'd be no reason for her to run away. She'd never do that. Look, Mr. Abernathy, the district's policy makes no sense to me and I don't care what it is. I want you to call the police now, not later. Please call them now."

"I'm afraid I can't. It's the district's policy. I'll get in trouble for violating it."

Rebecca ran her hand through her hair. Bureaucrats, she detested them. They only do something that's in their best interest, only actions that secure their position. She could tell by the tone of the principal's voice that he would not violate the district's sacred policy.

"We're here, ma'am," the cab driver said as the right rear door opened and a hotel bellman grabbed Rebecca's carry-on.

"Ok, Mr. Abernathy. Don't worry about it. I'll take care of it. I wouldn't want you to get in trouble by doing the right thing. We're only talking about my child here." Rebecca held the phone away from her ear and looked at the bellman. "Give me a moment," she said, putting the phone back to her ear. "Ok, Mr. Abernathy, you keep yourself out of trouble and I expect you to call me if you hear anything."

"I will. I—" the principal started, but Rebecca had already hung up.

"Welcome to the Wilford Hotel, ma'am. How long will you be staying with us?" the bellman asked as Rebecca got out of the car after paying the driver.

"What? Oh, I'm not sure how long I'll be here. I've got it," Rebecca said, reaching out to take the carry-on from the bellman. *Breathe, ok think. Oh my God, what happened to her? Where is she? How could the school not be calling the police?*

She pushed her way through the revolving door into the main lobby and stood there, stunned by the turn of events. Everything seemed to be in slow motion. Walking through the lobby, she made her way to a bench and sat down, putting her head in her hands crying. The only time she'd ever felt this kind of sorrow was when, as a young teenage girl, she'd learned her father had been killed. But this loss and fear was different. This had to do with her daughter. The more she processed it, the more questions came up. Sitting upright and wiping her eyes and face with her hands, she reached into her purse and pulled out her phone.

"Harper here."

"Are you here? I've left messages for you…"

"Yes, I'm here at the Wilford. I need help. My daughter is missing from her school. I just talked with the nanny. She came up missing around 10:45 this morning, Arizona time. I'm not staying, I'm going to catch the first flight I can back to Tucson. I…"

"Are you sure she's missing? She didn't go over to a friend's house or something? You're only talking a few hours here. I'm sure there's a good explanation of where she is," Nottingham said, interrupting Rebecca.

"No, she wouldn't just take off. She's not like that. Someone has had to have taken her. There's no way she would have just walked away from school."

"Have they checked everywhere? Tell me what happened?"

"As far as I know, they've checked everywhere. The school's handling of this is a joke. They haven't even called the police yet, and it's been over four hours." Rebecca explained the school's story about the explosion at recess, moving the kids into the multi-purpose room and the discovery of her missing.

"You catching a flight and heading back right now will do nothing. I understand you're upset and worried. I'd be too, but kids always have a way of showing up. Go check into your room and then find what flights are available back to Tucson. It's getting late, you may have a hard time finding one for tonight."

"Look, the recess thing… the explosion… What if that was a diversion for someone to grab her off of the playground? The principal at the school told me Kimyung's friends said she was at the south end of the schoolyard when it happened. Maybe someone was on the sidewalk next to the schoolyard. Maybe the explosion was a distraction to give someone just enough time to grab her. Maybe there was a car right there. Maybe…"

"Slow down, Rebecca. Breathe. Let's look at this one piece at a time. Are you saying your daughter was targeted?"

"I don't know… maybe. Maybe some pedophile just wanted to grab a little girl. Maybe someone has a thing for young Asian girls. Hell, I don't know. I just know she's missing. I want you to activate the missing children's unit in Tucson. Let's get an

Amber Alert going and quickly," Rebecca said, fighting back another wave of fear and nausea wiping at her eyes.

"Ok, there's a lot of 'what ifs' right now. We can't do anything until the local PD down there contacts us. You know we don't have control over the Amber Alert system, that's the Department of Public Safety's jurisdiction. And if we did, there are certain procedures that have to be followed before they can activate it. Let me help you with this, get your room, check on flights. In the meantime, I'll have one of your agents contact the Tucson Police Department and see if we can get them involved sooner than later. Let's talk in an hour. Keep me posted if you hear anything before then. We're going to find her, Rebecca!"

"Ok, I'll check in and then find out what flights are available. Thank you, Ben," Rebecca said, feeling relieved to have Nottingham step in to help her. Here, it was good to have someone taking charge and telling her what to do. Getting up from the bench seat, she put her phone back in her pocket, grabbed the handle to the carry-on and went over to the check-in desk. Walking there she thought about the critical forty-eight-hour window of time in the recovery of missing persons. It'd been almost twenty-four hours since her daughter went missing and, so far, no clues.

# 1:18 PM
# Captain Sanchez

"Mario, we've got the girl. We'll be heading your way. Should see you in about twenty minutes," Captain Sanchez said, watching the dust cloud of Victor's car heading back to the main highway. He looked back at the pickup, seeing Kimyung sitting in the front seat, straining to see over the dash. He hated delivering her to Mario. It wasn't Mario he was concerned about; it was their mutual boss's penchant for young girls. Hopefully, this wouldn't be the case for this little girl and she'd stay in the care of Mario and his wife. He was skeptical, though. He looked down the road again toward the main highway and turned, walking back to the pickup.

"You've got the girl? I don't understand," Mario said. The captain explained what'd happened and also that he had money for him and Juan.

The night before, the Captain and his men were ordered by Juan Ortiz to drive to the Pemex station and be nearby when the girl was handed over to Mario. That night, it'd rained heavily and the desert road they were travelling had intersecting washes to be crossed but deep running water made them impassable. Because of this, they were forced to wait it out before crossing the receding water. It was pure chance that he and his men came upon Victor and the girl. Had it not been for the rain, they would have been at the Pemex station waiting for the handoff. The Captain worried for the girl. Juan Ortiz was a psychopathic murderer and a pedophile. His only hope for the girl was that her stay with Mario would be short and she'd be returned to the

United States before Juan's impulses dictated a different outcome for her.

"Mount up, hombres," the captain called out to his men. He watched as the two young men who'd held their rifles on the gringo climbed into the pickup bed. Walking over to the passenger side door, he opened it, looking at the girl.

"Are you taking me home?" Kimyung asked.

"Not yet. I'm taking you to a nice man who's going to let you stay with him and his family. They're going to take good care of you until we can get you home. They're nice people and have children around your age. ¿Hablas español?

"Sí, señor. Me llamo es Kimyung. Soy nuevo anos."

The captain smiled, listening to Kimyung's flawless Spanish.

"I'm impressed, señorita. Where did you learn how to speak Spanish?" the captain said in Spanish.

"My nanny taught me. She only talks to me in Spanish and I only talk to her that way. It's fun. My mommy has a tutor for me so I can learn Mandarin, too," Kimyung said, sitting up and smiling at the captain.

"Are your parents Chinese?"

"Yes, but my mother adopted me from China when I was six months old. She says it's important that I know my native language and know my roots and the culture I'm from."

"Your mother. Well, what about your father?" the captain said, curious why the girl had mentioned nothing about her dad.

"She's not married. She's says she hasn't got time to put up with the nonsense of a man. She said she's never found one that rocked her boat. I always wonder about that because we don't have a boat."

"I don't think that's what she meant, when she talked about a man rocking her boat," the captain said smiling at Kimyung. *Should I explain to her, I'm sure her mother meant she'd never fallen in love with a man… nah?* "It sounds like your mother is lucky to have you as her daughter. Does she work or does she take care of you all the time?" the captain asked.

"She works. She catches bad people."

"She catches bad people? Do you mean she's a police officer?"

"No, she works for the FBI. She's what they call a special agent. She's the boss of all the other agents in her office."

"An FBI agent? What's her name?"

"My mommy's name is Special Agent Rebecca Harper."

"That's something. I'm sure she's worried about you. I'll call her and let her know you're ok. What's her number?" He pulled out a pen and a small flip pad from his righthand shirt pocket and handed it to Kimyung. "Write her phone number down for me," he said to Kimyung, knowing he wouldn't be calling her. He took his cap off and ran his hand through his hair

127

and put it back on. He hated lying to the girl, but he wanted to give her a little hope, so maybe she'd feel better.

Kimyung wrote Rebecca's number down and handed it back to the captain. He looked at it and put it the notepad back into his pocket. *Special Agent Rebecca Harper. Harper… Harper… Where have I heard that name before? Damn, that sounds awfully familiar. I know that name.*

He got into the truck and looked back at his men to make sure they were secured inside the bed.

"Ok, head to the highway and turn left when we get there. We're going to the Pemex just down the road," he said, looking ahead then down at Kimyung, patting her on the head.

"Everything's going to be ok, Kimyung. You'll see," he said, looking back down the road. He was no longer smiling.

# 1:23 PM

It pissed him off that he'd lost control of his mission. Victor wasn't angry at the captain and his men for pointing guns at him. He understood. Being outmanned and outgunned is just that… being outmanned and outgunned. He appreciated moments like this, where having to think or ponder on a decision isn't an option. Those moments in life when everything is clear—no grey, just black or white… simple pure choice. To choose life over death sometimes requires removing your emotions from the decision-making process. Like craving ice cream, but there's only two flavors to choose from: chocolate or vanilla. Choose, motherfucker. With the barrel of a gun pointed at your head, it's a simple choice… At least, in that moment it was.

He banged his fist against the steering wheel. How could he allow himself to feel any kind of compassion for the young girl's crying and need to pee? Stupid. He could have just pulled into the Pemex, handed the girl over to the guy in the Escalade, and let him deal with her. Why should he care or have any kind of understanding about the girl's suffering? He'd never had children of his own, or at least none that he knew of, in all his globetrotting around the world. Besides, he was uncomfortable being around children and wanted none of his own. He was famous for leaving loving relationships the moment he felt vulnerable. But with this young girl, it was different. He felt bad about kidnapping her and taking her into Mexico. He wondered what would happen to her. The vibrating of his phone interrupted his thoughts.

"Victor here. Talk to me."

"Victor, it's me, Hector. I'm just checking in. When do you think you're going to take care of things for me?" Congressman Hector Granada asked.

"It's done, man. I'm in Mexico, heading back across the line."

"Jesus, man. I didn't think you were going to do it so soon. So, Mario has the girl now?"

"No."

"What do you mean, 'no?' The girl's still with you?"

"No. Ran into a problem. I didn't meet Mario and give her to him. I ran into some Mexican Federales and they got her. I didn't have a choice. Sorry."

"Oh my God. Mexican Federales? What the fuck? What are they going to do with her? Where were they taking her?"

"I don't have an answer to either of your questions. Look. It was a bullet in my head or turn her over to them. It was an easy decision. Either way, they were going to take the girl. I'm sorry, Hector. In my business, sometimes things don't always work out the way they're planned."

"What if they bring her back up here and turn her over to U.S. Customs? I'm screwed if that happens. Oh my God. This is not good."

"Calm down, congressman. I'm sure it'll be ok. Why don't you call your buddy, Mario? I'll be in touch," Victor said, ending the call. As far as he was concerned, Congressman Hector

Granada was a worthless piece of shit, but he had promised to turn her over to Mario. He pushed aside the notion of somehow helping the young girl, out of feeling bad for her. *No… I gave my word. It's as simple as that, nothing more. She's just a little girl.* Slowing down, he waited for the oncoming car to pass before he made a U-turn. Pulling his phone out, he hit the green call icon.

# 1:38 PM
# Pemex Station

The tan camouflaged Chevrolet pickup approached from the north. Mario rolled up his window, avoiding the dust enveloping his Escalade. He waited until Captain Sanchez opened his door before he got out to greet him. Standing at the back end of his Escalade he looked at the captain and then at Kimyung, sitting inside the captain's pickup.

"Hola, captain. ¿Cómo estás?" Mario said, reaching out to shake the captain's hand. He liked the captain and suspected he, too, had a disdain for his cousin, Juan Ortiz. It was more of a gut feeling than anything else. They'd never talked about it. Captain Sanchez also had a wife and children and, like Mario, would do anything to protect them from Juan Ortiz. It was a straightforward choice; either comply with Juan's demands, or risk having your wife tortured, raped and killed in front of your children. After that, if you had daughters of any age, they'd rape them, make them bleed, didn't matter. Once they'd had their fun, they'd kill your entire family and then tear you apart... one piece at a time.

"I'm good, Mario. Ok, here she is. I understand she'll be staying with you and your family for a few days before returning to the U.S.," the captain said, looking down, shaking his head and looking back toward Kimyung.

"Yes. The other day, I got a call from my wife's uncle, Hector Granada, asking me if I could do this. I called Juan first to get his approval before I said yes. You know how he is. So yes, she'll be staying with us in Hermosillo at our house. When she's ready to go back, Juan said you and your men would take her back up to the line."

"Sí, that's what he told me to do. Did your wife's uncle say how long you're to keep her?"

"He said just a few days. I'm not comfortable with this, but I agreed to it. He's paying me and I can always use the money. Besides, if I said no, I didn't want him calling Juan. I'm sure he would have. He thinks Juan owes him because of the money he gave him for the missiles."

"I understand. Smart on your part to include Juan. Let me guess, he demanded Granada pay him more money than you," said Captain Sanchez, laughing.

"You know him well. I don't like this. She's got to be scared to death," Mario said, looking at Kimyung, who was now sitting on her knees on the seat looking at both of them.

"She is. I feel bad for her. Do you know why he had her kidnapped and brought here? It is kind of strange. Did you know her mother is an FBI agent?"

"What? No, he didn't tell me the mother is an FBI agent, just why he had the girl kidnapped. Something about her mother implicating him in what we did two months ago with the Stingers. Hey, he's a drunk piece of crap. Anyway, it is what it is… Fuck! Hopefully, you can take her back to the U.S. soon. Juan's expecting a call from me once I've got the girl."

"I know all too well how he is. She seems like a very sweet girl. Very smart. Be careful what you say around her. I asked her

133

something, and she answered in Spanish, smart little girl. She also told me her mother is having her learn Chinese. I guess that's where she's from. She told me she was adopted. Did Juan say anything about taking her to him?" Captain Sanchez asked.

"No, he didn't. I hope he doesn't; I promised Granada she'd be safe."

"Look, between you and me... we both know how he is. If Juan tells you to bring her to his hacienda, let me know. I'll do my best to look after her."

"I will. Thanks, Captain," Mario said, feeling a bond beginning to grow between the two of them. Neither of the two men were bad, in their core they were good men with the dark cloud of Juan Ortiz hanging over them.

"Kimyung, this is Mario. This is the man I told you about that you'll be staying with. He and his family will take good care of you," the captain said, talking to her through his open door, pointing at Mario.

"But I want to stay with you. Please take me home. I want my mother. I don't want to go with this man," Kimyung said with tears welling up in her eyes.

"I can't take you back right now. I promise I will... soon. It's ok. He's a good man. You'll like his wife and their children. Come on, we got to go," the captain said, reaching in and gently grabbing Kimyung's hand, pulling her towards him.

"I don't want to go," she said, wiping tears from her face.

"It's ok. You're going to like my family. My kids are going to like you and you're going to like them and their mother," Mario said, looking at the captain and back at Kimyung.

"That's a good girl," the captain said, walking her to the big Escalade and opening the door to let her into the back seat. Mario watched as the captain leaned over and adjusted her seat belt.

"I'll see you soon, Kimyung," the captain said, closing the door.

"Thanks, captain. Hey, I meant to ask you—what did you do with the gringo?"

"I gave him a choice to leave or stay with a bullet in his head. He left," the captain said, smiling. The two men laughed.

"Smart gringo. Did he pee his pants?" Mario asked.

"He should have. I gotta tell you, Mario… that gringo… there's something about him. I think maybe I should have put a bullet in him," the captain said, tightening his jaw.

"Why do you say that?"

"He was too calm and collected. I think maybe he's a former special forces guy or something. I don't know… very fit looking and cool. Even though he displayed no emotions, I could tell he wasn't happy with us taking the girl. You know, you see a dog chewing on a bone and you just know not to take it from him because you might get bit."

"Sounds like you should have put a bullet in his head. I'm sure he's on his way back to the U.S. Hey, we'll take good care of the girl, that I promise," Mario said, looking at the captain and then at Kimyung.

"Yeah, I'm sure he's on his way back, too," the captain said, looking north up the road.

"Ok, Bueno, captain. Thank you for bringing her. I'll see you soon, when you take her back to the line," Mario said, noticing the look of concern on the captain's face as he spoke about the gringo.

"Yes, let's hope you'll see me soon so we can get her back to her mother. She's a nice young lady. Don't want anything bad happening to her. I don't like this business. Don't like it at all. Hey, here's the money the gringo gave me to give to you. I guess yours and Juan's is in there," the captain said, motioning to one of his men to bring the blue duck cloth bag to him.

"Remember what I said about calling me if Juan wants her to come to his hacienda."

"I promise you I will," Mario said. The two men shook hands, and he got into the Escalade, started it up and drove to the highway, heading south to Hermosillo. Five minutes down the road, Mario heard a small voice from the back say, "I'm hungry."

In the rearview, the Pemex station got smaller. Mario didn't notice the red car trailing a quarter mile behind him… nor did the captain notice when it drove past the Pemex two minutes after Mario left with the girl.

# 3:34 PM
# Food Court, Southwest Regional Mall

Doug Redman and his wife Liz had been to the matinee at the movie theater inside the Southwest Regional Mall. The same place, two years prior, had been the scene of a vicious terrorist attack. They killed and wounded scores of civilians.

"Memories," Doug said, putting his arm around Liz as they approached the frozen gelato counter. Turning, he thought about Carter Thompson, the friendship they'd formed and the other events they'd survived together since that day.

"Sir, would you like a sample?" asked the girl behind the counter. Doug looked at her. She reminded him of the girl that had been helping his daughter Kellie at the cell phone kiosk. Kim nudged his shoulder.

"Honey, what do you think? Let me try the cherry vanilla and also the salted caramel," Liz said, looking back at the young girl waiting for Doug's response.

"Ok, sure. Dark chocolate, let me have a taste of that," Doug said, Liz's warm hand on his shoulder bringing him back to the present. As he was reaching into his back pocket to get his wallet, his phone buzzed.

"Excuse me, hon. I've got to take this," Doug said, pulling it out and looking at it. He stepped back twenty feet from the counter.

"Alex, how the hell are you doing?"

"I'm good, brother. You know, still limping, but cruising along, riding a desk. You?" Alex said.

"I'm good. Still adjusting to civilian life but hey, you know, a few forays here and there with an assist from you have kept me from being bored. Been enjoying the quiet since that last little ditty we did two months ago. You know how it is," Doug said, scanning the food court area and beyond. Alex, a fellow Delta Force brother, had been badly injured on a mission and forced to retire. For several years, he'd been at the National Security Agency. They'd been on many missions together and shared a deep connection forged on the battlefield.

"Listen, brother. Something's happening. I waited to call you until I could confirm it. Congressman Hector Granada had that FBI's agent's nine-year-old daughter kidnapped."

"What? When did that happen? Wait a minute, are you talking about agent Harper that saved Carter and me?" Doug asked, looking around. Reaching down with his right hand, he felt the grip of the Glock 48 on his hip, concealed under his shirt

"This morning. Some guy named Victor took her to Juan Ortiz's cousin, Mario Quintana."

"Mario Quintana? He's up here? Why the hell would Granada have her kidnapped and then give her to Mario? What the fuck?"

"No, Mario's not here; he's in Hermosillo. This guy Victor snatched her from school and took her down there and is supposed to deliver her to Mario."

138

"Why? I don't get it. What in the world for?"

"I think it has to do with Hector Granada. Harper knows about his involvement with the Stingers and terrorists. Granada is hoping to keep her quiet by threatening her daughter," Alex said.

"Son of a bitch. That fat piece of garbage can't stoop low enough. Does Dax know about this?"

"No, I haven't called him yet. I wanted to talk with you first. He's going to be pissed... killer pissed. I guarantee it. Rebecca Harper is like a daughter to him."

"Yes, she is. Thanks for calling me. We owe her, owe her a lot. Not only did she save our lives, but you know... she's been running cover for us. Any other info you have besides that? Hey, not that I should ask, but I'm going to anyway... how did you get the heads up on this? Somebody's been listening in?" Doug asked, watching his wife look at him, smiling, while licking her frozen gelato cone.

"Fair question. After what went down at the border with the missiles, and since I had a feed on Granada's phone, I thought I'd leave it in place. I've been recording and checking on his conversations. This morning I caught one between Mario Quintana and Victor this morning. It matched up with a conversation between Granada and Victor from the other day. But you know the drill, I can't do anything about it because I'm violating Granada's Fourth Amendment rights... or, I should say, the NSA is. I wanted to make sure it was happening, and it did this morning. This guy Victor, he's good. How the hell do you snatch a kid from a school that's in session, in broad daylight, and no one calls the cops?"

"How do you know no one called the cops?" Doug said, looking at Liz and raising his hand with index finger pointing up She lowered her head down, looking at him, and took another playful lick.

"I set up a little back door to the Tucson Police Department's communication system. Trust me, they haven't been called yet. An Amber Alert hasn't been issued yet. Nothing. I don't understand it.

"Do you know if Rebecca Harper knows her daughter's missing?"

"Don't know. You'd think so, but then again, I've heard no chatter on it. You'd think there'd be some buzz amongst law enforcement, but nothing yet," Alex said.

"This is terrible. I feel bad for her. If she doesn't know already, I can't imagine what's going to go through her head when she finds out. Hey, wait a minute. Besides you, does anyone else know her daughter's on the other side of the line?"

"Probably not. I mean, if it hasn't been reported to the police yet, or even if it has, there's no way anyone knows where her daughter is. I think they're going to figure it out; it's just a question of when," Alex said.

"Someone's going to contact Agent Harper and it won't be Granada. Somebody's going to threaten her daughter, so she backs off, implicating Granada with the Stingers. This is going to be a big problem if the girl's in Mexico. I mean, the FBI handles kidnappings but they can't run down to Mexico. This is bad. Terrible. I think you should let Dax know. Not that he can do anything, but if nothing else for him to be there for Agent Harper," Doug said.

"Ok, I'll call him. I'll keep you posted. Out." Alex said.

"Roger that. Out," Doug said, walking over to Liz, attempting to smile.

"Everything ok, honey? I mean, the kids are at school and it's kind of early. You know, maybe we could run home…" Liz said, licking her gelato again and then her lips.

"Everything's fine, honey. Sorry, old war buddy of mine."

"Did you decide what flavor you'd like, sir?" the young girl behind the counter asked.

"Chocolate, plain cone, then my sexy wife here," Doug said, nudging and looking at Liz.

"Ok, chocolate. Coming right up," the girl said, turning red.

# 8:53 AM
# Surveillance

It's what he'd consider a modest neighborhood… by his interpretation of Mexican standards. The houses, all box-like, were painted white with an occasional pink, turquoise and blue home sprinkled in. All had wrought iron over the windows, wrought iron doors and six-foot wrought iron fencing in the front with sharp spikes at the top of each post. In the back, the houses had tall white painted walls with razor barbed wire running along the top. It reminded him of some parts of Somalia and Afghanistan… siege mentality ruled in this neighborhood. In fact, at least in this part of Hermosillo, every block seemed to have the same security. Fair to say the population of Hermosillo was awake to the possibility of robberies coupled with extreme violence.

He thought about crime-ridden areas of the United States and couldn't remember ever seeing this amount of security around every house. But then again, the United States has the Second Amendment and the people of Mexico did not. The Second Amendment gives the law-abiding citizen in America the advantage of being a potential threat to the bad guys. Woke American Citizens understand the adage; 'When seconds count, the police are only minutes away.'

Putting his binoculars down, Victor rubbed his eyes after watching who he assumed was Mario's wife putting children into a soccer mom van and driving off. From the uniforms the children were wearing, it was obvious they were off to school. The vehicle he'd trailed from the Pemex gas station south of Hermosillo the day before, Mario's Cadillac Escalade, sat idle in the driveway. It'd been a long night for Victor, moving his vehicle to different vantage points three times in an attempt not to draw attention from neighbors. He reminded himself... this is Mexico and not the U.S. People don't call 911 every time they hear a strange noise. In fact, a call to the police in Hermosillo was avoided. The residents didn't trust them... most were afraid of them. Better they handle things themselves and don't say a word.

He awoke to tapping on the driver's door window. Looking up, a welcome and familiar face smiled at him.

"It's about time your ugly ass got here," Victor said, grinning.

"Sorry I couldn't get here sooner. I had to find another set of wheels to drive down here. Fast car, but it stands out. I didn't want to get nailed at the border crossing. You look dead tired, dude. I thought you were coming back as soon as you handed off the girl yesterday. I'm glad you called me," Hal said, looking down the block and around.

"Get in. I'll bring you up to speed and then I'm going to get a room at the Fiesta Americana and catch a few winks. I only slept two hours last night while keeping an eye on things. The girl's in there," Victor said, pointing to Mario's house.

"What the fuck? Wasn't that the plan, for her to be staying with a family here in Hermosillo?" Hal said, grabbing the binoculars.

"Yes, that was the plan, but things changed," Victor said. For the next few minutes, he ran down everything that had happened the day before, including the run in with the Mexican Federales and the captain.

143

"So, your ego took a bruising by you not delivering the girl to your contact down here," Hal said with a wry smile.

"Yeah, ego for sure, but more of a matter of honor for me than anything else. I've never failed to keep my promises when doing a job. Besides, something's bothering me about this whole affair. I don't know, I got to know the kid a little. She's very strong willed, smart and tough as nails. Not shy about saying what's on her mind either..."

"Sounds like you developed a soft spot for the kid. Don't let it cloud your judgement, Victor," Hal said, looking at him.

"Maybe so on the soft spot thing. I've never had to snatch a kid before... She was scared out of her mind when she woke up. You know, calling for her mommy and carrying on about it. Look, she's supposed to be kept down here for two days and then taken back up across the line. I want to make sure that happens. I mean... that she gets back into the U.S. safely. There's lots of child sex trafficking going on. I don't want her ending up being sold to some man or group of men so they can get their sick rocks off. I'm just not going to let that happen."

"Ok, I'm with you, brother. It is pretty bad to be snatching a child right off of their schoolyard. What's the deal anyway? Why her and why now?"

"Her mother is investigating one of America's corrupt politicians. Apparently, he's been involved in some serious criminal activities. I don't know all the details. Anyway, the person who hired me wants to use her daughter as leverage, so the agent keeps her mouth shut about her knowledge of his activities. I think this is some serious shit, Hal, and my gut tells me it's a level of corruption that extends deep into Washington, D.C.," Victor said.

"Holy shit, man. The corrupt politician part doesn't surprise me," Hal said.

"Doesn't surprise me either. But then there's this little girl, Kimyung. I'll be straight up with you. I regret taking the job… Water under the bridge. I'm going to do my best to see she gets returned to her mother… It's the right thing to do. There's no need for her to get hurt because of some dirty politician's greed and lust for power. Fuck him," Victor said, looking down the street, gritting his teeth.

"I understand. You can count on me. Just let me know what you need me to do. We'll get her back across and do what we can to keep her safe. In the meantime, why don't you get some shuteye. I'll monitor things here. Keep your phone close to you. I'll give you a shout if I see they're moving her."

"Thanks, and thanks for helping me. I know you didn't need to. You're a good friend," Victor said, watching Hal get out of his car making his way back to his.

"Don't mention it… That's what friends are for. Now go get some rest. I got this shit covered," Hal said.

# Jade Lounge
# Washington, D.C.

The weather was hovering in the forties with gray overcast skies. Hector Granada, five minutes late for his meeting, was glad to get inside and out of the elements. Congressional staffers, along with a sprinkling of congressmen, dominated the scene. His eyes moved down the row of patrons near Ritz's usual spot and walked in that direction. Hector Granada felt insignificant and unsure of himself around the man. Saul Ritz was well educated with a law degree from Harvard. Hector barely made it out of high school. The senior senator from New York, one of the most powerful men in Washington and deep connections in every quarter that mattered in The Swamp. Because of Saul's arrogance and narcissism, Hector was convinced the senator didn't like Mexican-Americans, especially those from Arizona.

Nearing the back of the bar, he eyed Ritz from behind. There was no mistaking him. He was shorter than Granada, with an irregularly shaped body. Hector thought he looked more like Humpty Dumpty than an actual human. Despite everything he detested about Saul Ritz, he was his lifeline to helping him get out of the mess he'd created for himself. Granada stood behind him, waiting for a pause in the conversation he was having with a woman lobbyist who worked for a big pharmaceutical company.

"Hey, Senator. How's the world treating you?" Granada said, interrupting their conversation with a feigned smiled.

The senator paused and turned to his left, then looked up and down at Hector like he'd just interrupted something important.

"Mary, this is the manner-less Congressman Hector Granada of Arizona. Your district is near Yuma, right? Where the fuck is Yuma anyhow? Sand dunes and Indians… right?" the senator said, lifting his shoulders, laughing, while looking at Mary Hufault. The senator downed his martini and turned, waving his hand to the bartender for another round. Hector looked down, shifting on his feet, clenching his fist.

"No, my district is not near Yuma. It's northwest of Phoenix, Prescott. You're thinking of District 2, in the southern part of the state. Different district, different congressman."

"Yeah, ok, whatever. It's all desert, cactus and rattlesnakes to me. What are you drinking, congressman? A margarita?" Saul Ritz said, glancing a smile at Mary, who looked down into her drink smiling.

Hector looked at the senator sitting on the bar stool and then down at his feet, dangling a foot and a half off the floor, and then at Mary Hufault.

"Whatever you're having is good enough for me. Pleasure to meet you, Mary," Hector said, extending his hand.

"Nice to meet you, too. I bet you'd rather be in Arizona right now than here in this shit cold and miserable D.C. weather. Years ago, my husband and I stayed at the Tanque Verde Guest Ranch on the eastside of Tucson. We met Paul and Linda McCarthy at dinner one evening. It was quite a trip. Love Arizona. Beautiful state and incredible weather… except in the summer from what I hear," Mary Hufault said.

"I'm familiar with the Guest Ranch. It's been in Tucson for as long as I can remember. It's one of the last of the dude ranches in the area," Hector said, grateful for Mary steering the conversation away from Saul's belittling.

"Senator, your table is ready," the hostess said, interrupting the moment and pointing to a two-person table in the back corner.

"Well, gentlemen, I've got to run. It was nice to meet you, Hector. Saul, try to stay out of trouble. I'll catch up with you soon on that item we were discussing," Mary Hufault said, extending her hand to Hector and leaning over to give Saul a hug.

Hector watched the fifty-something, tall, attractive blonde walk toward the front door. *Nice ass... how I'd like to...*

"Here you go, gentlemen," the bartender said, placing two martinis in front of them.

"Congressman," Saul said to Hector, raising his martini waiting for Hector to reciprocate.

"Thank you, Saul. Shall we?" Hector said, lifting his glass toward the waiting hostess. Saul Ritz awkwardly eased himself off of the bar stool, landing on his toes. The two men followed the hostess to the table.

"So, tell me, what the fuck is going on with the FBI agent in Tucson and her daughter? You met with Victor right, worked out a plan like we talked about?" Saul asked, draining the martini glass and catching the eye of the passing waiter.

"Yes, I met with Victor but, as far as I know, he's still in Mexico," Hector said.

"What the fuck do you mean he's still in Mexico. Did he snatch the agent's daughter?"

"We, I mean, yes, Victor did. Yesterday morning."

"Did he call Agent Harper, explaining her options?" Saul asked.

"I don't know if he called her. I haven't talked with him since he crossed the line yesterday."

"Well, did he have the girl with him?"

"Yes, he was going to meet Juan Ortiz's cousin, Mario Quintana, and give him the girl to watch for two days. But he ran into some trouble."

"Trouble? What kind of fucking trouble?" Ritz said, looking Hector in the eye.

"He ran into some Federales and they took the girl, but..."

"Some Federales got the girl? Do you have a clue where she is now?"

"Yes, that's what I wanted to talk with you about. I got a call from Mario. A captain with the Federales took the girl from Victor. Turns out he also works for Juan Ortiz. He knew she was being brought to Mario and his family. What are the odds? Anyway, Mario and his wife have the girl," Hector said.

"Well, why the fuck haven't you spoken with Victor? Isn't he supposed to call the agent and warn her about what'll happen to her daughter if she doesn't keep quiet about what she knows about you, your little slut girlfriend and the missiles? I mean, wasn't that supposed to happen? Didn't that happen?" Saul said, leaning back as the waiter put his third martini on the table.

"I don't know if he's talked with the agent or not. I haven't been able to reach him since we spoke yesterday. He was supposed to call me last night after he got back into the country. Jesus fucking Christ, this is fucked up. I don't know what to do.

What do you think I should do?" Hector said, fidgeting with the salt shaker and looking around.

"Ok, toughen up. The important thing is you get a muzzle on that agent or we're all fucked. Somebody's got to call her. Second, after she's agreed to keep quiet, get the daughter back to her right away. Nothing can happen to that little girl. Do you hear me?"

"I hear you. I just hope nothing has happened to Victor."

"You're worried about Victor? You better hope to God nothing's happened to that little girl. I've never known him to not call in when he's on a job. Go outside and call him right now. No wait, order first, then go call him. I'm fucking hungry," Saul said.

"Ok," Hector said, watching their waiter walk towards their table.

After ordering his dinner, Hector got up and made his way outside, bracing himself for the cold. Stepping around the corner of the restaurant to get out of the wind, he hit the send button. After four rings Victor answered.

"Victor?" Granada said.

"Who wants to know?" Victor said.

"Victor, it's Granada. What's going on? Are you back? Did you call her mother? Did you…"

"Slow down, amigo. Hey, I told you—don't use my name or yours or anyone else's on the phone. You never know who could be listening. No, I'm not back across the line yet and, no, I haven't talked to her mother yet. I tried yesterday, but all I got was voicemail. Been a problem getting a signal… since you got through it seems it's working ok now. I'll call her in a little while."

"I spoke with Mario and I know about the captain taking the girl. Why are you still in Mexico? What the fuck? Do you know if the girl's ok? I want nothing happening to her. Just want to send a message to her mother… You know, scare her into keeping her mouth shut."

"I know what to do. Take a deep breath and chill out. I'll take care of it. I'll let you know after I get through to her," Victor said, shaking his head.

"You've still got the number I gave you, right?"

"I've got it. Talk soon."

Hanging up, Hector turned and went back into the restaurant, walking to his table.

"Well, did you reach Victor?"

"I did. It's being taken care of," Hector said as the waiter placed a medium rare ribeye with a fully loaded baked potato in front of him.

"It better be or we're all fucked!" Saul said, downing his martini.

# Saturday, 10:39 AM
# Tucson International Airport

They crowded the room with men, all talking at once. Rebecca couldn't quite make out their faces. Through a closed door on her right, she heard Kimyung screaming for her. "Mommy, help me, mommy. Make them stop mommy. They're hurting me." She tried moving toward the door, but the throng of men blocked her path. She reached for her badge but couldn't find it.

"I get her first. Back off," a deep voice said as the door started to open.

"Mommy, he's hurting me. Mommy, help!" Two men lurched back into Rebecca, pushing her to the floor.

"I get her next," another man said. Rebecca tried to holler that she's an FBI agent, but she couldn't get the words out. *Kimyung…* Someone was tapping her right shoulder.

"Ma'am, please put your seat up. We're about to land," the flight attendant said, bringing Rebecca out of her nightmare. Rebecca sat up straight, looking around the cabin. The cold grip of her department issued Sig Sauer holstered on her right side pressed into her hip.

"I'm sorry. I must have fallen asleep," she said to the flight attendant, taking a deep breath. She wiped the tears from her eyes.

"It's ok, ma'am. Please move your seat back up. Are you ok?"

"I'm fine… thank you," Rebecca said, looking down and burying her face in her hands. She pressed the button on the armrest, moving her seat into position. *Where are you, Kimyung? I'm coming for you.*

The jolt of the Boeing 737's wheels hitting the runway brought her further to alertness. She hadn't slept since she'd left Tucson the previous day, except for dozing off for an hour. It wasn't a restful nap one would want. It was a nightmare to Rebecca, a dream that fed her worst fears about Kimyung.

Rebecca felt the big aircraft come to a gentle jolt of a stop at the breezeway. As if on cue, the other passengers got out of their seats in front and back of her. She heard the sound of the aircraft door opening and saw the light from the walkway streaming in. She sat back, listening to the chorus of overhead bins being popped open. With both hands on the seat in front of her, she pulled herself up. She stood there looking around and grabbed her carry-on bag out of the overhead bin. Ahead of her, people starting moving to the exit. Being exhausted didn't matter to her. The only thing that mattered was finding her daughter.

As per school district protocol, yesterday the school had waited until hearing from CPS to call the police. Because of the waiting, it wasn't until 3:58 in the afternoon when the principal put a call into the Tucson Police Department. As per police department policy, they wouldn't issue an Amber Alert until the officer arriving on scene had spoken to the principal and CPS. Because the police were short three-hundred and fifty-eight patrol officers, it'd be another two hours before an officer could interview all parties. It wasn't until 7:07 PM when they finally issued an Amber Alert.

"Rebecca, I'm over here," Special Agent Sylvia Granada called, standing next to seated passengers waiting to board the same aircraft to Las Vegas.

Rebecca wasn't in the mood to deal with the enthusiastic Sylvia Granada, but resigned herself to it. What mattered to her right now was getting to the Tucson Field Office and taking charge of the investigation looking for her daughter.

"Agent Granada, any word on my daughter?"

"I'm so sorry about what happened. Here, let me take your bag," Sylvia said.

"Sylvia, any word on my daughter?" Rebecca said, pulling the handle away from Sylvia's outstretched hand.

"I'm sorry. No."

"Ok, let's go. Take me to the office."

En route to the field office, Rebecca placed a call to her former partner, Trevor Blake. Six months previously, he'd been put in charge of the Kidnapping and Missing Persons Unit. Trevor, former military, was as solid as they came and, like Rebecca, a no-nonsense field agent. Since he'd taken over the unit three months prior, they'd had an eighteen percent increase in the recovery of victims. Most of the cases handled by the Tucson Field Office were Latin Americans who'd illegally crossed into the country. The coyotes, once arriving at a drop house in Tucson or Phoenix, would hold them at gunpoint, demanding money from their families. It had become so commonplace in Arizona that Phoenix had become the number two kidnapping capital of the world. If ransom wasn't paid, the children and younger women would then be sold into the sex-trafficking trade in the United States.

Rebecca listened as Trevor brought her up to speed on the progress of the investigation.

"We found a witness who reported seeing an older, large black sedan with a push guard in the front. Sounds like a Crown Victoria. It pulled up a block east of the schoolyard, and a man got out, then walked onto the sidewalk in the school's direction. The witness is an elderly woman who was walking her dog. Unfortunately, her dog got off the leash and ran in the other direction. She doesn't know what happened after that because she chased after her dog," Trevor said.

"Do they know what the source of the explosion was?"

"TPD and our explosive unit say it was two cherry bombs and nothing more."

"I picked up a black Crown Vic on a security camera at a gas station heading southbound five minutes later. The Amber Alert issued late yesterday and has produced some leads, but nothing that has panned out. Although one person reported seeing a car matching that description stopping on a side street two miles from the school. A man got out, carrying something in his arms, which he put in a red car. The red car headed towards twenty-second street and the Crown Vic made a U-turn heading the other way. I wish I had more for you, Rebecca."

"I know you do. Thanks, Trevor. I know you and your team are doing your best. Did you check with Customs to see if any of their cameras picked up the car going across the line?" Rebecca asked.

"We did and nothing. Rebecca, we're going to find her. We will not stop until we do," Trevor said.

"Thanks, Trevor. I'm on my way in. Should be there in twenty minutes. I'm with Agent Granada. She picked me up at the airport."

"Ok, see you soon."

"Agent Granada, on second thought, take me home. I need to get out of these clothes and take a shower."

To Rebecca's relief, Sylvia Granada was silent during the twenty-six-minute ride from the airport to Rebecca's house.

"Thanks for the lift, Sylvia. I'll see you at the office in a little bit," Rebecca said, grabbing her carry-on from the back seat. She made her way up the walkway to the front door. Pausing and taking in a deep breath, she reached into her pocket and put the key in the lock, turning it slowly. The silence inside hit her like a dark wave, absent of the soul and energy of nine-year-old Kimyung. Stepping through the doorway, she wiped away the welling tears in her eyes. Closing the door behind her, she dropped the carry-on bag and made her way down the hallway. Pushing the door open and stopping in the doorway, she looked around her daughter's room. A row of stuffed animals neatly arranged on a bookshelf to the right of the window looked back at her. She felt the firmness of the mattress as she sat on the edge of the bed. *Oh God, please keep her safe and please help me find her.*

Sobbing, she gathered herself, sitting upright wiping the continuous tears away from her face. *Harden up, woman. It's time to get to work. We're going to find her and when we do, I'm going to kill them.* Rebecca was never one to wallow in emotions, but when her daughter came into her life, she'd discovered feelings she didn't know she had. The sense of loss was not something that she'd allow to overwhelm her and take her away from the task at hand. Standing up, she walked down to the end of the hallway. In her room, she took her clothes off and got into the shower. Fifteen minutes later, she was buttoning her blouse and reaching over to put her hand gun into the holster on her belt. As she pulled an old blue sweatshirt over her head, with wet and disheveled hair her phone rang. . Normally she ignored any unknown callers. Even the FBI gets robo calls but in this case...

"Hello," Rebecca said.

"Agent Harper, your daughter is in our safe keeping for now. To make sure she stays that way, forget about the people involved with the border incident last month. Don't dip your toe into political waters where they you don't belong.   Do you understand? Agree to this and you'll see your daughter again." The electronically altered voice said.

"Where's my daughter? Who and what is it you want to me to forget about?" Rebecca said, trying to keep the only link to her daughter on the line. *Who and what are they talking about? Political waters? What the fuck?*

"You know, Rebecca. Two months ago, at the border. The missiles, the people involved. One important person in particular. I will not spell it out for you. But think about it, Agent Harper, and think about how much you love your daughter. She's a pretty little girl. There are lots of men who would pay good money to have their way with her. You're a smart woman… Listen to what I'm telling you."

"You motherfucker, if anything happens to her, I swear, I'll find you and make you suffer."

"Now, now, Rebecca. You know we want nothing to happen to her. Just do what I'm telling you, then you can have your daughter back. And remember, if you get her back, don't pursue this. Do you understand, Rebecca?"

"Yes. Ok, I'll do what you ask. I just don't know who you're talking about," Rebecca said, struggling to remember everyone involved in that incident when she killed the two terrorists and what led up to it.

"Come on, Agent Harper. Sure, you know. What's yellow, tells a story and lives in the dark? Don't let a little politics get in the way of you seeing your daughter again. Taking your daughter was just a warning to you. We can take her again, anytime we want, and we will if you don't do what I'm telling you. You can't protect her twenty-four hours a day. Do you understand? And don't tell anyone about this call, not even at your office. If you do, you'll never see your daughter again. We'll sell her to the highest bidder. This isn't hard to figure out, Rebecca. Think."

"What the fuck are you talking about? W'what's yellow, tells a story and lives in the dark?" Rebecca said, but the line went dead. She'd felt anger before, but nothing like the rage boiling inside of her. *What's yellow, tells a story and lives in the dark?* Her sadness about Kimyung turned into determination to figure out the clue the voice gave her. Whoever the voice was… they enjoyed teasing her… wanting her to figure it out. She took a deep breath, making her way down the hallway and to the door leading to her garage. Frustrated by not knowing, she was encouraged by at least hearing from the kidnapper. It gave her hope that Kimyung was ok.

*What's yellow, tells a story and lives in the dark? Fuck!* Rebecca hurried out of the house to get to her office.

Arriving twenty-three minutes later, Rebecca saw her office had become a hub of activity… all having to do with the search for Kimyung. Trevor greeted her, giving her a hug.

"Nothing yet and nothing on the black Crown Vic. It's early still. We'll find her," Trevor said.

"Thanks, Trevor. I know everybody's doing whatever they can," Rebecca said, fighting the urge to tell him about the call she'd received. She turned and went into her office, half closing the door behind her, sitting at her desk and desperately wanting a cigarette. As she had on so many occasions since she quit smoking, she unlocked the righthand file drawer where she kept confidential items and reached for the pack of cigarettes nestled in between a short stack of case files. On top of the files was her yellow legal pad she used to make random and sometimes important notes. Grabbing the open pack, she brought it up to her nose and inhaled. *If there was ever a time to light up, it was now.* She looked back down in the drawer, looking for the red disposal lighter she knew was in there. Reaching down, she pushed aside the legal pad, and felt for the lighter with her fingers. When she found it, she moved the legal pad back into its place and began flicking the flame on and off, staring at the legal pad. *Son of a bitch!*

Rebecca picked her phone up off her desk and scrolled through the directory until she found the name she'd been searching for. There was only one person she could talk to and trust about the phone call she'd received. She pressed the call button before getting up and walking over to close her door.

Sylvia Granada, approaching Rebecca's office, stopped fifteen feet short of the door, watching it close. Turning, she walked back to her desk.

## 11:43 AM
## Rebecca's Office

"Dax," Rebecca said, crying, sitting at her desk struggling to get her words out.

"I know why you're calling, Rebecca," Dax said as Rebecca interrupted him.

"How… how did you know?"

"Doesn't matter. Listen, honey. She's down in Mexico. Hermosillo."

"Hermosillo? What the fuck—Hermosillo? She's in Mexico? *Hermosillo?*" Rebecca said, catching her breath from the sobering information.

"Yes. A source of mine alerted me to it last night. I tried reaching you but wasn't able to. As far as we know, she's with a guy named Mario Quintana, the cousin of Juan Ortiz. If you recall, he's the head of the Magdalena Cartel. Our understanding is that she's at Mario and his wife's house in Hermosillo. Her uncle is a congressman, Hector Granada," Dax said.

"What? None of this is making any sense. Hector Granada's niece is the wife of Mario Quintana and they've got my daughter? Wait, that's Sylvia's older sister. Son of a bitch. Why would Mario and his wife want my daughter? Are you saying Mario came all the way up here and kidnapped her from school and drove back into Mexico with her? Why?"

"I don't know. Think, Rebecca. Does Sylvia know about your knowledge of her uncle's involvement in the Stinger missile shipment?"

"Why would… Wait a fucking minute, it's all making sense now," Rebecca said, telling Dax about the phone call with the hints and her yellow legal pad with the notes about the congressman and the Stingers.

"That makes total sense, Rebecca, but it wasn't Mario who took her; it was someone else, hired by Hector Granada. Rebecca, didn't you say his niece is an agent in your office?" Dax said.

"Yes, that's who I'm talking about—Sylvia Granada, she's a new agent in my office. I remember her telling me about having an older sister living in Mexico. But there's no way she'd know about her uncle's involvement with the transport of Stingers to the terrorists. I have told nobody because of your guys' involvement in the operation. How could she possibly…"

"Think hard, Rebecca. I know it's difficult but maybe she somehow found out he was involved a couple of months ago, when you shot those two assholes and saved Carter and Doug. You singlehandedly prevented the Stingers from falling into the wrong hands with people at the Madkow Mosque. Think. There's got to be a reason. Is it possible she could have gotten into your office and snooped in your desk?"

All the pieces fell into place for Rebecca, like dominoes falling in unison. *Politics, notes… my legal pad. That time I found my desk drawer ajar. Granada. My legal pad…it'*

She remembered about two or three months ago, in her office, her yellow legal pad with notes on it, which included Sylvia's uncle, Congressman Hector Granada, and his involvement with an illegal arms shipment being brought into the U.S. to be picked up by a group funded by ISIS. Ever since college, Rebecca had made a habit of writing notes on a yellow legal pad, just like the one she'd kept in the locked drawer in her desk. That was the day she'd rushed to go get Kimyung at school because she'd been injured, and left her desk drawer unlocked.

Rebecca explained her mistake to Dax and couldn't rule out the possibility that Sylvia may have been in her office and looked in her desk. In fact, it was the only explanation that made sense. She'd shared the information on the congressman with her boss, Nottingham, who was the Tucson Field Office Supervisor at the time. When he'd demanded to know the source of her information, she'd told him it was from a CI (confidential informant) and wouldn't share the person's name. Rebecca urged him to start an investigation into the congressman, but Nottingham, over her objections, told her to leave it alone. Because Granada is a congressman, Nottingham didn't want to rock his career climbing the ladder in Washington. It was all she could do to contain her anger.

"I don't know, Rebecca. Could have been Nottingham running his mouth, boot licking, but then again, it could have been Granada's niece. Anyone else know about the intel on Granada? It sounds like the only logical explanation for how Granada found out you knew about his illegal activities. Whoever told him about your accusations is irrelevant to getting your daughter back. Granada is sending you a message. We'll deal with him later."

"You're right, Dax. Whether it was Sylvia snooping or Nottingham running his mouth doesn't matter," Rebecca said, gritting her teeth and shaking her head at the thought of her sloppiness in not locking the drawer. Unless, again, it was Nottingham.

"Rebecca, U.S. law enforcement cannot pursue this because she's in Mexico," Dax said.

"We've got an agent in Hermosillo, working with the Federales on drug and human trafficking intervention. Maybe he can get some help down there," Rebecca said.

"I wouldn't count on that. Besides, you've got to figure out a way to inform your team that you know she's in Mexico without revealing the source," Dax said.

"I'll think of something. I'll tell them you're a confidential informant and that I don't know your name… I don't know… something like that. They will not care. We'll reach out to our guy in Hermosillo and see what he can find out."

"Ok, good luck with that. I don't have a lot of faith in the idea. It's not that your guy in Hermosillo is dirty, it's just that I'll bet you dollars for donuts the Federales he's dealing with down there are on Juan Ortiz's payroll. Nothing happens in Sonora without Ortiz knowing about it, and nothing happens like this without him being a part of it. If she's at his cousin's house, then Ortiz knows about it. Guaranteed."

"Maybe so, but I've got to give it a shot, Dax. I don't know what else to do. Thanks for the heads up on this. I'll keep you posted," Rebecca said.

"Alright kiddo. I'm here. Call me later and let me know what's happening with your guy in Hermosillo."

"Dax, thanks for being there for me."

"Always."

## Sunday, 7:38 AM
## FBI Field Office
## Tucson, Arizona

She steadied herself, waiting for the team to assemble. With the coffee cup in her left hand, she covered her mouth with her right, wanting to yawn though she couldn't. Rebecca rubbed her eyes with her free hand, wiping away tears. Looking over at Sylvia, she reflected on the short time she'd known the new agent. Rebecca had pushed her early on, letting her know what she expected out of any new agent. Everyone knew that the only reason Sylvia Granada was accepted into the FBI Academy was because of her congressman uncle, Hector Granada. Rebecca had accepted this. After a few stern conversations in the past with Sylvia Granada, Rebecca at this point was not pleased with her lack of progress. Now, in her position as the head of the Tucson Field Office, she'd make do with her. But now with the kidnapping of her daughter by Sylvia's uncle, the only question now was could she be trusted? Did she know about his activities? Rebecca looked at her as Sylvia took her seat. *I wonder if she got a hold of my legal pad?*

"Many of you have given up your day off to come in and help. Thank you. I'm going to get right to the point. I have it on good authority that my daughter…" said Rebecca, looking down at the floor and catching her breath with her lower lip trembling. She turned to her right, wiping her eyes and taking a constricted breath. "Sorry, my dau… my daughter is across the line. She's… as of this morning, reported to me by one of my CI's… she's being held in a house in Hermosillo, Mexico. Unless any of you know differently, that's where we're going to focus most of our attention. I don't want to abandon any leads up here though. Keep working your sources."

"Any idea why somebody would take your daughter?" one agent in the middle of the room called out.

"I don't know if they targeted her because she's the daughter of an FBI agent or if it's something else. So far no one has contacted me," Rebecca said, hating to lie to them but feeling the need to for her daughter's safety.

"I'll contact George Young. He's our agent in Hermosillo, attached to the consulate. Hopefully, he's got some trusted contacts and can do something. Do you know the exact location of the house?" Trevor said.

"I do. Here it is. Why don't you give Young a call?" Rebecca said, tearing off a page in her yellow legal pad and giving it to Trevor. She watched as he turned and punched numbers on his phone before walking back to his office.

"Maybe my uncle can help. I mean, we have family on the other side and my uncle is a congressman. I know he knows people in Hermosillo. Do you want me to call him?" Sylvia Granada said.

"No... this is agency business," Rebecca snapped at her.

"Ok, I won't," Sylvia said with everyone in the room looking at her.

"Ok, that's all I've got right now. Keep doing what you're doing. It means a lot to me and my daughter. We're going to get my daughter back," Rebecca said. She could see the frustration on everyone's faces, now that they'd learned Kimyung was in Mexico.

Everybody knew it was out of their jurisdiction. All hope now was on George Young.

# 8:07 AM
# American Consulate
# Hermosillo, Mexico

George Young flipped the page of the major newspaper of the State of Sonora, Mexico. El Imparcial. George knew, as the citizens of Hermosillo knew, that if the newspaper were to tell the truth about Magdalena Cartel… the editor wouldn't live to see another day. The last editor to tell the truth had his body parts distributed throughout the city. George Young kept informed on local events so he could be tapped into the buzz of the city. Reaching for his coffee cup his phone rang. The caller ID read; 00857994589389

"George Young here."

"Hey, George. This is Trevor Blake at the Tucson field office. We're hoping you can help us with something. Rebecca Harper, our station boss… her daughter was kidnapped on Friday and we have information that she's being held at a house in Hermosillo."

"I read about it on the wire. Ok, let me see what I can find out. You know my hands are tied down here. I've got some good contacts, but I'm not sure if I can trust them. Give me a good number to get back to you. Do you have an address for where she's being kept?" George Young said.

"I do. Ready to copy?"

169

"I am, go ahead," George Young said, writing the address and Trevor's number down. He was familiar with the area. It was a ten-minute drive from the consulate.

"Thanks. Call me as soon as you can," Trevor said.

George put the phone down, tapping his coffee cup with a pen, and leaned back in his chair.

"What's going on? You look worried," George's wife said, having watched his expression change during the call.

"I am worried. Somebody kidnapped the daughter of the station supervisor for our Tucson office on Friday. They believe she's being held in a house close to here. I got to get on this right away," George said, looking away from his wife and scrolling through his phone directory until he came to the number he was looking for. General Yeppes. The head of the Mexican Federales in the state of Sonora. Except for Juan Ortiz, he was the most powerful man in the state of Sonora. George also knew the general was on Juan Ortiz's payroll. Finishing up his coffee, he hit the send button to the general's phone. *Fuck… what if Juan Ortiz knows about this? Could he be involved in the kidnapping? That makes no sense at all. Ortiz may be a homicidal psychopath, but he's not stupid enough to bring the heat of the U.S. government down on him. Son of a bitch… I wonder who's behind this?*

"General, buenos días. This is George Young over at the American Consulate. How have you been?"

"Good morning. You've never called me on a Sunday morning before. It must be important," General Yeppes said.

"It is. We've a problem I'm hoping you can help me with," George said, explaining the details of Rebecca's daughter's kidnapping along with the suspected location of her whereabouts.

"I see. Do you know for sure she's being held in the house?"

"As far as I know... At least, the most recent information shows that."

"What would you like me to do?"

"What I'd like is for you to investigate it, maybe send some of your men to the house. The U.S. government would appreciate your efforts," George said, curbing his tone since he didn't know if the general would offer help or not.

"Maybe I can. I need to make a few phone calls. Let me see what I can do," General Yeppes said.

"Ok, I'd appreciate it. I don't mean to pressure you, but could you do it this morning?" George said, knowing to put a bit of urgency into his request so he might, and only might, make the general move a little faster.

"I'll see what I can do. I'll call you back and let you know if I can do anything."

"Thank you, general. I appreciate you tending to this right away. The U.S. government and myself are very concerned for her safety. I'll await your call," George said, knowing how to play the game of push but not too hard. He also knew if the general wanted to, he could, after finishing the call, gather some of his men and go to the house. He'd give the general until after lunch and, if he hadn't heard from him by then, he'd call again. George Young loved the culture of Mexico and its people, but hated the level of corruption amongst with the government and politicians. Being assigned to the Hermosillo post wasn't a plumb assignment… but it was a wrung up the ladder in his career with the bureau.

# 11:30 AM
# The Compound
# Hermosillo, Mexico

Commander Yeppes learned years ago not to call Juan Ortiz before ten in the morning on a Sunday. The commander, like everyone else, lived in fear of him and took care not to rile him. In the Mexican state of Sonora, federal police officers were leaving in droves because many were targets of violent crimes committed by the Magdalena Cartel. They had already killed sixteen police officers this year. Under Yeppes command, the numbers of active officers needed were down forty percent. He knew that a good number of his officers were, like him, on Juan Ortiz's payroll and feared him.

With the second hand on his Rolex hitting eleven-thirty, General Yeppes sighed and tapped the green button on his phone.

"Commander, ¿cómo estás? What has you calling me on a Sunday morning? Got a problem with your girlfriend or maybe your wife?" the awakening and sobering up Juan Ortiz said, laughing.

"I'm good amigo. I got a call earlier this morning from a George Young, the FBI agent assigned to the U.S. consulate here in Hermosillo..."

"I know who he is. Is he causing trouble for you? I don't give a fuck if he's American FBI or not. Just let me know and I'll have him taken care of. You know, just like we did with Kiki

Camarena when we were younger men. That mother fucking puta," Juan Ortiz said, emphasizing the name "Kiki."

Commander Yeppes was more than familiar with the torture and killing of U.S. DEA agent, Enrique "Kiki" Camarena. As a young Federale, he and others witnessed his torture and murder. A rival cartel and Federales brutally beat, dismembered and killed the DEA agent. The mention of it by Juan Ortiz turned Yeppes's stomach. He'd carry the image, smells and sounds of Kiki's torture and death to his grave. The commander's upper body twitched.

"No, señor, nothing like that. He's been no trouble for us. We use him when we need to. He told me about a young nine-year-old Asian girl who was kidnapped on       Friday in Tucson and is being held at a house here in Hermosillo. He even gave me the address of where he said she's being held."

"These fucking gringos… always spying on someone. I mean, how do they know the exact address?" Juan Ortiz said.

"I don't know how he knows, but he does. He asked me if I'd take some men over to the house and, if she's there, he wants me to rescue her. I didn't want to do anything before talking with you."

"You're a smart man for talking with me first. Why so much trouble over a little girl? Plenty have been taken from the other side, brought here and trained, then sent back over to make us money. Anyway, I know all about it. My cousin Mario and his wife are looking after her."

"Her mother is an FBI agent. She's the head of the Tucson office. They're going to put a lot of heat on me for an answer," Commander Yeppes said, knowing that the sex trafficking of young women and children a part of Juan Ortiz's operation.

"Oh, her puta madre is an FBI agent? That's heat on you, not me commander. I know you can handle it. Do nothing. She's an FBI agent's daughter? Don't worry, I'll see she's taken care of," Juan Ortiz said.

"Ok, señor, but I know these gringos and they're always in a big hurry. I'm sure George Young will call me this afternoon. What do you want me to tell him?"

"Tell him you sent men to the house, and she wasn't there," Juan Ortiz said, hitting the end button.

Dax, getting up from his chair, walked over and picked up a log and pulled the screen back, throwing it onto the fire on his way to the kitchen. He never drank over two cups of coffee in a day and looks forward to his second cup. After leaving the agency, he enjoyed sitting around on a Sunday, catching up on reading the WSJ and watching a sporting event or two. In his decades of service to the country, he'd never had the luxury to do so until now. His time was now his own, and he enjoyed the lack of responsibility and urgency of the moments he lived in. Outside the kitchen window, the thermometer read forty-two degrees. He loved his home, his life and being able to just sit enjoying the fire and a cup of coffee. Reaching over for the TV remote, his phone vibrated on the table next to his chair.

"Dax here."

"Dax, Alex here, how are you doing?"

"I'm still here," Dax said. Years earlier, when Dax would call his ninety-one-year-old mother and ask her how she was doing, her response was always, "I'm still here." Now, approaching seventy-seven, he understood why she'd said that.

"Indeed, you are. I just picked up on a conversation between Juan Ortiz and Captain Sanchez. He's ordered the captain to go to Mario's house tonight and pick up Agent Harper's daughter and take her to Ortiz's compound. The captain didn't sound enthused about it."

"Not good. Did Ortiz call Mario?"

"No, he told the captain to call him. I haven't picked up anything on that yet. I'll let you know when I do," Alex said.

"Ok, keep me posted, Alex."

"Roger that, out."

"Out," Dax said, hanging up the phone and taking a long draw of coffee. Staring at the flickering flames, he thought about Rebecca and the pain she's going through. Rebecca... given the opportunity she would kill whoever kidnapped her daughter. After her father's death, Dax became like a father to her and her like the daughter he'd never had. Rebecca and the FBI, with Kimyung being in Mexico, were powerless to do anything meaningful. He assumed there was a senior agent assigned to the American Consulate in Hermosillo, but so what. Having to deal with the Mexican Federales to get anything done would be a waste of time. Everyone knew the Federales were on the payroll of the cartels.

Standing orders from the president wouldn't allow U.S. law enforcement to intervene in the sovereign laws of another country. To make matters worse, the U.S. military was prohibited from operating clandestine operations in Mexico. Unless the agent in Hermosillo could pull something off, Rebecca and her nine-year-old daughter were on her own.

Dax finished his coffee, got up and walked to the large picture window looking out at the Granite Mountain to the west. He knew getting Kimyung back and unscathed from an official point of view was hopeless.

He turned and headed to the kitchen. After rinsing his cup out, he opened the refrigerator, pulling out some ham, swiss cheese and mayo. Placing it on the counter he turned opening the loaf of whole wheat bread sitting on the counter and pulled out two slices. After putting the sandwich on a plate, he walked back to his chair and sat down, taking a bite out of it. He needed time to think.

Fifteen minutes later, after thinking about options of helping Rebecca and rescuing her daughter... there was only one. Picking up his phone, he found the number he was looking for. *They're the only chance we've got. Please be available and up for it.*

# 12:03 PM
# Back Porch

Mario sitting on his back porch watching his children playing on the swing set lifted a Pacifico to his lips and took a large swig of it. Kimyung sat by herself on a plastic horse attached to a large spring anchored in cement.

"Come on kids, lunch time. Come over here Kimyung," Adela said, putting a tray of sandwiches and chips on the picnic table underneath the canopy on the right side of the yard. The children stopped playing and ran over to the table. Kimyung got off the horse and sat down at the end of the bench seat at the table.

"Here, have a sandwich. It's good ham and cheese," Adela said to her.

"I want to go home. When am I going home?" Kimyung said, looking up at Adela.

"Soon honey, I'm sure soon," Adela said, stroking Kimyung's long black hair, looking in Mario's direction. She turned away from the girl and made her way back into the house to get drinks for the children.

The look on Adela's face was painful. She was a wonderful woman and even a better wife. She'd been patient with him ever since he'd taken over Reggie's job of being Juan's guy to call to take care of business when needed. Mario had been a content man when Reggie was alive and doing the job. Now everything fell on him. Juan constantly had him on the move between towns in

Sonora, checking on his operation. On more than one occasion he'd witnessed men dying at the hands of his cousin Juan. Putting the drinks on the picnic table, Adela made her way over to him, sitting down beside him.

"How long Mario?" Adela said looking at Kimyung who was wiping tears from her face. One of their daughters had her arm around her and holding a sandwich with the other hand.

"Soon. I think soon. I'm just waiting to hear from your Uncle so we can send her back." Mario said.

"Send her back, what do you mean? Send her how? She's a nine-year-old little girl. You just can't drop her off at the border and ask her to walk across. How the hell are you going to get her back to her mother?"

"Not sure yet, we'll find a way. Maybe send her across with one of the coyotes. I don't know, we'll figure it out. It should be soon."

"Send her with one of the coyotes. Are you losing your fucking mind? They'll rape her and then sell her to a sex trafficker. This is dirty business, Mario. We should have told my uncle no. The poor little girl, I feel so bad for her. She's such a sweet and innocent child. Mario, promise me you'll protect her and make sure she gets back across to her mother alright."

"I will, Adela, you have my word on it. And your uncle? I had to say yes or he would have gotten a hold of Juan. At least she's safe with us. Juan is a sick pedophile, I'm sure it won't be long. If I don't hear from your uncle by tonight, I'll call him in the morning."

"Alright, I guess that's all you can do for now. But please Mario, we've got to help this little girl. This is not right." Adela said looking at Kimyung and her daughter sitting next to her.

"We will, and for now we'll take care of her Adela," Mario said, getting up from his chair going inside and getting another Pacifico. Walking through the screen door to the kitchen, his phone vibrated in his shirt pocket. Before answering it, he looked relieved not to see his cousin's name, Juan Ortiz, on the caller ID.

"Captain Sanchez, how are you doing? What are you up to on this Sunday?"

"Your cousin called me. The young girl I found with the gringo on Friday that I brought to you... Juan wants me to pick her up and take her to his compound. I'll be there at seven."

"Take her to his compound? Tonight? But what if Hector calls and I have to take her back across the line?" Mario said looking out through the kitchen window hearing the children's muffled voices from outside. He knew the captain knew of Juan's penchant for young girls and didn't imagine for a moment the captain liked the idea. But the captain worked for his cousin and he had to be careful what he said.

"I know Mario. Look, I don't like it any more than you do. If you want to call your cousin and talk him out of it go ahead. I'm just doing as I'm told. I'll be there at seven."

Pressing the red end button, he placed the phone back in his pocket. He could call his cousin but passed on the idea, thinking about the safety of his wife and children. *Adela's will not like this.*

181

# 12:05 PM
# Tucson, Arizona
# On Hold

"Honey, when you come back out, would you mind bringing me the glass of water I left on the counter?" Doug Redman said, leaning back in his chair with the Sunday paper. It was a biased newspaper, but he enjoyed reading the local news. Almost every page was devoted to bashing the president. In the Op-Ed section was an article calling for his resignation. But then again, Doug knew the *Arizona Red Star* did not differ from most of the newspapers in the country.

"Ok, are you hungry?" Liz called out from the kitchen.

"Sure, I could eat. What do you have for your poor starving husband?" Doug said, enjoying civilian life and being able to spend a lazy Sunday afternoon at home.

"We've got some leftover pizza from last night that the kids didn't eat. Want me to heat a couple slices up for you?"

"That'll do. Thanks, honey. Where are the kids?"

"They both went to the movies with some friends and won't be back until later this afternoon. Why do you ask?" Kim said, rubbing her tongue behind her upper lip and glancing over in Doug's direction.

"Hmm.... just wondering. Sounds like we're alone for a few hours."

"Sounds like it to me, too," Kim said, knowing her husband's familiar conversation of foreplay.

"I've got an idea for some fun after lunch."

"I bet you do… Let's hurry and eat then," Kim said with a smile.

"Hmm… I've got a better idea—let's have fun first and then eat," Doug said, putting aside the paper. His phone vibrating on the coffee table interrupted Doug's thoughts of lust with his wife.

"Damn, be right there, honey. I've got to take this call. Dax, how the hell are you?" Doug said, knowing from the caller ID who it was. A call from Dax was a sharp crack back into reality from his thoughts of being under the sheets with Liz. In less than a nanosecond, he went from being aroused to full on, head-on-a-swivel alertness. Dax was not only a comrade-in-arms to him, he was also the older brother and mentor he'd never had. Dax only called when something bad had happened.

"Hey, Doug. How are you, Liz and the kids?"

"They're great, Dax. How are you doing? Enjoying retirement up there in Prescott?"

"You know, retirement has its moments… none of which are ever exciting. Not like the old days. I miss them. But, what the hell. I've still kept my toe in the pond. Doug, I'll get to the point. You know the FBI agent who saved you and Carter's bacon? Rebecca Harper?"

"Great lady. I hope I get to meet her someday. She's been our guardian angel for the last year and a half. What's going on?"

"Friday, her nine-year-old adopted daughter, Kimyung, was taken right off the schoolyard in the middle of morning recess," Dax said, his voice breaking.

"What the hell? What happened? Did they get her back?" Doug asked.

"No, they haven't. We know where she is, but Rebecca and the bureau can't get to her?"

"What do you mean 'can't get to her?' How come they can't rescue her?"

"The girl's in Mexico. Last known location she's being held in is a residential house in Hermosillo. As far as we can tell she's been there since Friday afternoon."

"Mexico? Why her? Why is she being kept in a house in Hermosillo? How do you know for sure she's in Hermosillo and at the house still? Do you have some eyes in the field down there?"

"Alex has a handle on it. It's not guaranteed she's still at the house, but probably she is. Alex has heard nothing to the contrary. He's got surveillance on calls to and from Hector Granada, Mario Quintana and Juan Ortiz. And no, we've got no eyes on the house. The Bureau has an agent at the consulate in Hermosillo. He's reaching out to the Federales' commander in charge, but I wouldn't count on the commander doing anything. Guarantee he's on the payroll of Juan Ortiz."

"Wait a minute, slow down a minute, Dax. Are you telling me Juan Ortiz orchestrated the kidnapping of Rebecca's daughter? And Hector Granada's involved?"

"No, he didn't say Ortiz did the kidnapping. It was Granada—"

"What the fuck? Granada? Do you know what for and why?"

"We think it has to do with the last operation you and Carter ran on the Stingers in Nogales."

"Ok, you mean he's punishing her for stopping his Stinger shipment from reaching the terrorists? Are you kidding me?"

"Not exactly. Rebecca knows about his involvement with the Stingers, but has kept quiet to protect you guys. I'd let her know months ago what Alex discovered about Granada," Dax said.

"Oh man, that's terrible. Rebecca's got to be beside herself. God help whoever did this if she gets a hold of them. The woman shows no mercy on evil. I've seen that firsthand. What's the FBI in Washington doing about this? I mean, something has to be done," Doug said.

"The president's been informed and my understanding is he's spoken with the president of Mexico about the situation and trying to avoid an international incident. Problem is, the new Mexican president isn't tough on the cartels. His philosophy is hugs, not bullets, when it comes to them. Since it sounds like it involves Juan Ortiz, I can guarantee the Mexican president won't lift a finger to help rescue the girl," Dax said.

"That's fucked up, Dax, but I get it… It is what it is. Do you think the president will allow a black ops operation to rescue the girl?"

"No… listen, Doug. After the Stinger event in Nogales, the president is aware of what you guys did and recognizes me as the point man, if you will. He knows I'm capable of putting together sanitized off-the-books operations."

"You say she's in Hermosillo? That's only four hours from here… Needn't say more, brother. I understand why you're calling me. Let me see if I can scramble the guys. You've got eyes in the sky up on the house where's she's at?"

"No, the president won't authorize any incursion into Mexico. Doug, I hope you guys can do something and quick."

"Needn't say more, Dax. Hey, even if it's just me, I'll go. Carter and I owe Rebecca. I'll call you back ASAP."

"Thanks, Doug. I knew I could count on you. I'm heading out and coming your way in thirty minutes. Should be in Tucson by late afternoon."

"You got it. See you this afternoon. Out."

Doug got up from his chair and made his way to the kitchen, coming up behind his wife and putting his arms around her waist. She pushed back into him.

"Honey, we've got to put our fun on hold. That was Dax. I've—we've got to tend to something right away. I'm sorry," Doug said, feeling Liz's right hand reaching around, touching him. He knew she wouldn't protest, wouldn't complain, wouldn't pry… only trust him to be safe.

"Oh, ok. You'll have to make it up to me," Liz said, turning around, resting her arms on his shoulders and gliding her tongue across her lips.

"I promise I will," he said, pulling her close and kissing her.

# 12:23 PM
# Carter Thompson's House

"Why don't we go get a bite to eat somewhere? I'm hungry," Carter said, turning off the TV and pulling Kim close to him on the sofa.

"Sure. Where do you want to go?" Kim said.

"Hmm… How about Tohono Chul Park? I heard they have a great brunch."

"Sounds good to me. Give me five minutes and I'll be ready," Kim said, kissing him before getting up from the couch.

Carter glanced at her as she walked to the hallway, grabbing the remote to turn off the TV. On the end table, his phone rang.

"Hey, brother. How are you doing?" Carter asked.

"I'm good. Something urgent has come up. Dax is on his way down from Prescott. Should be here this afternoon," Doug said.

"What's up?"

Carter listened as Doug explained the situation. Looking up from the phone, he watched Kim walking towards him. He looked at her as he made his way outside to the patio, closing the glass door behind him.

"Jesus, man. That's bad, terrible. After what that woman did for us… we owe her and we owe her big time. Even if we didn't, I'd be in. She's got to be out of her mind with worry about her daughter. I guess it's tag, we're it again. Count me in. I'll see if I can track down Garrett. My place is available this afternoon. If I remember right, Dax likes his coffee black," Carter said, feeling the hairs on his neck stand up. Looking through the glass door, he saw Kim smiling at him.

"Yes, Dax likes his coffee black. How's 4:30?"

"That works, I'll be ready and hopefully Garrett will be here, too."

"Great. I'll get a hold of Rocco, Mike and Conway. See you this afternoon. Out."

Through the glass door, Carter saw Kim pointing to her watch and rubbing her stomach. Amidst thinking about the expected mission, he smiled back at her. Holding up one finger, he mouthed the words "one second." Looking back down at his phone, he found Garrett's number.

"Hey, Garrett. How are you doing?"

"Doug, I'm good. And you? What's up?" Garrett said.

"Something's come up. We're meeting at my house at 4:30 today," Carter said, knowing there wasn't a need to explain all the details to Garrett. He knew Garrett well enough to know that he'd pick up on the urgency of the situation without needing to explain until he saw him in person.

"Damn… I can't. I'm in New Jersey at my niece's wedding. Hell, man, I'm sorry. What's up?"

"No worries, brother. It is what it is," Carter said.

"Hell, man, I could tell them an emergency of some sort came up and I'll catch the first flight out of here. Should be able to be back by late tonight or early morning, I'd think."

"No time. We're rolling out of here early evening. If all goes well, we'll be back by noon tomorrow. Who knows what's happening to that little girl? We have to get her out of there and back to her mother."

"Damn. I understand. Hey, is Alex overseeing this?" Garrett asked.

"He is. With any luck, we'll have some eyes in the sky on the house and surrounding area."

"Ok, good to know. Maybe he can keep me up to date on what's happening. I hate sitting this one out," Garrett said.

"I know. Next time. Enjoy the wedding and have a good time with your family. It's important to them and you. I'll give you a shout when we get back. We'll get together for a beer or something," Carter said. After the first operation in San Miguel and Chicago, both were given Alex's phone number.

"You're on. I'm buying. Be safe, brother, and give my regards to the rest of the team. Talk soon," Garrett said.

"You're damn right you're buying. I'll see you when you get back," Carter said, hitting the end button. Turning, he looked at Kim who, with a smile mouthed, "come on," tapping her watch again.

"I'm sorry, honey. That was Doug who called, and then I had to track down Garrett. Let's go to lunch. I'm hungry," Carter said, giving her a kiss. He knew the mention of Doug and Garrett in the same sentence alerted her. He hoped she'd continue to understand and support whatever he and the rest needed to do without asking questions. "I love you, honey," Carter said, putting his arm around her as they made their way out of the house.

"I love you, too. No need to explain… Besides, I'm hungry," Kim said, punching him in his ribs.

# 4:18 PM
# Of Mice and Men

Catching five hours of sleep in the middle of the day wasn't his style. But with two days without sleep, he'd welcomed Hal taking over his watch five hours earlier. After a quick shave and shower, he grabbed a cup of Mexico's finest dark roast coffee, along with two machaca beef, cheese and bean burritos. Carefully walking and sipping the coffee, he made his way out of the lobby of the Fiesta Americana to his car parked in the back parking lot.

Pulling up behind his car, he watched Hal looking into the rearview mirror in his car. The window to the driver's side door went down as he approached.

"Anything shaking?" Victor asked, taking a bite out of his burrito while handing one to Hal.

"All quiet. A few cars coming and going down the street in front of the house, but other than that... nada. Thanks, man. I'm fucking hungry," Hal said, reaching out with his right hand, taking the offering.

"Well, I guess that's a good thing," Victor said, looking through his binoculars at Mario's house, five hundred yards away.

"What's the plan, boss?" Hal said.

"Assuming all remains quiet and also assuming the girl is still in the house... I think tonight is as good a time as ever to go in and get her. Maybe around midnight or so. And, assuming that goes ok, we haul ass to the border and figure out how to get her back to her mother without exposing ourselves. The getting her back to her mother part should be easy… That is, assuming crossing the border doesn't include a search of my car. If that happens, I'm fucked, but at least the girl will get back to her mother. If we get that far and I get cuffed, just get your ass back to New Mexico. Don't worry about me. I'm entitled to my one phone call and that will be to my lawyer. In the meantime, why don't you cruise on over to the Fiesta Americana and get some rest. Be back here by ten," Victor said, taking his fourth bite out of the burrito and smiling. He continued to look in the house's direction. Taking one more bite, Hal looked up at Victor.

"That's one hell of a plan with a lot of 'assumes' in it. I'm sure everything is going to work out just peachy… no question about it," Hal said, looking up at Victor and breaking into laughter.

Victor couldn't contain himself thinking about what he'd just regurgitated to Hal under the guise of a so-called plan. Holding on to what was left of his burrito, Victor leaned against Hal's car and burst out laughing.

"Fuck, man. What can I say? You asked me what the plan was, and that's it," Victor said, trying to keep a serious face before breaking out into uncontrolled laughter.

"Sounds perfect to me, Victor. No big deal. We're only one-hundred-seventy-five miles south of the U.S. border in the capitol of the State of Sonora with a million people. It looks like an armed encampment with all the razor barb wire strung on the houses. Plenty of Federales and Mexican military cruising around with nasty looking men manning M60 machine guns. Oh, and that little ditty you told me that the cousin of the guy who's holding the girl is the head of the Magdalena Cartel. I don't see any kind of potential problem here… Noo… nothing."

"Yeah, that's right… a piece of cake," Victor said, finishing his burrito with a smile.

"Fine… fuck it. I'm all in," Hal said, taking his last bite and wiping his hands together.

"Ok then. Get the fuck out of here, go get some rest and see you back here at ten. Oh… and bring some coffee with you."

"You got it. See you at ten," Hal said, starting his car up. Victor watched Hal drive a block down the street, turning right at the corner. He got into his car, making himself comfortable in the driver's seat, and grabbed his binoculars. *So much for the best laid plans of mice and men.*

# 4:27 PM
# Hot Fudge Sunday

"Alright, honey. Don't spend too much money shopping," Carter said, pulling Kim close to him. He wiped the tears on the corner of her eyes away.

"Don't be gone too long… and come back to me all in one piece. No doubt whatever you guys are doing needs to get done. I just want nothing happening to you. I don't want you getting shot or catching any shrapnel like you did at the mall. Come back safe and sound… do you hear me?"

"I hear you. I promise I'll be fine and so will the rest of the guys," Carter said, knowing that he didn't know. *Was that to assure her or myself?*

As she pulled out of the driveway, Doug and one other figure sitting in the front passenger seat of his truck made their way up the driveway. Carter opened the front door and stepped out onto the landing, giving them a wave.

"Dax, how are you doing? Hey, Doug. Come on in," Carter said, stepping further out to greet them.

"Carter, you're looking good and fit. Kim must take good care of you," Dax said with a wry smile.

"She does," Carter said.

As the three men turned and began walking back to Carter's house, another truck rolled into the driveway with Rocco behind the wheel. They turned, greeting Rocco, Mike and Conway as they hopped out, making their way to them. Five minutes after entering Carter's house, everyone took a seat in the living room with coffee in hand. All eyes were fixed on Dax. Other than the first time these men came together to intervene on a problem when law enforcement wouldn't, Dax was now the catalyst for their gatherings.

"Thanks for coming on such brief notice. I don't know if Doug's filled everyone in on the details or not. A nine-year-old girl has been kidnapped and, as of two hours ago, she's being held in a house in Hermosillo, Mexico. She's the daughter of FBI Agent Rebecca Harper. Rebecca has been like a daughter to me and was the one who saved the lives of Doug and Carter in the Stinger operation. Also, as I think you know, she's hidden her knowledge of your past activities," Dax said, taking a sip of coffee.

He explained the details of Kimyung's kidnapping and the man and the black car last seen leaving the area. The details of Alex's involvement and his ability, through the NSA's resources, to track and monitor phone conversations between Congressman Hector Granada, Juan Ortiz, Captain Sanchez and Mario Quintana. There had also been another individual who Alex hadn't been able to identify by the name of Victor. He learned of him because of the conversations between Granada and him. Alex knew Victor was the one who'd taken the girl. They didn't know if he acted alone or had help.

"We were told to bring our gear and be ready to go… the only question I have is when are we leaving?" Rocco said looking around the room.

"Everybody have their gear and weapons ready? Combat load out?" Doug asked, getting up from his chair and walking forward to stand next to Dax. Carter looked around the room, seeing nothing but thumbs up, including his own.

"Ok, obviously this is urgent. Travel time to the target from here is about four hours. Normally, we'd be looking at close to four and a half to five, but we won't be stopping to do paperwork on the other side for visas. It's now four-forty-eight what do you all say we get out of here at the latest by five-thirty?" Doug paused, looking around the room with everyone nodding in agreement.

"How about five-twenty instead?" Carter said.

"That's good with me. We'll shoot for it, but we've some planning to do in the meantime. I'm not going to sugarcoat this, gentlemen. This is a perilous operation, way beyond what we've done in the past. We don't have the luxury of any kind of reconnaissance, and coming back into the country could be a problem. I don't want to leave our weapons and gear in Mexico, but it's a possibility. On the plus side, we've Alex covering our six as much as possible. We also have the element of surprise. Except for Alex, we're on our own. We're going into the interior of Mexico to a house that may or may not have security. Assuming we get into the house with no shots fired, we've got to get the girl, get out and head back to the border. Highway fifteen is the only road between Hermosillo and the U.S. border, and it's a long drive. Plenty of time for the Federales or cartels to be setting up roadblocks, ambushes… you name it. Once we get to the border, we've got to get across with no hitch with U.S. Customs. Separate from the five of us coming back across. We'll have the girl with us and no paperwork for her. Bottom line is we're going to figure this one out on the fly. First things first, we've got to get down there and rescue the girl," Doug said, looking around the room.

"That wouldn't be the first time, boss," Mike said.

"Ok, we'll be taking two vehicles. Carter, you and Rocco will ride in your truck. Mike and Conway will ride with me in mine. Ideally, we'll be in and out of Mexico in eight to ten hours. In case we get stopped, our cover is that we're heading to San Carlos to do some scuba diving and spearfishing. Did everybody bring the extra equipment I asked for?" Doug said, seeing everyone with thumbs up.

"Ok, good. We'll tie down six scuba tanks in the bed of Carter's pickup and lay your dive bags with gear in them on top. Make sure all of you have your mask, fins, snorkel and wetsuit on top. Put your AR, mags, handgun and the rest inside the dive bags for now," Doug said.

"I've been traveling down to San Carlos for over forty years. Just once did I have my bags checked, and that was a military checkpoint just north of Hermosillo. They half unzipped my dive bag and, seeing the wetsuit, that was it. Kim and I were down in San Carlos last year and, coming back, the checkpoint was there but they were waving gringos through. We both have Arizona plates, so I don't think it'll be an issue. But if it is, the scuba diving cover should work. Believable and enough room to hide our gear," Carter said, looking around the room.

"Ok. Keep your comms in the center console when approaching any kind of checkpoint. I talked with Alex and he'll continue to monitor phone calls and keep us posted. Questions?" Doug said, scanning the room.

"There's a thousand ways this mission could go wrong. I'll be working on getting you quick clearance back into the U.S., but no guarantees. From what her mother tells me, Kimyung is a very smart and tough little girl. Once you've got her, there's a code Rebecca told me for you to tell Kimyung. When you've contacted her, tell her Rebecca said, 'hot fudge Sunday.' Hearing that, Kimyung will know she's in safe hands. That's all I've got for now, gentlemen. Do what you need to do to keep her and yourselves safe. I know you're all more than familiar with the Magdalena Cartel. Remember who you're dealing with. They're no different from any other enemy... If the opportunity arises, show them no mercy. That's all I've got for now," Dax said.

"It's five-twelve. How about we're out of here in ten minutes? That'll put us into Hermosillo around nine-thirty," Doug said.

"How about five?" Conway said, grinning.

# 6:44 PM
# Four or More

Victor looked at his watch and then back toward Mario's house. The neighborhood was quiet except for an occasional car or pickup either turning in his direction or coming from behind. He'd duck down in his seat to avoid being silhouetted by headlights. Early in the business of surveillance work, to break up the monotony, he created a game of figuring out the average time of when a vehicle would pass by. After two days of surveillance, the average was a vehicle every fourteen minutes and thirty-eight seconds. This created a made-up purpose for being there besides watching the target. It takes a certain person who can sit in one place with little or no movements. Snipers have it and anyone that's in the spook business long enough has it.

"What's up?" Victor said, after sliding the green tab on his phone to the right and hitting the speaker icon. Answering the phone by putting it up against his ear at night time sent illumination onto his face and could give away his location. Keeping it on his lap, face down, and using the speaker function allowed him to use his hand or anything else to shield the light. It was one of the many little fine points of being in a hide. Victor played any little thing to his advantage.

"Where are you? Are you back in Tucson? I got a call from Mario. He told me Captain Sanchez of the Federales is coming to pick up the girl and take her to Juan Ortiz's hacienda. Fuck, man, this is bad. Mario and his wife were to bring her back tomorrow. This is bad, terrible," Hector Granada said.

"A Captain Sanchez is taking her to Juan Ortiz, the head of the Magdalena Cartel? Juan Ortiz?"

"Yes. Jesus, man. Where are you? Do you think you can do anything? I'll give you more money. You've got to help me. We've got to get her back. I just wanted to scare the agent. I don't want her daughter getting hurt or going missing. That wasn't the plan."

Victor listened to Granada, who sounded like he was on the verge of being in a state of panic and on the edge of tears. He would not reveal to him that he had his eyes on Mario's house. He wasn't about to let something happen to the girl. If it hadn't been for the incident yesterday with the Federales captain taking the girl, he'd be back in the U.S. But the incident happened. The image of that scene from yesterday played out in his head. The captain, his men and the barrels pointed towards him. Kimyung being taken and put into the captain's truck. The nametags on their uniforms. *That's got to be the same Captain Sanchez. What are the odds?*

"Slow down, take a breath of air and calm the fuck down. Let me think. You said the captain is coming to get her at seven? By himself?"

"Yes, seven is what Mario said. I doubt he'll be by himself. The Federales go nowhere without at least four men. What are you thinking? You haven't answered my question. Where are you?"

"I don't give away my location. How about I'm not where you are?"

202

"Well, how about it? Do you think you can get down there and get her back? If we don't get the girl back to her mother, I won't have leverage over her. She knows I'm involved in all of this. The threat of not getting her daughter back and something bad happening to her is keeping her mouth shut. It's my only leverage. How about it, Victor? Do you think you can do something? How much more do you want? Just tell me. I don't care. You're the only person I can turn to."

"I don't know. I'll be back in touch," Victor said, hitting the end button. He had to think. Yes, he could take on the captain and a few of his men. But if there were four or more... he knew it'd be better to wait for another opportunity. He knew he'd only get one shot at this and it'd have to be a good one. Looking at his watch, he saw that it was six-fifty-eight. *If Hal was here, maybe.*

He looked around, listening to a dog barking in the distance. The pungent smell of a fire somewhere in the neighborhood filled his nostrils. Picking up his binoculars, he brought Mario's house into focus. Headlights belonging to a camouflaged pickup truck appeared. Behind it, another truck with a gunner in the bed, manning what looked in the dark like an M60.

# 7:48 PM
# Highway 15
# Sonora, Mexico

"Alex, how are you doing? What's up?" Doug asked, five minutes south of Santa Ana, Mexico.

"I'm good. Two things. First, I wanted to let you know I'm getting a good track on you and Carter, who I can see is leading the way. Second, I just picked up a call between Granada and Mario Quintana. The congressman is freaking out about the girl being picked up by Captain Sanchez, who's taking her to Juan Ortiz's compound. He was screaming at Quintana. Sounded like he was shitfaced. After that, he made a call to the guy named Victor, who's in Hermosillo right now. This is not good. It's going to change your objective. I've some pics of Ortiz's compound taken from one of our birds last year. It looks like it's got a high wall surrounding it. No doubt he's heavy on security. Sorry to complicate things for you and your guys, but at least you'll have some idea of what you're dealing with going in. I've tracked the captain's phone and, sure as shit, he's almost there with the girl," Alex said.

"Not good at all. I assume you gave Dax a heads up?"

"I did."

"Ok, brother. Thanks for the intel. We'll figure it out. Keep me posted. Out," Doug said, rubbing his eyes from the glare of the oncoming headlights. He drove on in silence, knowing Mike and Conway would know from his side of the conversation that the profile of the mission just changed. And not in their favor.

"You don't look happy. What's up, boss?" Mike asked from the back seat.

Doug gave them a rundown of the call from Alex. He knew both men would do whatever was needed. Embarking on this rescue mission already had a strike against it; no eyes on the ground before they arrived. And now the rescue plan was out the window. The original target location wasn't a concern to Doug, nor would've been for Mike and Conway. What did concern him was that the new target location was probably fortified. Juan Ortiz would be sure to have men on the perimeter and within the walls. Then, once inside, and having neutralized any potential threats, there was the problem of finding the girl. Easy in a small house, which was the case for Mario's place, but a big hacienda?

"Sounds like a piece of cake to me," Conway said, laughing.

Laughter, when possible on the battlefield, was always good to ease the tension and fear of something about to happen that might not go so well. The gravity and potential danger of the task at hand wasn't mistaken.

"We've had worse odds. Remember that time in Afghanistan in the Korengal Valley. We're going to rescue that little girl and get her and us the hell out of there and back across the line," Mike said.

"Roger that. We'll save her. Ok, let me give the boys in front of us a call and give them the joyful news," Doug said. *Modify, adapt and overcome.*

# 8:03 PM
# Juan Ortiz's Compound

"Where are you taking me? Are you taking me home? I want to go home," Kimyung said, seeing the glare of the floodlights as they approached the main gate.

"I'm sorry. You can't go home right now. It's ok. We're going to a big house. You'll be there overnight. Soon, you'll be able to go home," Captain Sanchez said. He didn't enjoy lying to her. Now, because his boss was taking her, he didn't know if and when Kimyung would ever go home. Too many times he'd been told to bring teenage and younger girls to Juan Ortiz. Stories of Juan Ortiz molesting young girls, then discarding them to one of his coyotes to do with as they wished. The border in Arizona is littered with bras and panties, hanging from branches of "rape trees." He had no reason to doubt the stories. Juan Ortiz only wanted this girl for his own pleasure and, afterwards, would probably send her to the states for prostitution.

"I want to go home. I don't want to be here. Please take me home," Kimyung said, wiping tears from her face. The captain opened the glove box, pulling out tissues for her.

"I know, I know," Captain Sanchez said. He had two young daughters of his own. Pursing his lips, he took a deep breath just before the pickup came to a halt in front of two men armed with AK47s. Walking towards him, they squinted in the glare of the headlights. Dust drifted up from behind as the trailing pickup stopped behind him. Nodding his head at the men, the gate opened. The captain and Kimyung in his pickup and the car behind them moved forward along the tree-lined drive to the main house. He watched an armed man with a German Shepard making his way down the inside perimeter of the wall. Ahead, the well-lit area around the house revealed a wide set of wooden steps leading up to a porch that wrapped around the house. On the porch were two other men with AKs walking back and forth. They came to a halt. Captain Sanchez opened his door and walked to the left front side of the truck. Through the front door to the house, Juan Ortiz emerged with a drink in one hand and a cigar in the other. He stopped at the top of the steps, looking at the captain and then at the pickup.

"Hola, Captain. So good to see you. What did you bring me tonight?" Juan Ortiz said in a slurred voice, looking at Kimyung, who was straining to look over the dashboard.

Juan swayed back and forth and then steadied himself. He raised the cocktail glass to his lips, took a sip and lowered it, followed by a long pull on his glowing cigar.

"Hola, Juan. This is the girl you told me to pick up from Mario and bring to you. Can I have a word with you?" Captain Sanchez said, looking at his childhood friend from the streets of Aqua Prieta.

"Of course," Juan Ortiz said, glancing at the two men on the left and right of him. The two men on cue moved in opposite directions, giving Juan Ortiz and the captain privacy. Juan walked down the twenty steps and stood off to the opposite side of the truck from Kimyung.

"What's on your mind captain?" Juan said.

"Amigo. You know it's a U.S. congressman who's involved in the taking of this little girl, right?" Captain Sanchez said, walking over to him. Juan took a sip from his glass and then a long draw on his Cuban cigar, exhaling the smoke to his left.

"Yes, I do. So what? That fat ass Granada means nothing to me other than a payday now and again. That Stinger deal got pretty fucked up, didn't it? No matter, I got my money. And because of him and some fucking gringos, I lost men and so did you. San Miguel is no longer good for me. It's all because of that fucking Granada. Amigo... he owes me," Juan said, putting his hand on the captain's shoulder, leering at Kimyung.

"I know, but come on, Juan. She had nothing to do with that. She's a little girl and needs to get back to her mother. Her mother is the chief of the FBI office in Tucson. Did you know that?" Captain Sanchez said, looking back at Kimyung and then at Juan.

# Mommy, where are you?

Kimyung strained, looking over the dashboard and then to her right and left. To her right, one hundred feet were lit by lights, but beyond that, everything drifted into blackness. Looking again over the dash, she watched the two men talking, hearing their muffled voices. Undoing her seat belt, she gripped the door handle and slowly opened the door, keeping her eyes on the two men. Turning in the seat, she planted her feet on the floor, pushed the door open and jumped out, tumbling to the dirt in the driveway, then rolling to her feet. Using the body of the truck to hide her movements, she ran towards the darkness.

"Boss, she's getting away," yelled one man on the porch.

"Stop her," Juan Ortiz hollered, looking up at the porch.

The other man on the porch raised his rifle up.

Running, she fell, skidding in the dirt and rocks just as one round hit the dirt to her left and another one whizzed past her left ear. She scrambled to her feet.

"No, don't shoot her. Go get her, you fucking idiot. What a fucking moron," Juan said, turning to the captain. He looked over at the captain's men in the truck and back to him.

"Tell them to go after her. She's a feisty one. I like that… hey amigo, she's going to be lots of fun. Just like breaking in a horse!" Juan exhorted, as he drank the last bit of tequila and tossed the tumbler aside.

Hearing voices and footsteps behind her, she ran as fast as she could. Breathing hard, the light faded to darkness. Ahead, a stand of mesquite trees looked like ghosts in the night. She ran towards them and kept going until she tripped over a fallen tree. She scooted up against the back side of it, hoping not to be seen. The sound and breeze of one of the men jumping over the tree brushed her body.

"Little girl. Come back, we won't hurt you. It's dangerous to be out there on your own. There're coyotes and mountain lions. Come back. We'll take care of you," Kimyung heard a voice hollering twenty feet away from her. She was sure the man would hear her heart pounding. A fast, high pitched rattle sounded close to her head. Her primordial instincts for survival kicked in, causing her to freeze.

"Careful, I hear a rattlesnake over there," the man that'd been calling for her hollered to the others.

Kimyung knew about rattlesnakes from a field trip her school had taken the year before. She knew what they looked like, the sound they made and how dangerous they were. *Mommy, where are you?*

# 8:38 PM
# Not a Hacienda

Victor followed the three trucks to the gate leading into Juan Ortiz's compound, driving past the gated entrance, not looking in their direction. A half mile past the gate, he pulled off on a side road and turned around, then stopped and hit the green icon on his phone. A groggy sounding deep voice answered.

"Hey, Victor. What time is it? Did I sleep too long? What's going on? Everything ok?" Hal asked.

"We've a problem, or I should say we've a bigger problem. Federales in two pickups pulled up to the house and took the girl. I followed them to what looks like a large hacienda with a high wall surrounding it. It's well-lit with two men with guns standing out of the main gate. No doubt there're more men inside... I'm sure it's Juan Ortiz's hacienda. I'm sitting on a side road about half-a-mile south of it. Not sure what to do about getting the girl back. It's not looking good. After you've had your coffee, give me a shout and I'll give you directions on how to find me. No rush. I've got a bad feeling about this."

"Wow, that's fucked up, man. Ok, I'll jump in the shower and get moving. I'll call you in a little. Do you want some coffee and a burrito?"

"Another burrito? Sure, why not, and roger that on the coffee."

"Will do. See you soon," Hal said.

Victor tapped the red end button and rang Granada.

"Where are you? Did you get her? Are you back?" Congressman Hector Granada said.

"I'm across the line. No, I haven't gotten her... at least not yet. I've run into a problem," Victor said, explaining about the Federales picking Kimyung up and the situation at hand.

"Jesus, man. You've got to get her. You can't come back here without her. Oh my God, I can't believe this. This is so fucked up. When will you be back here with her?" Hector Granada said.

"As soon as I can. Look, I'm going to be straight up with you. I don't know if I'm going to rescue her or not. What about Mario Quintana? Have you talked with him? I mean, he's the one that was supposed to bring her back in the first place, right?"

"I'll call him and call you back."

"Ok, talk soon," Victor said, hitting the end button. Looking down the street leading back to the entrance to Juan Ortiz's place, there was no traffic. He looked at his watch. *This isn't a hacienda... this is a heavily armed compound... fuck...*

# 9:18 PM

"Hermosillo, 15 kilometers" read the road sign as Carter and Rocco drove by at eighty-five miles an hour. Ahead, the lights of the city of one million illuminated the sky against the backdrop of the cold and dark surrounding desert.

"Ok, brother. We're almost there. How are we doing on fuel?" Rocco asked.

"We're ok, but I need to hit the bathroom when we hit Hermosillo. There's an Arco on the main road just after we get into town. You can get some gas, but sometimes it's bad down here. Not like ours at all," Carter said, rubbing his eyes from the glare coming off the highway of oncoming traffic. I'm getting a little hungry too. How about you?"

"Yeah, I could eat. Let's give Doug and the guys a shout and see what the plan is," Rocco said, stretching.

"Good idea," Rocco said, hitting the send button. Through the speaker system in his truck, both men listened to Doug's phone ring two times.

"Hey, brothers. How's it going up there?" Doug said.

"We're good. Thought we'd stop and take a piss when we hit Hermosillo. Gas up if you need to, but Carter said we're good, so we won't take the time. He has long-range tanks. Also, the aging entrepreneur here is getting hungry," Rocco said, laughing.

"Ok, good idea. I think between Liz and Kim we've got plenty to munch on. After, let's find a place where we can pull over and figure out what we're going to do. When we do, I'll see if I can get Alex on the horn to advise."

"Sounds good, Doug. There's a park not far that we can go to. It should be quiet at this time of night," Carter said, as overhead highway lights began to appear. Ahead in the distance, the faint green glow of a traffic light greeted them. 'Bienvenidos a Hermosillo' (Welcome to Hermosillo) read the sign as they crossed the city line. Within five minutes, the lights of the intersection with the Arco station shown ahead. Pulling in with Doug's truck right behind them, an attendant greeted them. In the rearview mirror, Carter watched another one approaching Doug's truck.

"This is nice. I miss the good old days when gas station attendants came out to handle the gas, check your oil and clean your windshield," Carter said. Even though both pickups were parked in front of the bathrooms, the man with a sponge on the end of a long pole began moving it back and forth across the windshield.

"Yeah, I read about that in an ancient history book," Rocco said, laughing.

After explaining to them in broken Spanish that they were only stopping to use the bathroom, Carter thanked the man and gave him two dollars. Doug, watching Carter, did the same with his guy. Fifteen minutes later, both trucks pulled into the park with Carter in the lead.

# Hugs Not Bullets

Shivering, Kimyung lifted her head, looking around in all directions. It'd been over thirty minutes since she'd heard the voices of the men looking for her. Keeping her eyes on the shadowy serpent three feet from her, Kimyung put both palms on the ground, pushing herself away from the coiled rattler. After getting a safe distance away, she sat up, stretched her cramped legs in front of her and looked around. She could make out the glow of the lights surrounding the big house. Listening, she looked around one more time and eased herself onto her feet. Brushing herself off, she walked deeper into the mesquite grove. Before long, she came to a tall wall. Moving to her left, she walked, hoping to find a way out. It was impossible for her to see the ground sensor twenty feet in front of her.

All sections of the wall lit up from the floodlights mounted on three-foot poles above the eight-foot wall.

"Señor, she's over there. I see her," one of the two men with AKs slung over their shoulders said, running in her direction.

"Get her. Tie her up and bring the young feisty puta to me. Captain, have your men join mine. Come at her from both angles. ¡Muy rápido!" Juan Ortiz said as the Captain turned, barking out orders to his men.

"Juan, I think she's going to be more trouble than she's worth. Why don't you let me take her back to Mario and get her back to the states? Because her mother's an FBI agent, I'm afraid the American president is going to put a lot of pressure on our new president to do something. We don't want the military getting involved looking for her," Captain Sanchez said, hoping to persuade Juan not to keep her.

"Fuck our new president. I'm not worried about it, amigo. Besides, he's said his new policy towards the cartels is 'hugs, not bullets.' He likes the money I and the rest of the jefes give him. Plus, I heard he doesn't like the American president. I'm keeping her for a while… When I'm done with her, you can have her. You like little girls, don't you?" Juan said, putting his arm around the captain. Captain Sanchez sidestepped away from his embrace.

"I don't like this, Juan. Come on. This is bad for business. I'm telling you this is going to be trouble."

"I think what you need to do, Captain San… Sanchez… is just do what I tell you," Juan said in a slurred low and threatening tone.

The captain stared at him. He'd seen Juan like this just before he'd do something horrific to anyone going against him. He thought about the scared little girl out in the dark, then thought about his daughters and what he'd do if it was one of them out there. What if Juan wanted one of his daughters? The captain took his gaze off of Juan, who'd been swaying, staring back at him.

"Hey, amigo… You have two young daughters, don't you?" Juan said, staring at the captain while running his tongue across his lips.

The muscles in the captain's jaw quivered. He stared back at him. This was no longer the mischievous childhood friend he'd grown up with. How much longer could he tolerate putting up with him. How much longer did he want to live in fear of his family being tortured and killed if he stepped out of line. No, in that moment, Captain Sanchez saw Juan Ortiz for what he'd become: a violent and evil psychopath whose only purpose in life was to spread darkness wherever he went. He and the other cartel jefes were all the same. A brotherhood of cruelty and evil. With every cell and fiber in his body, the captain restrained himself. He knew Juan Ortiz, and there was no mistaking the threat and message he'd just given him. He turned right, hearing voices coming from out of the trees. Two of his men approached them, holding Kimyung by her arms.

"You have good men. Bring her to me. Carlos, go get Maria," Juan said, watching as Kimyung and the two Federales came into view.

"Yes, I have outstanding men," Captain Sanchez said, turning to Juan and back toward Kimyung. *I'm going to kill that bastard one of these days.*

Kimyung resisted as best she could against the two grown men's grip on her small arms. Walking up to her, Juan put his cigarette in his mouth and reached down with his right hand, feeling her long black hair.

# Shampoo

"Yes, señor," Maria said, walking up behind Juan Ortiz, looking at the young girl and back at Juan.

"Take her up to my room and get her ready for bed. You know what to do," he said, looking down at Kimyung without looking in Maria's direction.

"I'll take her. It's going to be ok. You can come with me," Maria said, taking Kimyung's reluctant hand.

"Where are we going?" Kimyung said, looking up at Maria.

"It's past your bedtime. Let's go upstairs," Maria said.

Once in Juan's bedroom, Maria turned down the bedsheets and fluffed the pillows.

"You must be a tired little girl. Why don't you take a quick bath and I'll get you some milk and cookies? Huh? Wouldn't that be nice?" Maria said, leading her into the bathroom and turning on the tub.

"When am I going home?"

"I'm sure soon, maybe in the morning," Maria said with her fingers under the faucet, making sure the water wasn't too hot. "Let's shampoo your hair, and here's some soap for you to wash yourself," Maria whispered, pushing Kimyung's head under the running water and then squeezing shampoo onto her head. After washing her hair and rinsing it off, Kimyung stood up, soaping herself down, then sat back into the water to rinse off. Maria handed her a large white towel and picked up her shoes and clothes. She put them on a small chair in the back corner of the bedroom. Coming back into the bathroom, she handed Kimyung a small bathrobe, instructing her to put it on.

"Come on, let's get you to bed. Things will be better in the morning. You'll see."

A yawning and tired Kimyung made her way to the bed and climbed up into it, pulling the covers over her.

"Go to sleep, young child," Maria said, walking to the door and the light switch. She looked back, seeing Kimyung was already sleeping.

# 10:47 PM
# Ortiz Park

"Ok, Alex downloaded a rendering of Juan Ortiz's hacienda. It's big and surrounded by a wall that goes for three hundred yards on all four sides. It looks like the distance between the house and the west wall, opposite the main gate, is around two hundred yards plus or minus. The house is two stories with a big patio and pool on the west side of it. We don't know if there're sensors for the wall or lighting… Assume there are. Also assume there are plenty of men with guns inside the walls. Because Alex tracked the captain's cell, arriving right on time at Mario's house, he's confident Rebecca's daughter is somewhere inside those walls. Oh, one other thing. It looks like on the grounds there have a lot of trees and brush. We need to get over there and do as much recon as we can. There's a large gate on the road on the east side with a long drive. Maybe there're some openings on the wall we can exploit," Doug said to the team assembled around a concrete bench.

"Sounds like a piece of cake to me. Any idea how tall the wall is?" Conway asked.

"Don't know. Let's get over there and figure it out. Also, other than the road that the main gate faces, it's open desert for a half mile or so in either direction. It makes access in and out of there difficult with our trucks," Doug said.

Carter sat listening to Doug and the others as they chimed in. His thoughts drifted to when he was a kid in Evanston, Illinois. There was a big house with a six-foot wall covered in ivy surrounding it. A water pipe running on the outside of the wall was high enough for them to climb up to get on top of the wall. Carter always went first because he was taller and could jump higher than the rest. Once he pulled himself up, he'd lay on the top of the wall and reach down to grab the next boy to help him up. Bobby, the smallest one in the group, always went second. Once Bobby was on top of the wall with Carter, the two of them would help the rest of the boys. On the other side of the wall was a barbecue area that was nothing more than a hop, skip and jump back over the wall. *I doubt this is going to be that easy.*

"Carter, any thoughts? You know this area better than the rest of us," Doug asked.

"I'm only familiar with the east side of Hermosillo. I've never been on the west end where Ortiz's compound is. Nothing but big homes and properties. Even though it's a big town, it's laid out simple. The road we came in on is the main one heading north and south. There's another one that heads northwest, all the way to Puerto Penasco, Rocky Point, on the northern end of the Sea of Cortez. Another way back to the U.S., if needed. One other road heads northeast, going to Aqua Prieta, right on the border with Douglas, Arizona. Another way back into the U.S. I've never been on either of those roads, so we'd be figuring it out as we go," Carter said to everyone.

"Ok. Let's hope this is an easy snatch and grab and we get back across the line without trouble. Like our other two ventures… except for Alex providing some help, we're on our own. Look guys, I need not tell you… do what you need to do. There are two parallel roads running on the north and south sides of the wall. When we get there, we'll split into two teams and work our way along the opposite walls, starting from the west, the backside. From there, Carter, Rocco and Conway will work the west and south side of the wall, looking for an entry point. Mike and I will do the same on the north side. Assuming both teams go undetected, we'll meet back two hundred yards west of the wall and complete our entry plan. It's not the best situation, but we'll make it work… We're not leaving without that little girl. Questions?" Doug said.

"Does Alex have any idea where the girl is?" Carter asked.

"He hasn't a clue other than somewhere inside those walls. Ok, everybody, let's do a quick radio check and then let's roll," Doug said.

# Victor and Hal

Victor looked down the road to the front of the compound. He could see any traffic that might turn on either of the roads running parallel to the compound.

Victor, thinking about how to rescue Kimyung, didn't notice the vehicle coming up behind him until the lights were right on him. The lights illuminating the inside of his car pulled him out of his thought process. For a fleeting moment, the thought of what happened the other day on the dirt road with the Federales pulling up on him and the girl drifted by. A cloud of dust floated over the rental. With his hand on the grip of his Glock, he started easing it out of its holster. The headlights went off, he heard the driver's door closing, and saw the silhouette of a tall man walking towards him. Exhaling, he relaxed his grip.

"You know, you could have let me know you were on your way. Get in," Victor said to the welcome sight of Hal. Hal walked back behind the car and around to the right front door. The small SUV swayed as he opened the door and put himself into the seat next to Victor.

"Sorry about that. Next time. So, what do you think?" Hal said, picking up Victor's binoculars and looking the half mile north down the road.

"I can see two guys down there in front of the gate. I'm sure they're armed?" Hal said.

"Oh yeah, they're armed. And no doubt more of them inside the wall, including at the main house," Victor said.

"AKs?" Hal asked as Victor looked over at him, panning the area.

"AKs and probably AR15s on the inside. I'm sure Obama and Eric Holder's so-called Fast and Furious Operation was a big help to guys like Juan Ortiz. They might even have some Barrett fifties. Who the fuck knows? But hey, that's ancient history now. Damage done. How many men with weapons behind that wall is a mystery... but I guarantee, whatever the number, it's a bigger problem than we can deal with," Victor said.

Victor and Hal sat in silence. The odds of the two of them rescuing her were about zero.

"Victor, I know Granada assured you the girl would be returned to her mother in two days or you wouldn't have taken the job. You believed him. Bad timing on the dirt road with Federales taking her at gunpoint... I know it turned this in a different direction. And now it appears she's in the hands of the cartel. Lord only knows what could happen to her now."

"You're right. Granada promised me she'd be ok. Should've known better than to trust a slimy politician. Fuck. If she doesn't get back ok... I'll hunt that fat pig down and do the country a favor," Victor said, gritting his teeth and gripping the steering wheel.

"I get it. What do you think... do you think we can pull this off? I mean, I'm here because you're my friend. You wouldn't have called me if there wasn't a serious problem. But, I got to tell you... trying to rescue her inside those walls sounds like a suicide mission. And then, if we got her, it's a long way back to the border. Only a few different ways to get there from here," Hal said, putting the binoculars down and looking at Victor.

Victor grabbed the binos, bringing him to his eyes. Another two minutes of silence permeated the inside of the small SUV.

"I hear what you're saying, Hal. I wish I'd never taken the job. Damn… I've got a bad feeling about the outcome for that little girl. Ortiz will have his way with her and then give her to one of his guys. From that point, she'll be taken back into the U.S. A nine-year-old Asian girl will bring a high price. They'll hook her on heroin. She'll never see her mother again and be dead before she sees her tenth birthday. Ok, look… let's hang out here until dawn. I need to think this through. You're right. This might be a hopeless situation. I don't know. I just don't like bailing out on her. It's because of me taking the job that put her into this situation," Victor said, shaking his head.

"Fair enough. I'm not going anywhere," Hal said.

In the distance, the lights of two vehicles closed the gap on the compound. One turned to their right, down the road on the north side of the compound. The other one kept coming in their direction and turned right, heading west on the road just to the south of the compound. Through his binoculars, Victor watched the closest vehicle go past the west side of the compound, continuing on. A mile past the compound, Victor could see the faint glow of red through his binoculars.

# 11:05 PM
# A Matter of Trust

The team worked all day and into the night trying to uncover leads. So far, nothing. The looming question was why her? Was Kimyung's kidnapping just a random opportunity for a passing pedophile who couldn't resist their urges? Or was it something more? Is it possible Rebecca was targeted and her daughter was to be used as a pawn to coerce her into doing something she didn't want to?

Fighting the urge to fall asleep, she finished her tenth cup of coffee for the day. What would it matter if everyone knew why her daughter was taken? It wouldn't change the fact that Kimyung was in Hermosillo. The reality was she knew it would matter if they knew why she was taken. She didn't care about any of it... She just wanted her daughter back, safe and sound. She'd promised the caller she'd keep quiet, and she would. Rebecca knew even after getting her back, Kimyung couldn't be protected twenty-four hours a day. She knew better than to think the FBI would provide twenty-four-hour, seven-days-a-week protection for her daughter. The caller had made it clear if she didn't keep quiet, she'd never see Kimyung again. And if she said anything after she got her daughter back, they'd take her again. Rebecca had no choice but to agree to the kidnapper's terms. Besides, exposing Congressman Hector Granada would expose Carter, Doug and the rest of the team. And right now, they were the only ones she trusted to rescue Kimyung.

It'd been ten minutes since she'd ordered everyone to go home and return early in the morning. Standing in her office doorway, she noticed a light on in a back office. It was Trevor, her friend and former partner. Turning and sitting at her desk, Rebecca looked at her watch and then down to her right. She opened the file drawer. It'd been a long time since she'd given them up. Her stomach tightened at the thought of where Kimyung was and that she was powerless to help her. She knew her daughter was tough as nails, but she was still a nine-year-old girl who had to be scared to death, wondering why she hadn't come to save her.

Someone frightening her daughter or doing something to her was almost too much to handle. Taking a deep breath, she looked at the red and white pack, sitting on top of the yellow legal pad. *Fuck it*. She grabbed the pack, pushing aside the legal pad and papers underneath it. The red Bic lighter was easy to spot. Rebecca made her way through her office door and outside.

# 11:08 PM
# West Side Wall

Driving a mile past the compound, both pickups turned around with their lights off and night vision gear deployed. Two miles to the west of the compound, both parallel roads intersected a road they'd overlooked that ran north and south. Carter flipped the kill switch that Mic had set up a year and a half ago. Doug's truck was similarly equipped. When engaged, the brake and interior lights would not come on when the brake pedal was pushed or doors opened. Carter left his finger on the toggle switch, thinking about Mic. It seemed such a long time ago when they went to San Miguel to help the Grimm's. Taking his finger off the toggle, he reflected on his good friend and fought off a wave of sadness. *Miss you brother.*

With lights off, the men drove a quick mile and pulled off a quarter mile from the west compound wall.

"We're turning off as planned," Carter said into his mike.

"Roger that, we're doing the same in five seconds," Doug said.

Carter opened his door and stepped out, looking around through the greenish glow of his night vision goggles.. Fifty yards away was Doug's pickup. He watched Conway taking their gear out of the back end. Five minutes later, wearing his chest rig with twelve loaded magazines and four extra pistol mags, Carter was ready. He looked at Rocco and Conway; both were looking at him.

"Ok, we're heading east as planned," Carter said again, scanning the area around him and east towards the compound. Inside the walls shown a green glow.

"Roger that. Time is 23:22, we'll meet back as planned at 23:42, fifty yards west of the wall. Out," Doug said.

"Roger that. Out," Carter said. The three of them gave a thumbs up and began moving to the east towards the compound with Rocco on point.

Carter took the middle position with Conway behind him, guarding the rear. Rocco and Conway were younger and quicker than him, and they'd done combat tours in more shitholes than they could remember. Being the leader was something he'd done in his mid-twenties when he started his first business, but never on the field of combat. Carter hadn't worked for anyone since he was twenty-six years old. At this point in his life, he was well past the point of having to be "the guy" all the time. He no longer owned any companies, having sold the last one years prior. He now was content coaching other business owners to succeed. This lifestyle was rewarding and allowed him the freedom to go on the occasional mission in the last couple of years.

Rather than the straight and easy path of just walking down the road to the compound, Rocco kept them fifty yards off of it, weaving through the desert fauna. Through his NVGs, Carter could make out the blinking infrared identifier on the top of Rocco's helmet. Carter looked around, up at the stars and straight ahead as they moved forward at a steady and methodical pace. He imagined Doug and Mike to the left of them doing the same. They'd be converging on the back wall within minutes. Rocco's right hand came up as he went to his right knee. In unison, without a sound, Carter went to a knee along with Conway. An elixir of adrenaline coursed through his veins. He welcomed and relished feeling alive, warm and alert. *This is where I belong, doing what I'm doing right now.*

"Rocco, what's your position?" Doug said.

"We're ten yards back from the tree line, running up to the wall," Rocco said.

"Roger that. Disregard the early plan and move to your left and let's form up. Stay behind the tree line."

"Roger that. Moving," Rocco said, turning left, raising his left hand, pointing toward Doug and Conway. Carter fell in behind Rocco, turning to verify Conway was behind him. Ahead, two IR lights moving as if suspended in air came into view along with Doug and Mike. Within two minutes, they huddled together in kneeling positions.

"Rocco, move up to the edge of the tree line and recon the back wall and corners, then get back here. Let's see what we're dealing with… On second thought, hold tight," Doug said.

Carter looked forward and around, feeling his right hand on the pistol grip and left hand on the front rail of his AR-15. He dropped his right hand, tapping the bottom of the magazine for the fifth time since they'd left the truck.

"It's clear, but there're lights on top of the wall along with three cameras. One on each of the corners and one in the middle. I'm sure there have to be motion sensors to go along with this.

Hopefully, the sensors are wired in series. If I take one out, they're all out," Conway said, taking a knee.

"Take care of it. Mike, go with him," Doug said, looking at Conway.

Carter watched the two men move forward into position with Mike taking a knee and Conway going into a prone position. Conway took his Ruger 22 Takedown model out of his pack, assembled it, attached the scope, mounted his NVG behind it and screwed the suppressor onto the barrel.

The quiet puff sounds reached Carter's ears as Conway worked his way down the wall, shooting out the floodlights, cameras and two sensors.

"Ok, I think we got them all. I think we're good to go," Rocco said.

"Let's hope so. We should assume there's the same light and camera setup on both the north and south walls. I don't want to take the time to deal with them. We'll do our entry here on the back wall. Rocco, I want you to go to the southwest corner and, Conway, you do the same on the northwest corner. Once you've reached the corners, I want you both to move along the wall towards each other to the center, looking for an entry point. See if you can find something we can exploit. That's a very tall wall. Anything you can find would beat having to go over it. The three of us will be set up along the edge here for overwatch. Once you meet each other in the middle, we'll move up to your position and go from there. Questions?" Doug said.

The five of them moved up to the edge of the tree line, going into combat kneeling positions. Rocco and Conway made their way to their respective corners. With Doug fifty yards to the right of him and Mike the same on the left, the three had the backside and two corners of the wall covered. In the distance, the howl of a coyote echoed in the cold desert air, followed by the incessant yapping of the rest of the pack. The green glow of the rest of Hermosillo and beyond the compound was unmistakable.

Arriving at the corners, Rocco and Conway turned, beginning their trek towards each other. Seventy-five feet from the corner, Carter watched Rocco linger over a spot on the wall and then continued his movement towards Conway.

"I think I've found something back towards the right corner," Rocco said.

"Roger that. We're coming to you," Doug said.

Listening through the radio, Carter, Doug and Mike hurried to meet up with Conway and Rocco.

"What did you find?" Doug asked in a whispered voice to Rocco.

"Back over there," Rocco said, pointing back in the direction of the southwest corner.

"Carter, stay here, Mike, go to the other corner," Doug said, nodding his head to Rocco to show him what he'd found.

That Black Friday at the mall, San Miguel and Nogales played over and over in his mind like a movie. Carter's mouth was dry. He reached for the feeder tube to the bladder in his pack, taking a long draw of it. *Stay frosty.*

# Day, 11:48 PM
# Sylvia Granada

Double checking the lock on the door to her apartment, she put the three empty soda cans on the tile floor next to the door. This was besides the door alarm she'd bought on Amazon that would make a loud wailing noise when activated. She didn't used to be like this, but after going through the FBI Academy and entering the world of criminals and violence, she'd put into practice what she'd learned at the academy. Assume the worst and always be ready.

Walking into her bedroom, she turned down the sheets on her queen-size bed and glanced over at a novel by Dean Koontz… *Ashley Bell*. It was a haunting and compelling story that she'd planned on reading more but, looking at the time, she passed on the idea. *Tomorrow night, I'm getting to bed earlier so I can read more of it.* At least that's what she'd been telling herself for the last eight days. Jumping up on the bed, her purring cat joined her, rubbing up against her leg.

Petting him, she thought about the recent events of Rebecca's daughter being taken. She felt terrible for her and wished somehow she could be the one to find her daughter. Then Rebecca would like her. Looking at the nightstand, she arranged the Sig Sauer pistol so she could grab it. Reaching to turn off the lamp on the nightstand, her phone buzzed. Holding the phone and laying back on the pillow, she took a deep breath. *I don't want to deal with him right now.*

"Hello, Uncle. How are you doing? What's up? Kinda late," Sylvia said.

"How's my favorite niece doing? Sor... Sorry, did I wake you?" Hector Granada said.

"No, it's ok. I was just getting ready to go to bed. What's up?"

"How's work going for you? Anything interesting happening?"

Sylvia listened to the odd question, wondering if he was drunk again. "Work's fine. What do you mean by anything interesting happening? I mean, kind of."

"I heard something happened to your boss's daughter. Kidnapped or something. Is that true?"

"Yes, but how did you hear about that?"

"You know, word travels fast. Do they know who did it or where she is?" Hector said, slurring his speech.

"No, I don't think they know who did it, why or where she is. Why are you asking?"

"You'd tell me if you knew who it was... riii... right?" Hector said.

"I'm not supposed to talk with anyone about any case unless someone is authorized for me to talk to. You understand, don't you?" Sylvia said in a serious tone.

"Ok, ok, just asking. I don't want you to get in trouble. Just checking to see how things were going... that's all. No harm in asking, right? I mean, it'd be ok to tell me... I'm a congressman...

right? Hey, listen, I may be in Tucson in the next few days. Dinner?"

Her mind went back to the incident while driving him to La Paloma, when he put his hand on her leg and wanted her to have a drink with him. She shuddered.

"We'll see, Uncle. They've got me busy right now. I've got to get up early so I'm going to run. Call me when you get to Tucson."

"Ohhh ok, I will. Good night to you, my pretty niece," Hector said.

"Good night," she said, hitting the end button. *Why the questions about Rebecca's daughter?*

# 11:56 PM
# The Wall

"Give me a minute," Rocco said, squatting down with a short tire iron he'd pulled from his pack, working a loose block at the bottom of the wall.

Carter watched Rocco wiggle the tire iron at the base of the wall, twenty feet from the corner. Rocco reached behind him with his left hand, holding an adobe block. Conway grabbed the first one, turning to his left three paces and placing it on the ground with Mike, then took the next one and repeated the process. Carter turned, continuing to look north down the wall, with Doug on the southwest corner of the wall. Five minutes later, a group of fifteen adobe blocks lay stacked at the base of the wall.

Welcome to the hacienda, boys," Rocco said, standing up and stepping back, looking down at the three by three-foot hole created by removing the blocks. "Fuck this shit of hopping over the wall. Thank you," Rocco said, kissing the tire iron and reaching behind, putting it back into his pack.

"Handy little tool... also good for cracking skulls in a pinch," Rocco whispered with a smile.

"Outstanding work. Ok, Rocco, take the lead; we're right behind you. I'll be last in, Carter. You go before me," Doug said.

Watching Mike wiggling through the opening, Carter went to all fours and then onto his stomach, working his way through with his helmet, rifle and pack going through first. Going to a combat kneeling position on the other side, next to Rocco, he adjusted his night vision goggles after putting his helmet back on. He thought it odd the area they were in was pitch black, but grateful at the same time. One hundred feet ahead, through the green glow, there was a swimming pool with furniture surrounding it. Off to the right of the area was a small building. Beyond that, the lights of the mansion illuminated the dark contrast of the compound.

"Spread out in a wedge formation ten yards apart. Rocco, take point. Conway you're left, Mike you're right, Carter rear and I'm center. Watch out for sensors, cameras, you know the drill. Ok, let's roll," Doug said.

Twenty yards short of the pool, Rocco raised his left hand in a fist. Two red glowing orbs danced like fireflies in the dark, close to each other. Two flashes from Rocco's rifle, followed by the crack of the 5.56 projectile breaking the sound barrier and smacking against skulls reached Carter's ears. The dance of the fireflies ended, falling to the ground behind the short three-foot wall surrounding the pool area.

Checking for life, one man was moving. Conway pumped two more rounds into his chest. The gurgling sound of a sucking chest wound filled the air. Then silence. Mowed grass with a cobblestone path lead from the pool to the house, fifty yards away. In front of the porch on the left side, a children's swing set, slide and picnic table sat silent.

Ahead, it was easy to see two figures on either side of the large double doors, leading to the back and out to the pool in their direction. Doug signaled for them to huddle behind the three-foot wall.

"Ok, Rocco, did you bring the fun stuff with you?" Doug asked.

"I did, boss, right here in my pack," Rocco said, nodding his head backwards.

"Work your way along the wall and throw one of your boom sticks over, towards the front of the property, then get back here. Let's see if we can draw some of these guys away from the main house," Doug said.

"Will do," Rocco said, turning, making his way to the wall to their right.

Carter watched Rocco make his way down the wall. Stopping, Rocco stepped back and hurled the package over the wall and turned, heading back to them. The ground shook from the muffled explosion on the other side of the wall.

The two men on the porch ran toward the wall and stopped. Someone came out from inside and the two men ran down the steps and turned, running down the right side of the house towards the front.

"Ok, let's get the girl," Doug said, pointing to the bushes in front of the railing on the porch.

# Monday, 12:21 AM
# Demon

Feeling the bed being depressed with someone laying down next to her drifted into her dream world. A hand stroking her hair, breathing into her ear, the warm stench of cigar and alcohol and the feel of lips on her neck. But she was safe. The room was lit and her mother was there. The warmth of the body pulling her close from behind… hands rubbing her chest, her stomach, moving down.

"Mommy. Mommy, you're here," Kimyung said, bolting awake. She tried to turn but couldn't. Wincing from the smell of the moist and hot stinking breath confused her.

"Do what I tell you," a slurred voice said, wrapping an arm around her throat.

"Mommy," Kimyung screamed, squirming out of the grasp of the stranger and slipping off the bed onto the floor.

"Come here, you little bitch. Get back in bed with me. I'm going to make you feel good," the deep voice in the dimly lit room said.

"No, I want my mommy. Leave me alone. Where's my mommy? She'll hurt you if you touch me," she said, turning, looking around the room for a way out.

"It's ok. I won't hurt you. Come on, give me a kiss, make me feel good. You'll like it," the dark figure said, moving off of the bed awkwardly, standing, swaying, holding on to the bedpost with his left hand and his right hand on his crotch. She stared at him and turned, running to the bedroom door. The knob turned, but the door wouldn't open. With both hands she twisted and tugged at it, turning her head, looking at the swaying naked demon with eyes rolled up in his head staring at her. Drool ran down the left corner of his sneering mouth. He stroked himself with his right hand. She pulled and kicked the door.

"Mommy! Somebody, help me!" Kimyung screamed, coming to terms with the unforgiving door. As she turned her back to it, the naked figure lurched forward, stumbling and landing hard on the floor. He grabbed her left ankle with his right hand. She yanked her foot back and kicked the creature in the face. She felt the soft flesh and cartilage of his nose give on impact from her heel. Turning to her right, she ran to the lone tall dresser in the room. He gathered himself off the floor, blood dripping from his nose. Wiping it with the back of his hand, he gritted his teeth and walked towards her. Before she could get away, he was in front of her, holding his penis with his right hand and smiling. She'd never seen a naked man before.

"Get away from me," she yelled, burying her right heel deep into his scrotum. The demon doubled over, grabbing his balls, gasping for air giving her enough room to run under the bed.

"Oh, you little bitch. I was going to be nice to you, but now I see how you are," he moaned, swaying back and forth with his hands still on his balls.

"Leave me alone or I'll kick you again. My mother has me taking karate… I'll hurt you again."

"The others weren't like you. When I'm done with you, you're going to make me money making other men happy, but I'm going to have you first," he said, going down on one knee, grabbing her right ankle as she tried to go under the bed, pulling her across the hardwood floor. He kept his head back as she kicked with her left foot. Her little fingers pressed into the floor. His other hand grabbed her left ankle, pulling her all the way out. Then, with both hands around her waist picked her up slamming her onto the edge of the mattress face down. His left hand pinned her down by the neck as she felt him spreading her legs with his right hand.

"You're hurting me. Mommy!"

"I've going to give you something that'll make it feel better."

The building shuddered followed by the force of something hitting the side of the house followed two seconds later by a muffled explosion. He turned, looking toward the door before releasing his grip. She scooted across the bed to the other side, down to the floor and under the bed.

"What the fuck was that?" he hollered to whoever might be listening. Turning, he moved towards the door.

"Where's Captain Sanchez? What the fuck was that?" the demon said, turning at the doorway and moving back to the bed. She watched him grab his wadded-up bathrobe off the floor and his feet step into a pair of slippers. Heavy footsteps moved towards their room with black boots arriving and stepping through the doorway.

"Sir, there was an explosion on the south side of the wall along the street. Our men are on their way," a man said as two more men arrived.

"Captain, find out what's going on. Are we under attack?" the demon said as the black boots moved back towards the door and out.

"Juan, where's the girl?" a man's voice asked.

"Don't worry about it. She's under the bed… the noise scared her. Come on, let's go. I'll be back in a little, young Asian beauty," said Juan Ortiz, seeing her foot sticking out from underneath the bed on the right side. Stepping out, he pulled the door closed behind him, locking it from the outside.

Coming out from under the bed, Kimyung ran to the door, trying to turn the handle to no avail. Turning around, she looked around the room for somewhere to hide. Tears running down her face and pressing hands together in front of her with fingers pointing up, she dropped to her knees, looking up. *Please, God, send angels to help me.*

# Boom

"What the fuck? What was that?" Hal asked, turning to Victor.

"Man, I don't' know. That was some serious shit, judging from the noise and size of the flash. Let's sit tight and see what happens," Victor said, looking through his binoculars in the blast's direction.

Two Federale pickup trucks raced through the open gates, turning right, heading towards them, then turning right onto the road running towards the site of the explosion. Red brake lights glowed in the darkness.

"Fuck, man. That's a lot of heat. I don't want to get tangled up with a pickup that's got a mounted machine gun in the bed. If you know what I mean," Hal said, bringing his binoculars down.

"I hope the girl's ok. I don't have a clue how we're going to rescue her. They've way too much firepower for us to go up against. This is fucked up. They're moving. One truck is turning around," Victor said, watching one set of headlights go back to the road and turn right, heading straight for them.

"We're screwed, dude," Hal said.

"Fuck," Victor said, taking his finger off the engine start button as the headlights of the pickup sped towards them. Two hundred yards from them, a blinding light bar mounted on the front of the truck came on, casting shadows on Victor's rental.

"What do we do?" Hal asked, looking at Victor.

"Nothing. We do nothing. There's no way we can shoot our way out of this. Ok. We're two dumb gringos who don't speak Spanish… We got lost trying to find our way to San Carlos. Put your gun under your seat," Victor said, reaching down with his, tucking it underneath his seat as the pickup skidded to a halt ten yards in front of them. Holding his left hand up to shield his eyes from the lights, Victor squinted as four shadows jumped from the bed of the pickup, shielded by the blinding lights. Two men on each side positioned themselves five feet away.

Victor rolled his window down, only to be met with the front end of two rifle barrels a foot away from his face. Hearing tapping on the passenger side window, Victor looked over at Hal.

"Roll it down," Victor said, looking back at the Federale holding the rifle on him and the other man standing a few feet behind him to his right.

"What are you two doing here?" a voice said in English.

"We were looking for the main road heading south to San Carlos and got lost. We'd turned off the main road to find a restaurant on Trip Advisor that sounded good, and now we're not sure where we are. Can you point us in the right direction so we can get back to the main highway going to San Carlos?" Victor said, looking at the man standing behind the one with the rifle. Squinting and continuing to shield his eyes, he couldn't make out the features of the one who'd spoke. *That voice sounds familiar… Oh, fuck.*

"Not a likely story, Victor Livingston. Who's your amigo on the other side of the car?" the voice said.

"Hal's his name. How do you know my name?" Victor said, feeling a sinking as he realized it wasn't a good idea to put their guns out of reach.

"Remember, we met yesterday? I don't forget a face or a name. Especially when they've got a nine-year-old girl with them on a dirt road in the desert, miles off the main road," the voice said.

There's was no longer a question in Victor's mind who the voice belonged to... the dots connected.

"Oh, it's you. How are you doing, captain? Imagine that, running into each other twice within a couple of days. Small world," Victor said, smiling. The captain took three steps forward, bringing himself into view.

"Ok, now, what are you really doing here? Please don't tell me it's because you're trying to get to San Carlos. We both know that's not true. Was it the two of you who set off the explosion?"

If this was a game of chess, then the captain just put Victor and Hal into check... maybe... checkmate. Victor's mind raced, trying to look for an out. Time to just go to the heart of the matter. The captain let him go the other day. Maybe he'd do the same again.

"Can we talk in private Captain?"

"It's ok. My men don't speak or understand English. I'm listening," Captain Sanchez said, stepping closer, putting his left hand on the hood and his right hand on the grip of the gun on his hip. "You've been sitting here for a while. Your hood is cold," the captain said, looking at the hood and then Victor.

"Ok, I'll be straight up with you. I followed you after you took the girl from me to the Pemex. I watched as you gave her to another man who drove away in a gold Cadillac Escalade. I assume that was Mario. Then I followed him to a house in Hermosillo, which I believe is his house. My friend here and I set up surveillance on the house, trying to see what was happening with the girl. Then I saw two Federales pickups pull up and take the girl. We followed the trucks to here and we've been sitting here since then. No, we had nothing to do with the explosion," Victor said, looking at the captain who'd stepped close enough so that he could see his features and eyes. Victor knew that sometimes the best strategy for getting out of a jam was just to tell the truth. He didn't move his eyes off the captain, who he suspected was weighing whether to believe him.

"Ok, gringo. I believe you, but my boss who lives behind those walls might not. Do you know who he is?"

"Juan Ortiz? Where's the girl, captain?" Victor said, maneuvering to take control of the conversation.

"She's in there," the captain said, nodding his head in the compound's direction.

"Ok. Why is she there?" Victor said.

"You're in no position to be asking questions, gringo. Ok, I understand you following us, but why are you still here?"

Victor looked over at Hal, then back up at the captain, taking a deep breath. So far, they were still alive and would keep telling the truth to the captain.

"We're trying to figure out a way to rescue her and get her back across the line. She's a good kid. She was supposed to be down here for only two days and then taken back. I have to be honest with you. You pissed me off when you and your men found us on that road. I've never lost a package. Call it a professional thing or whatever, but I've never snatched a kid before. I don't like it and want to make sure she gets home safe. I'm trying to make this right," Victor said, looking at the captain.

"Ok I understand. But do you think you're just going to walk into Juan Ortiz's compound and take her?"

"No, that's the problem. I..." Victor stopped short as the sound of another explosion from the other side of the wall reached them. Off in the distance, the muffled staccato sound of an AK-47 reached them.

"Corporal, you and Moro, stay here and guard these two men. Shoot them if they try anything. You and your gringo amigo next to you... don't move. I'll be back," the captain said, turning and running back to the pickup.

The driver in the pickup backed up, making a quick U-turn, throwing dirt and rocks toward Victor and Hal's car.

"Fuck, dude. What do we do now?" Hal asked, lighting a cigarette.

"We have two options. Sit tight and wait for the captain to return, or we kill these two guys and make a run for it. When the captain returns, I'm not so sure he's going to let us go. If he doesn't, my guess is we'll end up inside those walls surrounded by cartel. I don't think that'll end well for us. If we shoot our way out of this, no doubt the whole Mexican police force and the military will look for us. I don't know. What do you think, brother?" Victor said, talking softly.

"I'll follow your lead. Make the call. I'm right behind you," Hal said, taking a drag off his cigarette and looking at the barrel of the rifle three feet from his head, then up at the young man holding it.

Their options sucked, but Victor was confident he could grab his handgun under the seat and shoot the kid holding the rifle in the forehead before the guy reacted. He knew he could kill the other Federale too. But it wasn't just him. There was Hal and his life to consider. Whether Hal could drop his guy before the guy reacted was a big question. He felt responsible for him… and then there was the nagging feeling of responsibility for Kimyung. *Fuck.*

# Bindings

Forming a V formation, Doug took point, going up the wide porch steps with Conway and Mike to his left and Rocco and Carter to his right. The subdued sound of men's voices and vehicles idling were on the other side of the south wall.

"Porch clear," Doug whispered through all of their headsets. Stepping forward, he opened the two big wood and glass doors leading into a great room, flanked on either side by stairs leading to the second floor. To the right, at the front of the room, a man holding a phone to his ear ran to a hallway to their left. Doug held up his fist... the team froze in position with their rifles up. Arriving at the hallway, the man turned right, heading to the front of the house.

Doug gestured for Carter and Rocco to take the stairs to the right, pointing at Mike to cover the ground floor great room, and motioned that he and Conway were heading up the stairs on their left.

Reaching the top of the landing, Carter looked down it to the end. A wooden banister ran the length, making a U shape over to Doug and Conway on the other side. It reminded him of saloons depicted in old western movies. On their floor to the right were three doors spaced twenty feet apart. The side that Doug and Conway were on had the same arrangement. Carter looked down to where Mike was and ahead to where the man had disappeared. At the front, on the second floor in the middle, was an eight-foot-wide alcove, recessed back four feet with a door. Looking down at the floor on both the right and left sides were stairways leading to the ground floor.

Glancing to his left, Carter spotted Doug and Conway stacked against the first door they'd come to. Stopping and turning, he and Rocco did the same with Rocco in the lead. Coming through the door, Rocco button hooked left with Carter slanting right, both men's rifles up, triangulating their firing position in the room. A king bed with a canopy over it sat against the back wall in the middle with fresh blood stains on the mattress Rocco ducked into a door, leading to a bathroom, and backed out. The room was a square shape, maybe twenty by twenty feet. Leather ankle and wrist bindings were attached to the bedposts. To the right was a nightstand with a drawer. Carter, pulling the drawer open revealed a black leather hood and a red rubber ball with a leather strap attached to a buckle on one side.

"Sick fucks. Carter, let's go," Rocco said, nodding his head and rifle back to the doorway to the landing.

"Room clear, moving to the next," Doug said over the radio.

"Room clear here and moving to the next," Rocco said, returning the message.

Coming out of the second room, Rocco held up his right fist, freezing Carter in his steps.

"Hold up. Someone's coming out of the door at the front center top," Rocco whispered into his radio, peeking his head out, looking right. Across the way, Doug and Conway stopped short of their doorway. Carter imagined Mike down below, moving to cover. A man in a bathrobe came out, yelling in Spanish, heading to the stairs at the front of their landing.

"Moving," Doug said on the radio.

After clearing the last room on either side, Doug, Conway, Carter and Rocco moved to the alcove in the center with the door.

"Carter, you watch the stairs to the right. Conway, do the same for the left," Doug said on the radio.

Taking up a position at the top of the stairs, Carter thought about Kim. He wondered what she was doing at the moment. A door opening and voices below reverberated off the walls, up the stairs. Leaning into the corner, he pointed his rifle down the stairwell.

# Gringos

"Where're your other men, captain?" Juan Ortiz said, standing in the main door entrance as the captain walked up the front porch steps.

"They're down the road to the south. We found two gringos parked facing this direction. I left two of my men to watch them," Captain Sanchez said.

"Two gringos, sitting on the road a half a mile from the explosion? Did you see anyone else? What did they say they're doing there?"

"Didn't see anyone else. They said they were on their way to San Carlos and took a wrong turn looking for a place to eat. I don't think they had anything to do with the explosion. They wouldn't have been able to make it back to their car in time unless they set it off with a remote device. I don't think that's the case. They look like two tourists, nothing more," the captain said.

"Do you believe them?" Juan said, swaying to his right and catching himself.

"I think they're ok," Captain Sanchez said, not wanting to reveal what he knew about Victor. He respected Victor for not lying to him. Neither man wanted harm to come to Kimyung.

Juan Ortiz stepped out onto the porch, pulling out a pack of cigarettes from his robe. He leaned forward and put one into his mouth, and one of his men appeared, holding a lit lighter.

"Maybe they're telling the truth? Bring them to me. We'll see if they're on their way to San Carlos or if they had something to do with the bomb going off. I think it's strange for you to find them on the road like that. That's what I'm thinking, captain," Juan Ortiz said, exhaling his first puff of the cigarette, looking at the captain.

"I agree it's very coincidental. Maybe it wasn't a bomb. Maybe it was just some local kids fucking around… You know, trying to prove their manhood by messing with you. Besides, it can get messy if two Americans go missing in Hermosillo… bringing unneeded attention to you," Captain Sanchez said, trying not to be overly persuasive with his boss. He took a step and a half back from the smoke drifting his way.

"Who said they'd go missing? I just want to make sure they're telling the truth. My men and I will help them with that. Go get them," Juan Ortiz said, staring at the captain with heavy eyes.

"Ok," the captain said, turning and walking down the steps to his truck. *Shit, I should have just told Juan what they said… If he finds out I didn't… Fuck. I'm sick of living like this. This is all wrong. The little girl, all the torturing and killing.*

"Let's go," the captain said sharply, getting into the truck with his man behind the wheel.

# Uncontrollable Urge

"I'm going to grab the binoculars off the dash and lean through my door to look in the compound's direction. When I raise them up, I'm going to drop them on the outside of the car. My guy will step back, but I'll play the dumb gringo and open my door. It'll be a distraction for him. When I drop them, lean back. I'm grabbing my gun and taking your guy out first," Victor said, looking straight ahead.

"Holy shit. Ok, whenever you're ready."

Victor weighed the different scenarios of how this could turn out for the two of them. None of them were good. If they ended up being taken into Juan Ortiz's compound, he knew they wouldn't come out alive. Being tortured and having his limbs and head cut off or whatever the fuck they'd do was not very appealing. Shooting their way out of this, though a long shot, seemed to Victor to be the best option. *Time to drop back and punt.*

With his right hand, Victor felt for the outer rubber coating of the binoculars. Bringing them up, he leaned left towards the open window but stopped short.

"Fuck," Victor said, looking toward the lights illuminating them coming off of the two fast approaching Federales' trucks. He put the binoculars down between himself and Hals seat. Within thirty seconds, dust engulfed them, coming in the windows, followed by the sound of the doors on both trucks opening and closing.

"Well, so much for the best-laid plans of mice and men," Hal said with a dejected tone.

"Hang tight, brother. We're going to get out of this one way or another," Victor said.

Two more Federales, one on each side, joined the two men that had been left to guard them, approaching with their rifles up and barrels pointed at them. Behind, Captain Sanchez followed.

"Both of you get out of the car, take three steps forward, put your hands on the hood and spread your legs," the captain said.

His tone, though not threatening, wasn't friendly. Both Federales on either side frisked Victor and Hal, then put their hands behind their backs, cuffing them. They walked the two to the captain's truck and put them into the back seat.

"If you value your life, listen to what I'm going to tell you. These are dangerous people. Don't tell them what you told me about following us here and wanting to rescue the girl. Stick to your story about getting lost. Play the dumb gringos. Do you hear me?" Captain Sanchez said as the driver turned the pickup around and headed back to the gates.

"We hear you… Why are you helping us, captain?" Victor asked, looking at Hal who shrugged his shoulders.

"That's not important. If you're lucky enough, he'll let you go… If I were you, if you value your life, forget the girl. Get back across the border as quick as you can. Do you hear me?" the captain said, continuing to look forward as they turned, going through the gates.

"We hear you," Victor said, looking ahead as they rolled down the long drive to the well-lit house.

Both the rear doors opened within moments of the truck stopping in front of the house. Victor and Hal were yanked out and thrown to the ground, landing hard from not being able to break the fall with their hands cuffed behind their backs. Victor winced as a boot went hard into his stomach.

"Get them up. Let's see what they have to say for themselves," Juan Ortiz said, standing at the bottom of the steps.

They pulled both men to their feet. Victor took a series of shallow breaths, trying to regain his composure. An almost uncontrollable urge to laugh, looking at Juan Ortiz standing in his bathrobe with a lit cigar, drink and bedroom slippers on, swept over him. The entire scene was comical. They were in Hermosillo, Mexico, past midnight, handcuffed, standing in front of the head of a dangerous and powerful Mexican cartel, who was puffing on a cigar surrounded by his goons and Federales. All of them armed to the teeth with guns. Victor bit his lip to keep from laughing.

"You two, get back to your positions on the back porch," Juan Ortiz said, looking at the two

"Sí, señor," the larger of the two said, nodding his head to the other men. Victor watched the two of them ascend the steps and disappear into the house. Moments later, the sound of gunfire erupted from inside.

"Go," Juan Ortiz shouted to three of his men, pointing to the steps.

"Go with them," Captain Sanchez said to four of his men.

"Captain, leave one of your men with these two. I'll deal with them later," Juan Ortiz said, turning to make his way up the steps to the porch with his lit cigar still in hand.

Victor looked at Hal, the captain and then at the sight of Juan Ortiz making his way up the stairs in his bathrobe. Still cuffed and catching his breath from the boot in the gut, he smiled.

"Stay here," Captain Sanchez said to the corporal and turned, heading up the stairs.

# Tango Down

With his left hand, Doug gripped the door handle leading into the room the man in the bathrobe came out of. Slowly turning it each way, he felt it come to a stop, not allowing him to open the door. Doug stepped back as Conway went to a knee in front of the door with a lockpick.

"Stand by," Doug said into the radio, looking down at him. Conway got up, resuming his position behind his boss. Turning the handle, Doug moved through the door opening, button hooking left with Rocco slanting right.

With the room covered, Doug sidestepped left through an open bathroom door and reappeared, scanning the room. The bed was disheveled with the top sheet and blanket pulled to the opposite side. At the foot of the bed, a black padded bench seat with restraints attached to it sat empty. Leather restraints hung from the four bedposts. On the other side of the room, Conway pointed to the bed while taking three steps back, raising his rifle up. Doug followed suit with both men holding their rifles at the ready. In unison, the two went down on one knee, moving forward with their left hand to meet the floor, going prone. The two men pulled their rifles back and looked at each other, then back under the bed.

Kimyung, naked and curled up in a fetal position, looked at Doug with her almond-shaped terrified eyes.

"It's ok. We won't hurt you. Are you Kimyung?" Doug asked, laying there looking at the frightened young girl. He looked over at Conway and then back at her. He felt tears welling up, imagining if that had been Kelli, his young daughter. Taking a deep breath, he suppressed the emotion. An overwhelming urge to find the man in the bathrobe and beat him to death with his bare hands came over him.

"Boss… you ok?" Conway said, looking at Doug.

"Yes, I'm Kimyung. Do you know my mommy? I want to go home," the girl said, tears streaking down her face.

"Your mommy said to tell you, 'hot fudge Sunday.' Do you understand, 'hot fudge Sunday?' We're here to take you to her. Come out from there and let's get you dressed. We've got to move quickly before those men come back," Doug said, staring into her frightened eyes. Conway turned, retrieving her clothes and shoes. Kimyung hesitated for a moment, then scurried out. Conway handed her clothes, one piece at a time. With her shoes on, he slung his rifle over his back, scooped her up in his arms and nodded to Doug. The three headed to the doorway and stopped. With a quick peek, looking right and left, Doug was assured to see Carter to his left and Rocco to his right at the top of the stairs, looking down. Taking three steps to the railing, he looked down, seeing Mike positioned in the back near the doors leading to the outside. The sounds of voices reached him as two men walked down the middle of the room, heading to the back, talking. Turning, he motioned with two fingers to Conway, standing in the doorway with Kimyung, and pointed down below. Looking over to Carter and Rocco, he did the same. Gunfire from the other end of the room erupted. Turning and looking down, Doug saw the two men drop. He knew Mike was compromised, otherwise he would have used quieter means to stop them.

"Let's go," Doug said to the others. Conway put Kimyung down and grabbed her hand. The three of them went to the right with Doug taking the lead and Conway and the girl following. Walking backwards, Doug kept his rifle pointed down towards the front of the room with Conway and Kimyung running to the back. Carter and Rocco remained on the corners at the top of the staircase. Halfway down the length of the second-floor landing, Doug went to a combat kneeling position, aiming his rifle between the banister slats and down towards the front.

"Covering," Doug hollered. Carter opened fire on the corner. Seeing movement at the bottom of the stairs on Carter's side, Doug waited until three men bunched up at the bottom of the stairs. Doug opened up on them, dropping two. He watched as a third one tumbled down the stairs, dispatched by Carter.

"Moving," Carter yelled, walking backwards toward Rocco. Carter tapped his right shoulder and the two men moved backwards, rifles up, in Doug's direction.

"Moving," Doug called out, heading to the top of the stairs in the back. Conway and Kimyung were at the bottom of the stairs across from Mike.

"Mike, move outside to the porch and cover the left corner. Conway, cover the right. Leave the girl in the stairwell, we'll get her," Doug said through his radio.

With Carter and Rocco moving backwards towards him, Doug took four bounding steps down to where Kimyung was standing. Looking back down the length of the room to the front and seeing nothing, he grabbed her hand.

"You ok? Do you want me to carry you?" Doug said, looking at her.

"No, I'm ok," she said, looking up at Doug.

"Good, you stay close to me. I won't move too fast. We're getting you out of here and taking you home," Doug said as Carter and Rocco arrived.

"Moving," Doug said, looking left to the front of the room. Seeing nothing, he and Kimyung made their way through the doors and onto the back porch. A bullet buzzed by his head and then he felt a sting on his left ear, followed by gunshots from the other end of the room. Carter and Rocco opened up, silencing the gunfire.

To his right and left, Conway and Mike fired their weapons down the side of the house.

"Moving," Doug said, grabbing Kimyung's hand and headed down the steps and to the cobblestone walk, heading back to the pool area.

"Moving," Rocco called out, followed in unison by Carter, then Mike and Conway on the corners.

The six of them made it to the pool patio without incident. Within two minutes, they were at the hole in the wall. Without a word, Rocco headed through the opening first, followed by Mike. The sound of muffled shots from the other side of the wall were followed by silence.

"Tango down," Rocco said into his radio.

"Carter, you go and then I'll pass her to you," Doug said.

On the other side, they spread out in a slant left formation with Kimyung behind Carter. They moved at a pace they hoped she could maintain. Seeing she was tiring, Mike picked her up.

"Double-time," Doug said, turning around to look back towards the outside wall of the compound. Moving beams of light and distant voices faded behind them.

# Uncuffed

Victor nodded to Hal, putting his head down and charging into the young Federale, hitting him in the sternum and knocking him to the ground. The young man tried calling out, but struggled to breathe from the force of Victor's head hitting his. The muffled sounds of gunfire and yelling from inside reached them as the Federale's right hand went for his handgun. Hal's right boot came down hard on his forearm, stopping him, followed by a harder kick to his head from Hal's left boot. Victor turned towards the unconscious man's belt, moving his hands to the keys on it. Victor knew this drill. In his early training, they'd practiced it many times. It didn't take but a moment for him to unhook the keys. Rolling to his knees and then onto his feet, he turned towards Hal.

"Turn around and give me your hands," Victor said, backing up towards Hal, feeling his hands and wrists and the cold steel wrapped around them. Within seconds, he found the handcuff key on the ring, put it into Hal's set and turned it, freeing Hal's right wrist. Hal turned and grabbed Victor's wrists, releasing him from the cuffs.

Victor bent down, taking the HK USP .45 caliber handgun out of the moaning young man's holster.

"You fucked him up... Nice work. Let's get the fuck out of here," Victor said, turning toward the Federale pickup parked behind the one they'd arrived in. Reaching in through the rolled down driver's door window to the steering column, he felt the dangling keys left in the ignition. Opening the door, a shot came from the top of the stairs.

"Motherfucker... I'm hit," Hal yelled. Using the space between the truck's door and cab as a shield, Victor steadied himself and unleased three rounds in the shooter's direction. The man slumped, tumbling a third of the way down the steps.

"Hold on," Victor said, running up the steps and relieving the man of his AK-47, then bounding back down to Hal. Grimacing, he held the back of his left thigh.

"I'm good, let's go," Hal said, getting into the cab with Victor's help. Closing the door, Victor ran around the front of the cab, hopped in and turned the key. Backing up, doing fast U-turn he floored it heading down the drive to the gate. Within moments the lights illuminated closed gates with two men with AK's standing facing them in front of it. Knowing they were in a Federale pickup might not alert the men, he stopped twenty feet short of them.

"Abre la Puerta, muy rapido," Victor hollered in Spanish, telling them to hurry and open the gate. He hoped the confusion of the sounds of the gunfight at the house and their means of escape in a Federale truck would do the trick. Standing in the headlights with the dust from the pickup drifting towards them, they looked at each other. After a brief conversation, the one on Victor's left turned, making his way to a post with an illuminated keypad.

"¿Qué fue lo que pasó en la casa?" the other man said, walking towards them on the driver's side, wanting to know what was happening up at the house.

"How are you doing?" Victor asked, turning to Hal and then back to the approaching man with his AK pointed to the ground in a relaxed position.

"I'm good. I'm not pumping blood yet," Hal said, wrapping a dirty towel he'd found stuffed in a side pocket on the door around his thigh.

"Stop," Victor said, opening his door and stepping out, bringing his rifle to his shoulder.

"Alto!" Victor shouted again after the man took three more steps towards him. Seeing Victor standing there with a rifle pointed at him, he stopped. The other man busy working the key pad looked over. Victor walked up to the closest man, taking his rifle, and pushed him back towards the other man with the end of the barrel of his AK-47. Stepping back four paces from the first man, he pointed it at the other.

"Ponga el rifle en el piso lentamente y abre la puerta," Victor said in Spanish to the other man to get him to slowly put his rifle on the ground and open the gate.

"No, señor. I don't know the combination," the man said to Victor. Taking three steps towards the first man, he butt-stroked him, dropping him onto the ground and pointing his rifle back at the one by the keypad.

"What? You don't know the combination?" Victor said, firing a round grazing the man's right ear. Holding the AK-47 with his right hand, he aimed at the man's chest and stooped down, picking up the other man's rifle with his left hand, slinging it over his shoulder and watching the man punch in the code.

Back-stepping to the pickup, he felt the door handle as the gate opened.

"Let's get the fuck out of here," Hal said, holding his leg.

"Roger that," Victor said, punching the accelerator. Twenty feet on the other side of the gate, he made a hard right, speeding to their parked cars.

"Look, we'll ditch this thing and get back in our car. This thing stands out too much. We'll leave your car here… I'll buy you another one when we get back," Victor said, smiling.

"Sounds good. Hopefully, we can make it to the border ok," Hal said in an energetic tone.

"They'll be expecting us to head north… We're going south. It'll be too hot heading north,"

"Ok, south sounds good. Where are we headed?" Hal said.

"A little more than an hour from here is San Carlos. Beautiful spot with lots of places to stay. It's a tourist hangout. Years ago, it was all Americans and Canadians, but now it's mostly Mexican Nationals. With all the violence going on down here, most of the Americans and Canadians are gone. Besides, there's been a growing middle class in Mexico the last twenty years and they love to party at seaside resorts. We'll get a room there and lie low for a couple of days. Think you can hang in there until then?" Victor asked.

"I'll be ok. Laying out by the ocean for a few days sounds good to me. You're paying for it," Hal said, wincing and laughing.

Victor skidded in the dirt, stopping the pickup and putting it into park. Jumping out, he ran to the other side, helping Hal and getting him his rental car. Closing the door, he got back in the Federale pickup, parking it behind their other car. Running back to their car, he got in. Relieved to see no sign of any vehicles coming after them, he hit the accelerator, doing a spinning U-turn and heading in the opposite direction of the compound.

"Talk to me, Hal. You good?" Victor said, looking over at him.

"Yeah, I'm fine," Hal said in a weak voice.

"When we get to San Carlos, I'll get you some medical attention. Not a hospital. I'm sure there's a doc I can pay to come to the room and check you out. Hang in there. You're going to be ok," Victor said, speeding a mile down the road, turning left onto a street he hoped would lead them to the highway to San Carlos.

# San Miguel

"Carter, you and Rocco take the girl in your truck. Mike, go with them. Conway, you're riding with me. Carter, since you know the area better than the rest of us, you'll lead, but keep your ears on. If we run into trouble, let Conway and me move ahead of you if you can. You doing ok? We're going to get you out of here and back to your mother," Doug said, looking at Kimyung and then Carter.

"Ok, heading north up Highway 15 won't work since we've made our presence known. How about we make a run for San Miguel? I think we've a good shot at it once we're out of Hermosillo and heading northeast. If we can get to the town of Cananea, we've a good chance of getting to San Miguel and north back across the line through the Grimms' old place. But we need to get moving. With any luck, we'll get ahead of them setting up roadblocks. They'll be looking for us," Carter said.

"Sounds good to me. Mount up, let's roll," Doug said.

Carter, with Rocco riding shotgun, listened to Mike helping Kimyung into the back of his pickup. They headed west on the dirt road, moving away from the compound. Coming to a road running north and south, he turned right. Eventually the two vehicles made their way onto Highway 15, heading to the exit that would take them to the mining town of Cananea. Thirty plus years ago, Carter traveled through Cananea on his way back into the U.S. through Aqua Prieta, the border crossing at Douglas, Arizona. It was a two-lane paved road taking them to Cananea. From there, it'd be an hour drive to San Miguel and across the border at the Grimms' old ranch. Once across, it'd be a straight shot up to I-10 and westbound to Tucson.

# Aftermath

"Juan, are you ok?" Captain Sanchez said, looking at this boss standing in the middle of the great room with a pistol in his hand. Spread out through the compound were lifeless bodies of his men and three of Juan's men. Smoke hung in the air like a ghost. The smell of blood and burnt gun powder stung his nostrils. Somewhere behind him, on the steps leading up to the second floor, the sound of moaning mixed into the scene.

"What?" Juan Ortiz said, slowly turning his head towards the captain.

"Are you ok?"

"Yes, I'm fine. Where's the girl? Who were those fucking guys?" Juan Ortiz asked.

"She's gone. They took her. My men saw them leaving in two pickups heading west, and then they turned right, heading north. I'm sure they're heading for the main road. I think they were gringos. They talked to each other in English," Captain Sanchez said, looking at Juan Ortiz standing in front of him in his bathrobe with a pistol in his left hand and half of a cigar in his right.

"Pinche gringos. Gringos, gringos—I'm sick of them fucking up my operation. How the fuck did they get into my compound and my house? Do we have a traitor among us?"

"They came in through a hole they punched in the wall in the back southwest corner. It looks like they shot all the lights and cameras out. They somehow disabled our sensor system. I think it was the same gringos who killed your men and mine in San Miguel."

"Why do you think that, Captain?"

"Just by the way they were moving. Their fighting skills are superior to ours. Those guys are pros… maybe American special forces. I don't know, just seems that way. They're going to make a run for the border. We'll setup roadblocks on the major roads heading north out of Hermosillo."

"Get a hold of Commander Yeppes. I don't want them getting out of the country. Tell him I want his men to bring them and the girl to me. I want them alive. Do you hear me? I want them and the girl alive… It'll be fun, punishing her and torturing and killing them… slowly," Juan Ortiz said to the captain, looking up to the ceiling and taking a puff on his cigar.

"Yes, sir. What do you want to do with the gringos out front?"

"Bring them in here. Go get one of those big blue plastic tarps and spread it out here," Juan Ortiz said, turning to one of his men and pointing to the center of the tile floor in the big room.

"Captain, they're gone and so is one pickup," one of the captain's men said, running and coming to a halt in front of the captain. The captain looked at him and then at Juan.

"Gone! What do you mean they're fucking gone? Go get me those fucking gringos that stole my girl and find those other two bastards. I'm going to skin them all alive and make belts for all of you. I want a drink. Somebody get me a fucking drink," Juan screamed, wiping the saliva from his chin with the back of his forearm. He turned and headed for the stairs on the right side.

Deep inside, the captain hoped whoever rescued the girl would get her back across the border and away from this monster. But, for the safety of his family, he'd have no choice but to capture them. Pulling his phone out of the pocket on the left side of his cargo pants, he punched in the number to his commander. Relieved with the sound of the commander answering, he explained the situation and what Juan was demanding. He knew Commander Yeppes would comply with Juan's demands. He also knew, within one hour of the phone call, the commander would have every well-traveled road heading north out of Hermosillo set up with roadblocks. Unless the gringos and the girl found a safe place to lay up for a few days, the likelihood of them making it out of Mexico were slim to none. *I wouldn't want to be them if they're caught.*

# 1:34 AM
# Exfiltrate

Doug was right behind Carter as he took the exit off of Highway 15, heading northeast. It'd only been twenty minutes since they exited the area west of the Juan Ortiz's compound.

"What are you boys up to down there? I picked up a conversation with Captain Sanchez and a Federales commander by the name of Yeppes. Sounds like you made a real mess out of Juan's casa. He wants all of you and the girl brought to him alive. Apparently, you left some of his guys and the captain's men face down in pools of blood. The commander is setting up roadblocks on all roads heading north, west and east out of Hermosillo. Good job rescuing the girl. Are you guys still in Hermosillo?" Alex said.

"Outskirts. We just took an exit off of the main highway and we're heading northeast. Carter, Rocco and Mike are in front of us with the girl. Carter's somewhat familiar with the area. We're heading to Cananea. Assuming we reach it, it's not much further to San Miguel and back into the country. Hopefully we go undetected," Doug said.

"Fuck, man, you guys are on your own. Have you talked with Dax?"

"No, not yet. I was getting ready to when you called. I'm going to see if maybe he can get us a set of eyes in the sky. Keep me posted if you pick anything else up. The next time we talk, we'll be across the line." Doug said.

"For sure. I'll let you know if I hear anything. Keep your head on a swivel. Out," Alex said.

"Out," Doug said, looking ahead at the taillights on Carter's pickup and back to his phone, hitting the send button.

"Where are you guys at? Were you able to get Kimyung?" Dax said in his usual straight-to-the-point style.

"Roger that. We're northeast bound, heading out of Hermosillo. She's riding with Carter, Rocco, and Mike. Conway and I are trailing behind them. The plan is to go through a town called Cananea and from there it should only be about an hour to San Miguel and across the border," Doug said.

"Have any problems when you found her?" Dax said.

"Nothing we couldn't handle. We made a bit of a mess out of Juan Ortiz's place. I just spoke with Alex. He picked up a call from Captain Sanchez to a Federale commander by the name of Yeppes. Not good. They're setting up roadblocks heading anywhere west, north and east out of Hermosillo. You don't have any A-10s loitering in the area you could send our way, do you?" Doug said, remembering the time in Afghanistan when Dax coordinated A-10s coming in and saving his and his platoon's bacon.

"Wish I did. But let me see if I can do something. There are Predator B drones operating on this side of the border. I'll see if I can pull in a few favors and get one down there to watch over you. Not likely, but if I do, it'll be unarmed and flown by one of the pilots out of Davis Monthan in Tucson. I'll be in touch. In the meantime, stay healthy," Dax said.

"Thanks, Dax. With any luck, we'll all get out of here in one piece. We're getting this little girl back to her mother... We owe her mother big time. Let me know if you get anything worked out with a drone. We'd welcome any help you might get us. We've got every Federale in Sonora after us. Out," Doug said, rubbing his eyes, looking ahead and down both sides of the road. The amount of lit buildings were disappearing as they made their way out of the edges of Hermosillo into the desert.

"Conway, how are you doing?" Doug asked.

"I'm good. How about you, boss?"

"I'm good, too. You ok if I catch a few winks?"

"No worries, I've got this."

"Ok, if I'm not stirring in thirty minutes give me a nudge," Doug said, looking at his watch and out to his right, to the east. *Not long before sunrise.*

# 1:37 AM
# San Carlos

"Hey, brother. How are you doing? Stay with me—don't sleep," Victor said, veering right onto the exit to San Carlos off Highway 15, heading south into Guaymas. Victor, seeing Hal had fallen asleep, nudged him.

"What? Ok, I'm good. This hurts like a bitch," Hal said, holding the back of his thigh with his left hand and rubbing his eyes with his right.

"Pain is good. Lets you know you're alive," Victor said.

"How very true. I never thought about it that way. There're lots of other ways to let me know I'm alive besides getting shot," Hal said, hitting the window switch to put his window down.

"Haven't smelled that in a long while. The Sea of Cortez. God, that smells good," Victor said.

"It smells great, but it's cold," Hal said, taking a deep breath in and hitting the up switch to the window.

The two men drove on, seeing the lights of San Carlos illuminate the sky a few miles ahead. To their left, a quarter moon revealed an occasional glimpse of the ocean.

"Ok, there are several hotels in San Carlos. I'll go in first and get us a room. Can you walk ok?" Victor asked, turning to Hal.

"I'm ok, I..." Hal said, just as Victor's phone lit up.

"I can't believe he's calling me right now. Probably drunk. What's up?" Victor said, putting the phone to his left ear.

"Wha... what's up? You fucking tell me what's up. Where's the girl?" Congressman Hector Granada said, slurring his speech.

"I don't have her. Last thing I knew, she was inside of Juan Ortiz's compound. There was an explosion outside of the compound and then a few minutes later a gunfight inside. Don't know what was going on. Long story short, we barely escaped with our lives," Victor said, looking at his watch as a center road divider with white-painted curbs appeared with street lights brightly illuminating the road. *One-thirty in the morning. This guy is off the deep end.*

"What? Oh, my God. You've got to be fucking kidding me. You're fucking with me, right?"

"No, I'm not fucking with you. Don't know where she is and the chance of getting her back is... It's not going to happen. Besides, we've got bigger problems. My partner took a round in the leg. We were able to escape while a gunfight was going on inside the compound. We're going to find a hotel and lie low for a day or two. I'm going to get my partner some medical help," Victor said, looking at Hal.

"No, fuck him. You've got to go back and get the girl. Nothing like this was supposed to happen. You've got to get her. Your friend will be alright. Go back," Hector said.

"No can do. Why don't you call your buddy Mario? Maybe he can help you? I mean, his cousin is Juan Ortiz... right?" Victor said, driving past a row of closed merchants, restaurants, scuba

278

diving shops, bars and real estate offices. Up ahead, a fork in the road loomed. Victor veered to the right.

"I paid you a lot of fucking money. Do your job," Hector Granada said, yelling.

"You did, but you didn't pay me to rescue the girl. You only paid me to deliver her to Mario Quintana. Trying to rescue her was something I was doing on my own time. I didn't charge you for a rescue mission. I kept my end of the deal up. I've got to go; we're pulling into a hotel. Call Mario," Victor said and hung up. He watched his phone light up six more times until it stopped.

"What was that all about?" Hal said, looking over at Victor.

"Our good congressman, drunk as usual and having a shit fit because of the girl. He didn't like the news when I told him about what happened. Fuck him. He's a worthless piece of garbage."

"Yeah, but what if he wants you for another job sometime?"

"Fuck him. I don't work for lowlifes like him. If I'd known, I'd never have taken the job. Listen, sit tight and don't fall asleep. I'm going in to see about getting a room," Victor said, opening the driver side door.

"Make sure it's a nice one with two women... for each of us. And tequila, don't forget the tequila. I could use a few shots right now," Hal said, smiling.

"I'll see what I can do. Be right back. Hang in there, brother," Victor said, getting out and closing the door behind him. He hadn't parked right under the main entrance, but rather back around the curve of the drive in along a red curb.

After securing their room, Victor made his way outside and started walking to the car. A security guard was standing next to the passenger side of it.

"Buenas noches. Como estás. Se habla ingles? Victor said loudly.

"Yes, I do speak English. I was trying to tell your amigo that you can't park here. Is he ok, he seems a little out of it. Maybe too much tequila? the guard asked.

"He wishes too much tequila. He got hurt, bad cut on his leg. Do you know any doctors that'd come to our room to take a look at him?" Victor said handing the man a crisp one-hundred-dollar bill. The guard took it and smiled.

"I think I understand. Yes, I do know a doctor… he's very good. Your friend wouldn't get any better care if you took him to the hospital and for the right price, he knows how to keep silencico," he winked.

"I'll take care of him. How do I reach him?"

"I'll call him. Go to your room. What number is it?" the guard said pulling out a small note pad and pen.

Victor knew at Mexican resorts it was either the security guards or the cab drivers that had all the connections you needed. But since there were no cab drivers around at this hour, Victor, concerned for Hal's worsening condition, weighed the options. Risk versus reward. *Do I trust this guy, or not?*

An hour later there was a knock on the door and a thin man with receding hairline and black bag introduced himself as Doctor Lopez. After giving Hal a local anesthetic and digging around in the back of his leg for less than a minute the doctor proudly displayed a 7.62x39 mm bullet. The doctor instructed Victor to monitor Hal's temperature, keep the dressing clean and to let the guard know if there were any complications. Hal was feeling no pain because, prior to the doctor's arrival, Victor had encouraged him to do multiple shots of mezcal, including the worm floating at the bottom of the bottle.

Before leaving, Dr. Lopez handed Victor a bottle of antibiotics with instructions for the slumbering Hal.

Victor put his head down for a much overdue rest. After five minutes laying there he knew sleep was not going to come because of the recent events racing through his mind like a movie. Sitting up, he grabbed the pack of cigarettes and Zippo lighter off the night stand and made his way through the sliding glass door leading to the outside balcony. Stepping into the cool ocean air he took a deep breath and lit up. After the damaged they'd inflicted at Juan Ortiz's compound, the Federales and cartel would be on the hunt for the two of them. For the next week to ten days trying to head north to get back into the U.S. would be a suicide mission. Taking another drag off his cigarette he looked over the balcony railing and down at the oversized swimming pool five stories below. *A week or two here? Margarita's and women walking around in bikini's... I think we can handle that.*

Victor looked out at the reflection of the moon off the Sea of Cortez, yawned and smiled.

"Boss, wake up… Boss." Doug heard Conway's voice somewhere in the distance. "Boss, wake up."

"Ok, I'm up. How long did I sleep? You were supposed to wake me in thirty minutes," Doug said, looking at his watch, stretching and raising his right hand to catch a yawn as they rolled to a stop behind Carter's pickup.

"I know… look ahead. We've a problem," Conway said, pointing down the road. Through the desert blackness, red and blue flashing lights a mile away blinked at them.

"Ok, sit tight. Carter, you guys with us?" Doug said into his radio.

"We see it… Not good," Carter said over the radio.

"We've two options. Take our chances that it's not a roadblock, and maybe a traffic accident, then drive on by. The other option is we turn around and head the other way. If we turn around, maybe they'll come after us or maybe they won't. My gut says it's not an accident," Doug said.

"Boss, two miles back around the curve in the road, I noticed a dirt road heading west. Probably a ranch road or something. How about we turn around and see if any headlights come our way? I say we go our night vision gear, hit our kill switches and go dark. If they follow us, we'll deal with it," Rocco said through the radio, turning to look at a sleeping Kimyung.

"I hear you. Six to one, half dozen the other… fuck it. I like the option of turning around. Whether they're looking for us up ahead or not, I mean, let's be realistic. What are five stinky gnarly looking gringos and a nine-year-old Asian girl doing on this road at almost three in the morning? We're going to raise eyebrows," Carter said, looking at the flashing lights.

"Ok, makes sense. Make a U-turn. We're right behind you. We'll keep an eye out to see if anyone down the road heads our way," Doug said, putting his truck into gear and following Carter, making a U-turn to head back towards Hermosillo.

"Headlights on, boss. Hard to tell how many from this distance," Conway said, raising the binoculars up to his eyes and turning back to get a better look.

"Ok, let's go lights out as soon as we go around the curve Rocco mentioned. I'll let them know up front," Doug said, queuing his microphone.

"Roger that," Rocco said hearing Doug's instructions.

"Glad things have settled down since we retired," Doug said, looking with a smile at Conway.

"Completely settled down. Plenty of time to take up golf now," Conway said, laughing.

Doug thought of Liz and his children at home asleep. Now, officially retired and no longer doing contract work overseas, he'd expected to kick back and live the good life. The two of them would raise their two children and, after the kids left the nest, they'd settle into growing old together. It was all on track until that fateful Black Friday.

Just past the curve, the taillights and headlights on Carter's pickup went black with Doug following suit, reaching down to flip the light kill switch. Donning his night vision goggles, Doug watched Carter slow down and make a righthand turn on a narrow dirt road heading northwest. Mesquite trees and prickly pear cacti dominated the landscape on both sides of the road. The downside to this maneuver was that the road was a straight shot heading northwest, or at least as far as they could see. Someone driving behind them would be able to see their fresh tracks on the dirt road. Within half a mile, the two vehicles came to a locked gate, preventing them from going further.

"We've a locked gate here. Anybody bring bolt cutters?" Rocco asked through his radio, looking at Carter.

"I've got to go to the bathroom," Kimyung said in a quiet voice from the back seat, sitting up from her nap, stretching and rubbing her eyes.

Doug watched the right rear door on Carter's pickup open, the young girl jumping the foot and a half to the ground. He thought about his daughter Kellie, though older than Kimyung, and how she'd be handling the situation. He was glad it was only a thought.

"I could use some relief myself," Mike said, getting out on the same side, behind Kimyung.

"I really have to go. I'm cold," Kimyung said, half jumping up and down with her hand below her waistline.

"Ok, we're going to go over there so you can go to the bathroom. But first, let me look around the area to make sure it's ok," Mike said, pointing to a stand of mesquite trees twenty yards off the right side of the road and handing her some tissues.

Doug smiled, listening to Mike tell her to stay put while he looked around the tree for rattlesnakes or anything else that could hurt the girl. Mike walked backed towards their vehicles as Kimyung disappeared behind the tree. After a few minutes, Carter, Rocco and Conway were gathered on the same side of the pickup that the girl got out of. She was in good hands. Any one of these men would lay their life down to protect her.

"I'm cold and I'm hungry. When will I be home?" Kimyung said, teeth chattering. Mike walked in their direction with Kimyung. Carter and Rocco stepped aside to let Mike open the door for her to get back into Carter's warm running pickup.

"We'll be taking you home soon. I've got something in my pack for you to eat," Mike said, pulling his day pack out and grabbing a chocolate-flavored protein bar. He opened it and handed it to her. In the distance, lights headed towards them.

"Fuck. Mike, get the girl and take her with you. Let's get back in those mesquites. Take up positions behind them. It looks like just one vehicle heading our way," Doug said out loud, looking toward the approaching vehicle.

It didn't take but thirty seconds for everyone to take cover in the trees. A shallow trench ran in front of the trees, angling back to the road and beyond the fence line. Carter and Rocco took positions in the trench ten yards apart, putting them off to the right of Doug, Conway and Mike's position in the trees with Kimyung.

"Ok, do you see that tree over there? I want you to go there quickly and get behind it. Stay low and cover your ears. Can you do that for me?" Mike said to Kimyung. The caring gentleness coming from of the big man surprised Doug. Kimyung scurried over to the tree, laying down and taking cover behind it. Mike had been career military and, as far as Doug knew, even though he was married twice, he didn't have any children. Like many men in Delta and other special forces units, the stress of him constantly being deployed proved too much for either of his wives. The glare of the approaching headlights pulled his attention back to the task at hand.

The beauty of going rogue is that they didn't have any rules of engagement... Anything goes for destroying your enemy. But this wasn't a bunch of vigilantes with happy trigger fingers. These were five American patriots doing the right thing. If they had any rules at all, there was one that stood out... Let common sense rule. If the vehicle approaching looked like regular Mexican citizens heading down the dirt road (doubtful), then they'd let them be. If they stopped and tried to break into their pickups, they'd let their presence be known and scare them off. On the other hand, if the approaching vehicle was a Federales pickup, and if they could convince the occupants to surrender their weapons, they'd zip tie them, take their radios and leave them on the side of the road. But if it was a Federales pickup with a machine gun mounted in the bed with a guy manning it... all bets were off.

The dust rolled forward as the Federales pickup came to a halt behind their two pickups. The driver and passenger in the cab, plus the three men sitting on bench seats in the bed, dismounted. The man on the M60 mounted machine gun remained in place. Holding their fire, Doug watched as the group of five Federales approached their trucks with rifles up.

"Oww, oww," Kimyung screamed, off to Doug and Mike's right.

The machine gunner in the pickup pivoted the M60 to his right. His head snapped back with the impact of Carter's 5.56 round hitting the side of the man's head. He slumped over the weapon, dropping to the floor of the bed of the truck. Doug and the others opened up on the remaining five. In less than twenty seconds, there were six dead Federales, having only fired three rounds from their weapons. The smoke hung in the chilled, windless desert air. The sound of moaning and gurgling met Doug's ear. The four of them moved from their positions, rifles up, shuffle stepping towards the downed Federales, checking each one and making sure they were silenced.

Getting Kimyung back to her mother was nothing they'd compromise on, including sparing the life of someone who'd do her harm if they had a chance. They would not be deterred from accomplishing their mission. A rising body count was all part of the journey.

"What happened?" Mike said, squatting down to comfort Kimyung, who was whimpering as quietly as she could.

"I don't know. Something stung me. It really hurts," she said, holding up her right index finger.

"Let me see," Mike said, holding the girl's hand.

"Can we leave? I don't like this place."

"I don't see anything. It's not bleeding… You probably got bit by a scorpion. Do you know what those are?" Mike said, looking on the ground and the tree.

"Yes, I know what a scorpion is and they don't bite. They have stingers on them. Last year at school we took a field trip to the Arizona-Sonora Desert Museum. They have a lot there in glass terrariums. They have a stinger on them."

"You are the smart little girl, aren't you? What do you say we get out of here?" Mike said, smiling at her. Taking her left hand, the two of them made their way back to Carter's truck.

"What do you say we grab the M60, boss? That might come in handy," Rocco said.

"What do you say we just get the hell out of here right now? We've a long way to go before we hit the border. Taking any major roads is going to be a problem. What are you doing? We've got to roll," Doug said, calling out to Rocco who'd already climbed into the bed.

"Just a minute, boss. Come on… let's take this bad boy with us, at least until we've made it across the border. It's got a bipod mounted on the barrel. I just need to yank it off this bed mount. Carter, Conway, help me with these ammo cans." The two ran over, each grabbing a can of the belt-fed ammo for the M60. They returned for one more load, putting all of it in the bed of Doug's pickup. Conway returned, taking the M60 from Rocco and putting it in the back of Doug's cab.

"Hey, I just remembered something. In college, a bunch of us went down to San Carlos. We ended up getting drunk and obnoxious. Two of our guys got in a fight with some locals over some señoritas. Fucked them up pretty bad. We had to make a run for it. When we got to Hermosillo, one of my friends whose folks had a house in Arivaca led us onto a dirt road heading north. It was a cattle ranch right on the border. If I remember right, where we crossed was the southern fence line of the ranch. When we reached the border, there was only a cattle guard and barbed wire gate separating Mexico from the U.S. We crossed and made it to his Dad's ranch and spent the night there. Great people, you know. Salt of the earth. His mom fixed us a meal. Arivaca is like twenty miles north of the border on the U.S. side. I remember the road we took was northwest out of Hermosillo. Eventually it turned north, where we stopped at this little town just south of the border. We were almost out of gas. It was a little place with a gravity-fed gas pump. From there, we trekked up a narrow dirt road through the hills to the fence line," Carter said, pursing his lips trying to remember.

"Do you think you can find it again? What was the name of the town?" Conway said, looking at Carter.

"It started with an S… that was a long time ago. I'll give it a shot; I think I can get us there. Can't be too many roads heading that way through the desert. Nothing ventured, nothing gained," Carter said, looking inside the truck at Kimyung.

# Interpreter

"Sergeant Ochoa, what's your position?" the lieutenant said into his radio for the second time.

After seeing the two vehicles stop and turn to go the other way, the lieutenant sent the sergeant and five of his men to investigate. Sergeant Ochoa was to report in every fifteen minutes. It'd been twenty-two minutes and no word. Captain Sanchez ordered the lieutenant, along with other Federales officers, to set up roadblocks on major roads heading east, west and north out of Hermosillo. They were to be on the lookout for two pickup trucks with Arizona plates. They'd been told that the men in the pickups were violent killers and to use extreme caution. Thus, the deployment of the pickups with an M60 gunner.

"Sergeant Ochoa, what is your position?" again the lieutenant said into the radio. In the last radio contact, the sergeant reported they'd lost sight of the two trucks around a bend in the road and were turning back to go onto a dirt road they'd passed that headed northwest.

"Sergeant Ochoa… report your position. Sergeant Ochoa, do you read me?"

The radio he'd taken off the sergeant crackled in Spanish. Rocco listened as he closed the front passenger door on Carter's pickup.

"We gotta get the fuck out of here. That's probably someone calling those guys on the radio. No doubt they'll start looking for them. I wish I knew what the hell they're saying," Rocco said to Carter and Mike.

"Rocco, stop using bad words… The man on the radio is calling for Sergeant Ochoa to report his position," Kimyung said, sitting straight up in the back. The three men looked at each other, smiling wide eyed, and then at Kimyung.

"You speak Spanish? No shi… I mean that's very cool. Where did you learn to speak it?" Carter said, nodding his head with a thumbs up to Mike and Rocco.

"My mommy has a tutor come to the house and my nanny and me only talk to each other in Spanish. I'm also learning Mandarin. I like it. I think it's fun. I'm hungry and thirsty," she said.

"Damn, we've got us an interpreter," Mike said with a chuckle, patting Kimyung on the head.

"Boss, when we hit the road, we need to double time it. Someone's calling for a Sergeant Ochoa to report his position. Wanted to give you a heads-up," Rocco said.

"Since when do you speak Spanish?" Doug said.

"I don't, but our young lady does. We've got us an interpreter."

"Outstanding. Let's get the hell out of here. Eventually they're going to find these guys and discover the missing M60. Might be a problem for us heading back to Hermosillo. I hope we can get across the main highway heading north to the west side of the city before they've time to deploy men to stop us. Balls in your court, Carter, lead the way," Doug said.

In short order, Carter turned right onto the road heading south, which would lead them back toward Hermosillo. Doug and Conway stayed right behind, following the outline of Carter's pickup in the dust cloud. Keeping the lights off and using his night vision goggles Carter accelerated to one hundred miles per hour.

"Sargent Ochoa!" said a voice on the radio they'd taken off of the body of one of the Federales.

# 4:23 AM
# Tucson, Arizona
# Dead Man Walking

*Mommy, mommy… help me, MOMMY,* Rebecca sat up in bed, staring into the dark.

"Kimyung, where are you? Kimyung," Rebecca yelled, confused by what the source of light was to her right. *Where am I? Where's my daughter?* She inhaled deeply realizing she was dreaming. Becoming conscious and focusing on the light, she realized it was the digital clock on the nightstand, partially hidden by her handgun. Moving it aside, she looked at the time… 4:23.

Laying her head back down, she pulled the sheet and covers over herself, wondering what was happening with Kimyung's rescue. All she knew was that, early evening yesterday, Carter Thompson, Colonel Doug Redman and three others headed to Hermosillo to save her. Dax promised her they wouldn't stop until they got her. It's not that she had any reason to question their abilities. She knew what they were capable of. She'd put her career on the line by keeping quiet about their past activities. Using lethal force to protect the people and country you love when the government won't is all the justification needed for her to look the other way. She was frustrated and angry because of the criminal behavior at the top rung of the FBI. It was now a different world and Rebecca felt that sometimes, under the right circumstances, breaking the law could be the right thing to do. Hell, she'd done it herself more than once.

She'd barely slept at all in the last couple of days. Ten minutes after laying there, she sat up and reached for the lamp on the nightstand. Looking at the clock, she thought about calling Dax, hoping to hear something. Good news or bad news… anything. Not knowing was driving her insane. She'd never felt this out of control in her entire life. Rebecca, a woman of order and strategies, was struggling and out of tears at this point. Something else had replaced her sadness and feelings of powerlessness. Anger, a growing rage, was now the only emotion available. She thought about Congressman Hector Granada and what she was going to do to him once she had her daughter back. Jail was too good for the piece of garbage. Maybe cut an ear off, a finger, his dick and balls—or maybe lodge a half-inch drill bit through his knees. The options were endless for her to think about. No matter what… in her book… he was a dead man walking.

She made her way down the hallway to the kitchen. Rebecca opened the freezer, taking out the bag of coffee beans. After filling the coffeepot up with water, she poured it into the coffeemaker's reservoir. She'd done it every day while talking with Kimyung about the day ahead. One, two, three, four scoops of dark brown beans went into the electric grinder. The familiar aroma met her nostrils, she inhaled. Putting the lid on it, she pressed down, oblivious to the sound of the beans being pulverized. *God, how good it'd feel to press his face into the grinder.*

The body of the grinder became hot, pulling her back to reality. Easing her right hand off the lid, she raised both hands up to her face and wiped two small tears away. *Fuck.* She'd call Dax at six.

Not waiting for the drip to fill the coffeepot, she pulled it off the hot plate and poured it into her cup. The steam rose from her cup and three drops of coffee splattered and danced on the hot plate with her standing there, coffeepot in hand.

Turning, she grabbed the pack of cigarettes laying on the kitchen counter. She fumbled with the plastic wrapping, trying to get a nail under it. Holding it at arm's length, she dug deep again, under the wrapping, tearing it back and lifting one out. Taking a deep breath, she held off a wave of nausea, put it into her mouth, grabbed the Bic lighter, her coffee and made her way to the back porch. Ten minutes later, after four deep drags on the cigarette, she eased into one of the chairs on the porch. Running her hand through her hair, she leaned back further feeling the cold metal back of the chair her back was resting on.

"Maybe after Kimyung gets back, it's time for me to hang it up and ride into the sunset. It's too dangerous for her. Hell, it's too dangerous for me," Rebecca said to the smoke ring she'd just made, drifting outward at eye level. In the righthand pocket of her bathrobe, her phone vibrated. Putting the cigarette in her mouth, she reached in, pulling it out.

"Dax, thank God you called. What's happening? Tell me."

"I just got a call a while ago… didn't want to wake you. They've got her…"

"Oh my God, that's good news. Are they back in Tucson?"

"No, slow down. They're not back in the country yet. In fact, they've a long way to go. They're heading out of Hermosillo running hard, trying to head north. They've got the cartel and every Federale in Sonora looking for them."

"Dax, anything you can do on your end to help them?" Rebecca said, pulling the cigarette out of her mouth.

"I'm doing all I can and wish I could send them some air assets, but the president was firm. No U.S. military or law enforcement of any type can operate in Mexico. I wish I could do more. They'll get her back. Those guys are unstoppable."

"Ok, Dax. Thanks for calling. Please, anything you hear... anything... promise you'll call me right away," Rebecca said.

"You know I will."

# 5:08 AM
# Hermosillo
# Flashing Lights

Carter hit the brakes, skidding into the righthand turn, causing him to fish tail and come to a stop at a 45-degree angle.

"Ahh... you overshot the runway a little there," Rocco said, laughing.

"Shut up... I know what I'm doing," Carter said, flipping Rocco off, laughing. He threw his pickup into reverse, turned the steering wheel hard right, put it into drive and punched it just as Doug and Conway made the turn, overtaking them.

"Nice driving," Doug said, laughing into the radio.

Ahead, the lights of Hermosillo, fifteen miles in the distance, illuminated the black western sky. The sign up ahead to the right, reading "Federal Highway 15, 13 KM," blew past them.

"Carter, what's the plan? We can't head up the main highway," Doug said on the radio.

"I know. We won't. We're going to cross the highway and go into the city. I'm trying to remember the name of the little town my buddies and I went through in college. I put in Arivaca in Google Maps, but it only gives us the route on Highway 15 and then into Arizona," Carter said.

"Ok, keep thinking," Doug said, letting Carter pass to take the lead again.

Up ahead, the sight of an overpass heading north and south loomed. Carter slowed down to blend with the increasing traffic. Behind, the first ray of daylight broke over the Sierra Madre Occidental Mountains. Carter was in the third row of cars stopped waiting for the light to turn green. The overpass had a clover leaf design to it, with the exit ramp on the northbound lane ending to the left of them. On his left in the distance, flashing lights entered the off-ramp racing towards them. Getting closer, it was easy for Carter to make out three Federales pickups. When the light turned green, they moved forward with traffic. Carter looked straight ahead as the first of the Federales trucks came to a halt in the righthand lane of the off-ramp. A half a mile ahead, there loomed another overpass. *Please don't notice us.*

"Damn," Carter said. Rocco kept an eye behind them, watching the Federales as Carter did the same in his driver's door mirror. On the other side of the next overpass, the light flashed green.

"Where are we going, Carter?" Mike said from the back.

"Straight ahead and we'll figure it out from there. Shit! They just turned and are heading our way," Carter said, looking for an opening in the early morning traffic to weave through and try to lose them in the surrounding neighborhoods. A little over a quarter of a mile separated their two trucks and the three Federales pickups. Behind him, traffic was pulling over to the right. Carter sped up through an opening in traffic, reaching the light just as it turned red. Without stopping, Carter made a hard righthand turn, flooring it with Doug and Conway right on their tail.

"Alter. That's it... fucking Alter," Carter said, slapping the center console with his right hand.

"Alter? Alter what? What the hell are you talking about?" Rocco said.

"Alter is the name of the little town I told you about. Alter. Punch that in your Google Maps and let's see what comes up," Carter said, speeding north as the Federales pickups with flashing lights made the turn behind them in his rearview mirror.

"Nothing's coming up," Rocco said.

"Alter. I'm sure of it because my sister—she's Catholic— was getting married the following weekend in Chicago. You know wedding... altar. Try it again... No, wait. Try Alter, Sonora, Mexico," Carter said.

"Got it. Two hundred yards ahead, make a left. It's going to take us into a neighborhood." Carter tapped the brakes, making the left turn in a four-wheel drift with the back of the truck fish tailing. Behind him, Doug and Conway followed closely, making the same maneuver and leaving a cloud of blue tire smoke hanging in the air. Carter counted the seconds, hoping the first of the Federales trucks wouldn't appear... It did. They were gaining on them.

"Hey, I didn't know civilians could drive like that," Doug said, laughing into the radio.

"Hell yeah. Piece of cake," Carter said back.

"Six hundred feet, turn right," Rocco said.

More than a quarter of a mile separated them from the Federales now. Five hundred yards after turning left, Carter hit the brakes as a trash truck stopped to pick up a load, blocking their path. Behind, Doug came to a halt with both his right and left doors opening. He and Conway jumped out, rifles up.

"Stay down," Carter heard Mike say to Kimyung, followed by the sound and pressure of the right rear door opening. Rocco was already out on his side.

"Stay at the wheel, Carter. If we have to, we'll leave Doug's truck as a blocker. They can pile in with us," Rocco said, turning, leaving the door open. In the rearview mirror, Carter watched Rocco and Mike move to the right behind a row of parked cars. As Rocco reached his position, the first of the pickups turned on to their street with Doug, Rocco, Mike and Conway laying down withering fire on the lead pickup. The second one behind slammed on its brakes and went into reverse, slamming into the third Federales pickup. The gunner in the bed of the lead truck got a two-round burst off of the M60 and went silent.

"Let's go," Carter said into the radio, watching the trash truck move forward, making a righthand turn up a short drive. Walking backwards to the truck, Rocco and Mike jumped in with their rifles up and pulled the doors shut. Carter floored the gas pedal, his wheels spinning for a second before grabbing the road bed and lurching them forward. In the left mirror, they caught the sight of steam coming out of the engine compartment of the first pickup. Doug and Conway trailed ten feet behind them.

"Make a left. Five hundred yards up and then a right. Three hundred yards after that," Rocco said. The end of the rutted paved road turned to dirt, dropping them down six inches. With the sun over the mountains, Hermosillo population of one million was coming to life. Carter made the righthand turn, speeding up to sixty miles per hour.

"Looks like straight ahead for seven miles and then a right turn and another left turn a half mile after that. Let's get the fuck out of here," Rocco said.

"You said a bad word," a small voice from the back seat said.

# 6:09 AM
# Pussies

"I want those motherfucking gringos. Where are they, Captain? Are you listening to me?" Juan Ortiz yelled into his phone.

"We're doing our best. They took the road to Cananea but turned around after seeing one of our roadblocks a few hours ago. One of our units pursued them up a ranch road turnoff. We found them all shot dead thirty minutes later with the M60 missing from the back of the truck along with the four cans of ammo. After I got the call, I figured they were going to head back to Hermosillo and dispatched three units to set up a roadblock just before Highway 15. My guys caught up to the gringos at a traffic light when they were coming down the off-ramp from Highway 15. They had a high speed chase into the western neighborhoods. Those guys shot up the lead unit, killing all four of my men. The other two units retreated," Captain Sanchez said.

"Retreated? What do you mean 'retreated?' What the fuck are we paying those guys for? Bunch of pussies. Should've had some of my men with them. It would have been a different story," Juan Ortiz said.

"Maybe, but most of our men are eighteen, nineteen, twenty-year-old kids. Whoever those gringos are, they're really good at what they do. My guys didn't have a chance against them. My guess is they're the same guys that I encountered in San Miguel last year. I lost too many men in that gunfight. Look, they've got to head north. They've got the girl with them and they're going to cross over to the U.S. I've sent thirty units into the western neighborhoods looking for them. Even if they're able to lie low for a day or two, at some point they're going to make a run for it. They've got to go up Highway 15. It's the only way out of the country unless they make a break to the northeast again," the captain said.

"What about them heading northwest, running towards Puerto Penasco?" Juan Ortiz said.

"I've got the coast covered. It's not likely they'd head that way because the country is too open. They'd be easy to spot. It doesn't matter. I've already set units up on the road leading north and south. We'll get them," the captain said.

"I want those pinche gringos alive. I want you to bring them to me. I'm going to peel the skin off each of them.... And the girl... I've a special treat for her," Juan said, putting his hand on his crotch and biting his lower lip.

"We'll do our best, Juan," Captain Sanchez said, hitting the end button, shaking his head.

# 7:53 AM
# Benjamin Hill

They'd made their way north until forced by a lack of roads to go east onto Highway 15. Turning left onto 15 North, it'd be an hour run heading to the town of Benjamin Hill, which had a Federales substation.

"Benjamin Hill, 15 Kilometers" read the sign as Carter and Doug passed it doing ninety miles per hour.

"There's a turnoff on the southern edge of Benjamin Hill we're going to take. It'll take us through the center of the town and, with luck, we won't run into problems," Rocco said.

"So far your navigational skills have been pretty good. Unusual," Mike said from the back, patting Rocco on his left shoulder.

"I'm hungry. When are we going to see my mommy?" Kimyung said.

"Hold on there. I'll get you something," Mike said, reaching into his pack and handing her another protein bar.

"That's what you gave me earlier. Do you have anything else?" she said.

"How's this?" Mike said, pulling out a Slim Jim.

"What's that?" Kimyung said, taking the long thin beef stick.

"Breakfast of champions. It's good. Take a bite," Mike said, smiling.

"Breakfast of champions? What are you talking about?" she said.

"It's a figure of speech. Go ahead, take a bite," Mike said.

Taking the exit, Carter steered them onto a dirt road turning towards the road running north to south through the center of Benjamin Hill.

"Turn left at the next block. I'm going to see if I can snake us through these neighborhoods without coming across one of those guys with an M60. Veer left," Rocco said as they approached a forked road on the north edge of Benjamin Hill.

"Got it," Carter said, looking in his mirror at Doug and Conway, trailing two hundred yards behind in their dust.

"We're going to come up to another left, taking us into a long running valley with a river in the middle of it. In about an hour we'll be making a righthand turn, taking us north through Alter. A whole hell of a lot closer to the border. Hey, brother, how are we doing on fuel and how are you doing? Do you need me or Mike to grab the wheel?" Rocco said, looking up from his iPad.

"We could use some gas. We're a little under half a tank. And yes, I could use a breather, maybe catch a few z's. Let's go a little further and we'll pull over and stretch our legs. Hey,

Kimyung, how are you doing back there with big stinky Mike?" Carter said with all of them laughing.

"Hey, boss, what do you say we find a place to pull over and take ten. We're going to spell Carter at the wheel and choke the chicken," Rocco said.

"Roger that. Sounds good to me. Just find a spot. We're right behind you," Doug said over the radio.

"Choke the chicken? What's he talking about?" Kimyung said, looking up at Mike.

"Never mind, honey, another figure of speech. Means nothing," Mike said awkwardly, trying to brush off the comment.

"What's a figure of speech?"

"I think what Mike's trying to tell you is Rocco just says funny things sometimes that make no sense," Carter said, looking over at Rocco smiling.

"Well, I think that's stupid," Kimyung said.

"Well... Rocco is kind of stupid," Mike said, laughing.

"Don't listen to them, sweetie. Isn't there a place coming up on the right? I feel like I'm getting roasted a bit in here," Rocco said, pointing ahead.

The three men burst out laughing. To the north of them was a range of mountains running north and south. The valley was being used for agriculture and was separated by large expanses of desert, dotted now and then with small buildings.

Mike helped Kimyung out of the truck, pointing her toward some bushes.

"What if there're snakes over there?" Kimyung said, retreating two steps.

"I'll go check it out for you. Sit tight," Mike said, walking around the bush then heading back their way.

"It's ok. No snakes," Mike said. She walked over to the bush, stopped and turned around.

"Don't look," she yelled and disappeared behind the bush.

After ten minutes, Rocco got behind the steering wheel of Carter's truck with Mike riding shotgun and Carter sitting behind Mike with Kimyung on his left.

"Hmm... I wonder what crops they're growing around here," Mike said five minutes into their drive heading west. Ahead on the right, waiting to pull onto the road, sat two large cargo trucks.

Carter looking at the trucks as they passed, noticing each had three men in the cab. Thirty seconds after they'd passed them, the trucks turned onto the road in their direction. Ahead, a green road sign with white letters announced the turnoff to Sáric, fifteen kilometers ahead.

"As I remember heading north, we stopped at Alter We got some gas there. They only had one little tiny store where we bought some beer. What a hoot that trip was. Anyway, I remember Alter, you know, like the word 'alto'… Spanish for stop. Just one of those crazy little details that stuck in my head. We're on the right track. We should stop there and see if we can get some gas and water. We're running low. Back there, when we stopped, I checked with Conway and they could fuel up, too," Carter said.

"Sounds good to me," Rocco said.

"Ok then. Wake me when we get there. I'm going to take a little siesta," Carter said, looking over at Kimyung. *We're going to get you to your mother.*

# 9:33 AM
# Sáric

"What the fuck is this place?" Carter heard Rocco say, pulling him out of his slumber. Rubbing his eyes, he looked around, trying to make sense of what he was seeing. He looked at his watch. *How long have I been sleeping?*

"Hey, what time do you guys have? Where are we?" Carter said, rubbing his eyes and again looking at this watch, struggling to orient himself.

"It's 9:33, brother. You've been out for about forty minutes. We're in Alter… At least, that's what the sign says," Mike said.

"Saric? Holy shit. This isn't at all what I remembered. It was nothing, just a few wooden buildings lining the streets and a gravity-fed gas pump. What the hell?" Carter said, looking at the small stores lining the streets and the people moving in and out of them. Shaking his head back and forth, he rubbed the top of it with his right hand and stretched. Rolling down his window, the smell of food carts made its way into the cab.

"There's a Pemex station up on the right. You're down to a quarter of a tank and I'm sure Doug and Conway could use some go juice, too," Rocco said, maneuvering their way through the slow moving traffic and turning into the gas station. Coming to a stop, a throng of young boys swarmed both sides of the cab. One jumped on the hood with a spray bottle, soaking the windshield, followed by a squeegee moving across the glass, removing the dust, grime and bugs. Another pass with the spray bottle, followed by a large rag the teenage boy pulled from his back pocket, left the windshield clean enough.

"Do you need to use the bathroom?" Carter said, looking left to Kimyung while opening the right rear door. It felt good to get out of the confines of the truck. Smelling the air with its mixture of gasoline and cooking foods pulled him back to another time in Mexico. Looking down the street in the direction they'd come, the two large cargo trucks rumbled past them. They drove a block north, making a left-hand turn, and went through a set of gates into a large yard. Bringing his attention back to Kimyung, who'd jumped out of the truck, Carter took her hand and walked her toward a sign reading "Baños". Walking around the corner of the building, they found two doors, one with a black and white sign reading "Hombres" and the other reading "Mujeres".

"Go ahead. I'll wait for you here," Carter said to her. Stepping a few feet back from the bathrooms, so he could get a better view, he looked down the side of the street they were on and then across to the other side. Across, there were stacks of black plastic gallon jugs. Next to them were backpacks, hats, shirts and what looked like shoes made of carpet. Everything was in black, dark green or brown. Further to the right, two men on a corner looked their way. Carter met their gaze, causing them to turn away.

"How she's doing?" Doug asked.

"Good. She's a smart, tough little girl. I can only imagine what must go on in her head," Carter said, looking at Doug and then back across the street at the two men, one now on a cell phone.

"That's good. Interesting shops along here. What the hell is this place? Lots of people, but why?" Doug said.

"It's a staging town. All this crap. Black water bottles, dark colored backpacks, hats and clothing. You see those things that look like shoes made of carpet. When they cross over, they put them over their shoes so they can't be tracked. All the supplies are so people can trek across the desert into the U.S. I've looked on Google Maps and, from here, illegals, drug runners and human traffickers go due north, where we're heading. They can also go northwest and cross over into the Sassaby area. That's what this place is," Rocco said, walking up to Doug and Carter.

Sáric, during the last four U.S. presidential administrations, had transformed itself from barely a dot on a map to a thriving business district. All of this catered to the needs of the Magdalena Cartel in its transporting of people and drugs. For those brave enough to cross the line and hike through the desert, everything they needed for survival and eluding capture was available in the local stores. But the coyotes of the Magdalena Cartel didn't spend money with the merchants. The people the coyotes snuck into the U.S., at two to three thousand dollars a head, kept the merchants in business. It was up to those people to outfit themselves, except for the young girls being trafficked into the U.S. Most of the young girls and women went on birth control before heading north just for that reason.

"There're two guys across the street at our two o'clock watching us. One on his phone," Doug said.

"I know, I've had my eyes on them, too. I think we need to get moving. Hey, did you guys see any sign of Federales while coming into town? We didn't," Carter asked.

"No. Strange," Doug said.

"I wonder if this is off-limits to them?" Carter said as a pickup with two men in    the cab and two in the bed with AK-47s drove by, looking their way.

"What do you think? How much longer before we hit the border?" Doug asked, looking around and then at Carter.

"The map say's its about fifty miles," Rocco said.

"As I remember… two hours or less. That was a long time ago," Carter said, turning to the sound of Kimyung opening the door and coming out.

"I got her," Mike said to Carter.

"Ok, let me hit the can and then we'll get out of here," Carter said, stepping into the men's bathroom.

When he left the bathroom, Carter noticed another pickup with two men drive by, staring hard in their direction.

"Rocco, I'm good to drive from here. Catnap did me well," Carter said, knowing if trouble came, Rocco was the best choice for riding shotgun. Besides, it was his truck, and he would be best behind the wheel.

Neither Doug nor Carter topped off their fuel tanks instead putting in just fifteen gallons each to save time. The sooner they headed north, the better. Waiting for an opening, Carter eased into the flow of traffic with Doug following. With only one road leading in and out of town, heading north to try and get back across the line was their only option. To the left looked like a large dirt parking area and a warehouse where the two cargo trucks had entered. Carter observed a group of men stood near three vans by the entrance of the warehouse. Four of the men were putting burlap bundles on their back with the help of some of the other men. On the ground were multiple stacks of burlap bundles.

Before long, the road took them beyond any buildings and curved gradually to the northwest. Just before the turn, Carter looked to his left as they passed the end of a long dirt runway, running parallel with the road.

"I'll be damned. I don't remember an airstrip... Almost nothing about this town looks familiar, other than the direction of the road we're on," Carter said.

"On Google Maps, it looks like you got us in the right place," Rocco said, looking to the runway on their left. Gradually the road turned right, heading north.

# 10:08 AM
# Juan Ortiz's Compound

He'd been used to sleeping late but today wasn't the day for it. Sitting upright on the edge of the bed, he grabbed the cigarettes on the nightstand. Jiggling it upward, he snatched one of two left in the pack with his teeth. Putting the pack down, he grabbed the lighter and brought it to the end of the cigarette. Taking a long drag, the acrid smoke filled his lungs. He held it for a moment then exhaled, throwing a cloud of smoke forward.

Hungover and only running on four hours of sleep put a raw edge on him, leaving him in a foul mood. It never took much to set him off. He was hungover with a headache and any little thing could send him into a fit of rage.. Thinking about the attack that killed several of his men, and how they took the girl, had put him over the edge. Standing up, he stretched, walked to the bathroom and took a leak.

Following that and his usual downing of tequila, he was good to go for another round of whatever came his way. Now, all he wanted was to know where the gringos and the girl were. Why weren't they bound and shackled in front of him?

"Pablo," Juan yelled after opening his bedroom door on the second floor.

"Coming," Pablo called out from down below.

"Any word on those fucking gringos and my girl?" Juan said.

"No, señor. Other than the incident last night on the road to Cananea and the shootout this morning in town, I know nothing," Pablo said.

"Where's Captain Sanchez? Get him for me. I want to know what the fuck is going on," Juan said.

"He left at about four this morning. Do you want me to call him?"

"No. What do you mean there was an incident last night on the road going to Cananea? Oh wait, I remember now," Juan said, adjusting his robe. "Make sure they clean up the mess from last night," Juan said, stepping back into his room and closing the door behind him.

"Where are you?" Juan said into his phone.

"I'm nearing Benjamin Hill," Captain Sanchez said.

"Where do you think they are now?" Juan said, undressing, preparing to take a shower.

"After the gunfight this morning in town… I don't know. Maybe they're holed up in the city somewhere. All the roads are covered."

"Find them," Juan Ortiz said.

"I will," Captain Sanchez said, hearing a knock on the door on the other end of the call.

"Just a second," Juan hollered toward his bedroom door.

"Sir, it's important. I need to talk with you," Pablo said loudly through the door.

"Captain, keep me up to date. Get them," Juan said and hit the end button. Not bothering to put his robe back on, he walked to the bedroom door and opened the door.

"What the fuck is it?" Juan said, standing in the doorway, glaring at Pablo.

"I just got a call from Fernando, one of our men in Sáric. They're there," Pablo said.

"Sáric? Who's there? The gringos? They're in Sáric?"

"Sí, the gringos and the girl," Pablo said.

"Sáric. Fuck, man. How did they get up there without getting seen? Son of a bitch. Get ready, we're leaving in thirty minutes and get ten of our men."

"Ok, sir, but there're only three of our men alive after what happened last night," Pablo said.

"Get who you can. Who do we have up in Sáric?"

"I'm not sure, maybe ten or fifteen men.. You know, the ones organizing the coyotes and mules. Maybe there's a few more. I'm not sure. They're not like our guys down here... I mean..."

"I don't care, they work for me and they'll do as they're told. Tell them to keep an eye on them and let us know where they go," Juan said.

"Ok," Pablo said.

"And tell the kitchen to fix me a burrito and some coffee in a thermos," Juan said, turning and hitting the call button on his phone.

"They didn't head east; they're in Sáric. How close are any of your men right now?" Juan said into the phone, leaning over, turning on the hot water in the shower.

"Right now? I've men in Puerto Penasco. They're at least three to four hours away," Captain Sanchez said.

"God damn it. I don't care. Send them now. I want those motherfucking gringos and the girl. I'm heading there in thirty minutes. Where are you right now?" Juan said, picking up his bottle of tequila and taking another long swig from it.

"I'm about thirty minutes south of Benjamin Hill," Captain Sanchez said.

"Ok, get over to Sáric. I'll see you there," Juan said, hanging up the phone.

# The Fence Line

Two miles after passing the runway, the road turned from pavement into a well-worn, rutted dirt track. Carter backed off on the pedal, easing the ride. Trailing behind them, a visible cloud of dust rose. Ahead, the road veered to the left.

"I'm not sure which one," Carter said, looking at Rocco as they came to a stop.

"Go left—it looks like the one we should stay on. Hell, man, we're almost there. GPS is showing us sixteen miles south of the line. I can't believe we've made it all the way through Hermosillo and Benjamin Hill to here without a problem. Good job, Carter," Rocco said, patting him on the shoulder.

On the right of the road was a mile or so of planted fields and, to the left, the desert gave way to rising hillsides. Just past the fields, with the road still climbing, Carter stopped at the peak before progressing gradually downhill. From their vantage point, between the two hillsides looking north, it was easy to see the mountains in the United States. Doug and Conway closed on them, stopping behind them just as Carter moved forward downhill.

"I think we might have a problem. A couple of miles behind us, Conway glassed three pickups heading our way. Whoever it is must be on a drug run or coming after us. Either way, it's not good," Doug said into the microphone.

"Roger that," Rocco said into the microphone.

"We better step on it. You said there's a barbed wire gate you guys went through?" Rocco said, looking at Carter and then back down at the GPS map.

"Yeah, as I remember, barbed wire strung to three short posts, acting as braces, with a wire loop where you attach it to the fence post," Carter said, picking up speed. Ahead, the road rose again. He hoped that when they were at the top of the next saddle, they'd gain distance on the pickups. Doug and Conway trailed behind them. With the dust coming off the two trucks, they'd be easy to track.

"How are you doing? We're getting close to getting you home," Mike said to Kimyung.

"I'm ok. When will we be there?" Kimyung said, looking up at Mike and craning her head to the right and left.

"Soon," Mike said.

As he was coming over the saddle and starting down the back side again, Carter looked in his rearview mirror, seeing Doug and Conway come to a halt.

"Whoever it is, they're gaining on us. Do your best to pick up the pace," Doug said on the radio.

Ahead, another small track to the right appeared. Carter looked over at Rocco.

"Stay on this, keep veering left," Rocco said.

Carter reached for the four-wheel-drive switch.

Appearing ahead was another turn to the right. With a nod of his head Rocco motioned Carter to stay left.

"Does this look familiar to you?" Rocco said, looking around and ahead, adjusting his AR-15, nestled between his legs.

"Kind of," Carter said as they passed a cattle pond on their right and another one on the left, one hundred yards further.

"Looks like some farming operation over there to the right. There're some buildings in the distance. Gee, I wonder what they're growing out here so close to the border?" Rocco said, pointing to the distant buildings with a sea of green crops in between.

"That I don't remember. I think most of this is cattle country, or at least used to be, judging from the cattle ponds we're seeing. I'm sure whatever they're growing is something you smoke," Carter said, laughing.

Ahead of them, the track continued its direction to the northwest. Within five minutes another fork in the road appeared. Carter, looking in the rearview mirror, could make out the ghostly image of Doug and Conway's car, coming up from behind.

"Go right."

"Right? Are you sure?" Carter said, looking at Rocco.

"Yes, for sure. Go right," Rocco said, pointing.

"Right it is," Carter said, looking at the hills rising to their right and left.

"We've only two miles to go. But I don't like this terrain. Great place for an ambush. Fuck, this is spooky. Reminds me of a bad time in the Korngold Valley in Afghanistan," Rocco said, shaking a bit as if shivering.

Carter knew better than to ask Rocco about the Korngold. He'd read Sebastian Junger's book, *War*. Rocco was jumpy, and Carter didn't want to add anything to his heightened state of alertness. Carter drove on, glancing in the rearview mirror to catch glimpses now and then of Doug's truck. He strained, trying to get a glimpse of the other vehicles he'd seen earlier, trailing behind them. Coming up to another saddle, they stopped on top. Below them, a quarter mile away, the barbed wire fence running east and west stood out. The other side of it was the United States.

"Hold up here. Let's wait for Doug and Conway to catch up," Rocco said, opening his door and stepping down. Carter put his truck in park, following suit, with Mike and Kimyung doing the same.

Carter grabbed his binoculars out of the center console, scanning ahead, looking right and left down the fence line. This part of the road he remembered because of the flat open area they'd crossed over, through the barbed wire gate, decades ago. On the other side of the fence was a wider and smoother road leading north. He'd remembered it because it'd taken them to his friends' parents' ranch house. At the time, they'd felt great relief getting back onto U.S. soil. The anxiousness of wanting to cross was no different now, except for a heightened sense of danger. Carter looked through his binoculars to the right and left of the fence line, looking for the gate. He kept coming back to their road, ending at a steel vehicle barrier. *Fuck*.

"We've got a problem," Carter said, moving his binoculars away from his eyes and down to his waist.

"What do you mean?" Mike said.

"The gate we went through… It's gone. There's a vehicle barrier where the gate used to be," Carter said, pointing down to the four-foot sections of rusting steel, crisscrossed in an X pattern.

"Fuck, that's a big problem. Oops, sorry, honey," Mike said, looking down at Kimyung.

"Damn," Rocco said, turning as he heard Doug and Conway pulling up behind them.

"Hey, pull ahead and down the hill a bit," Doug hollered, leaning out of the driver's window. Carter got back in his truck and pulled forward, stopping thirty yards down the other side of the hill. Doug and Conway stopped ten yards behind them.

"Those three trucks are still behind us. Where's the gate?" Doug said, closing his door and walking down the hill towards Carter.

"There isn't one. From the rust on the steel crossmembers, they must have put it in a long time ago, replacing the gate," Carter said, coming up to Doug, who continued walking ahead to the fence line.

"Fuck, that's a problem. A big one. Ok, we'll figure it out. But first, I want to see if those three trucks are still behind us," Doug said.

Carter walked alongside Doug, making their way to the top of the hill. Rocco was laying prone on the road with his binoculars up. He'd retrieved the M60 out of Doug's truck and had it on the ground with the bipod deployed.

"There were three trucks trailing about a mile or so behind us. Hopefully they turned off," Doug said, looking at Rocco.

Looking to the south down the road through his binoculars, Carter caught a glimpse of the sun reflecting off something in the distance.

"Bad. They're stopped. Looks like they're about a thousand yards out. Further down the road behind them is another trail of dust. Maybe some buddies joining them?" Rocco said with his eyes glued to his binoculars.

"Conway, you and Carter go down the road and find a way through. We'll sit tight up here," Doug said.

"Roger that," Conway said, turning and giving a nod to Carter. The two men made their way downhill to Carter's truck.

"Mike, take Kimyung and get her onto the other side of the fence up that road," Doug said.

# Chance Corral

"Rick, we need to get this thing working," Ranch owner Frank Chance said to his ranch foreman, pulling himself away from the engine compartment of the front-end loader. Though old, the loader had served him well over the last thirty years.

"Let me look at it, boss. We'll get it going," Rick said to the owner of the fifty-thousand-acre ranch. The Chance Ranch was the biggest one in the area. Frank Chance was one of the finest men he'd ever known, and by far the best boss he'd ever worked for.

It was a beautiful and rugged part of southern Arizona. The eastern border of the ranch butted up against the Buenos Aires National Wildlife Refuge. Like many Americans, Frank Chance was frustrated and angry the federal government wouldn't provide security in the area. His ranch, in the heart of the U.S. Border Patrol Tucson Sector, was a continuous hot spot for drug and human trafficking. He'd had congressmen and women down to the fence line and each one told him they'd do this, that and the other thing. To date, nothing had been done to secure the border. Two years prior, he took the head of Tucson Border Patrol down to the fence line, only to be told it was too dangerous for his agents to patrol the area.

"Pedro, when you're done welding that corral gate, I need you to go up to the storage building and get some fence wire. A short section is down in the western pasture. Damn drug runners," Frank said, hollering across the corral to Pedro, who was rolling an acetylene torch over to the broken steel pipe in the middle of the gate.

"I shouldn't be long, boss," Pedro said, stopping at the broken gate.

Frank turned and walked over to his pickup. Like his grandfather and father before him, and many ranchers along America's southern border, ranching had always been his way of life. As a younger man, he'd ventured off his father's ranch to Los Angeles before becoming a securities broker, eventually starting his own firm. He was so successful that he made more money doing that in a week than he could ranching in a year. But he couldn't get the open sky and Arizona sunsets out of his soul. Every Friday, he'd fly back to work at the ranch with his dad, returning to L.A. the following Monday. After five years making a fortune, Frank sold his investment firm to come back to the land he loved. That was thirty years ago. He hadn't left since.

Hearing a vehicle approaching, Frank looked north up the road, seeing his wife approaching with lunch for him and the men. The pickup rolled to a slow stop.

"Hey there, sweetheart. What did you bring us? I'm starving," Frank said.

"Nothing but lots of good stuff. What are you guys working on today?" Mary said, looking at her husband of fifty-four years.

"One of the mares got her leg caught up in the piping on the gate and broke some welds getting it out. Not a big deal. Pedro's over there getting ready to put a weld on it," Frank said, pointing at Pedro.

"What time do you think you'll be back up to the house?" Mary said.

"Should be around five. Got a leaky water pipe in the eastern pasture we've got to tend to first. It's making a mess out of everything and we're not able to pump water to the pond a mile north of it," Frank said, opening the door for her. Helping his wife out of the truck, he turned, going to the back to drop the tailgate. After doing so, he opened the cooler full of ice, drinks and sandwiches. Just as he lifted the lid on the cooler, gunshots rang out south of them. Curious, Frank grabbed the M1 Garand he'd left leaning up against the front tire of his truck and began walking down the road towards the sound. Five hundred yards away was a four-strand barbed wire fence, separating his ranch and the United States from Mexico.

"Frank, don't go down there," Mary called to him.

"It's fine, honey. Stay put. It'll be ok. Just some Mexicans shooting rabbits."

"Damn it, Frank. Rick!" Mary called out, turning toward Rick, who was leaning into the engine compartment of the loader.

"Rick, do you hear those gun shots? Frank's heading to the fence line—hurry and go with him," Mary said, looking back toward Frank. In the distance, more gunshots rang out.

"Rick!"

"Coming," Rick said, running past Mary to catch up with his boss a hundred yards down the road.

# Fence Line

"Come on, we're almost there."

"There's a fence there. How are we going to get through it?" Kimyung said, craning her neck to look up at Mike.

"Not to worry. We will. I'm going to pick you up and put you on the other side," Mike said, looking at the wide and flat open space on the other side of the fence. He'd cross the fence first and then lift her over it. Once over the fence, they'd have to run through one hundred and twenty yards of open flat ground to a road and tree line for cover. Turning to look up the hill, a high-pitched buzz blew by his ear, followed by two more hitting the dirt in front of them. He'd heard that buzz too many times in combat not to know that someone was shooting at them.

"Get down over there! Run," Mike said to Kimyung, grabbing her hand and pulling her towards the large bolder below them, ten yards from the fence line. Looking up the road, Carter's pickup stopped short of the vehicle barrier. Making a move to get her across the fence line was not in the cards at the moment. It was open ground between them and the fence and beyond. Raising his rifle up, Mike looked uphill through his ACOG scope for any sign of the shooters. He grabbed his microphone.

"Hey, boss? What's going on up there?" Mike said.

"We've got company. Maybe fifteen to twenty tangos. Not sure. There were three pickups, but then two more arrived. They stopped about six hundred yards down the road. What's your situation with the girl?" Doug said.

"A few rounds flew by us. Open ground between us and the fence and beyond. I wonder if they're going to get an angle on us up on the hill to our right. We're sitting tight for now," Mike said, watching Carter and Conway exit Carter's pickup. Conway turned, making his way to Doug and Rocco's position.

"What are we going to do? Please don't let me get hurt," Kimyung whispered, touching Mikes left hand.

"I promise we will let nothing happen to you. There's the United States, right there. You and I are going to cross over, but first we've got to wait until it's safe. It'll be ok," Mike said, turning back in the road's direction, looking up the hill to their right. As he was raising his microphone up to talk, a round knocked it out of his hands, sending plastic fragments into the right side of his face.

A hundred yards away on the other side of the fence, a man walked towards them with someone running up behind him. Mike leaned his back against the boulder, raising his rifle, looking at him. Through the four-power ACOG, what looked like an old cowboy carrying a rifle came into focus. The man running behind caught up to him. To Mike's right, forty-five yards on the other side of the fence, the hulk of a rusty car sat idle. The two men moved in the car's direction. Keeping his rifle trained on them, he kept his head down on the scope. *Please be good guys.*

"Kimyung, get behind me and lay flat on the ground," Mike said, wincing wiping the blood from his face and taking a deep breath.

# THE CAR

"It looks like those folks are in serious trouble. There's a little girl lying on the ground next to the man by the boulder. Up at the top of the road there are three more and another one down at the barrier. Hard to see them, but there're guys higher up shooting at them. I wonder what the hell is going on here?" Frank Chance said to Rick, pointing up the hill and back at the man with the rifle.

"Hell, boss. What do you think?" Rick said, popping his head up over the car and taking the whole scene in.

"Not sure, but it wouldn't be the first time I've seen people being chased by the cartel. They look like Americans to me and their trucks have Arizona plates on them. I think first we need to get that guy to put his rifle down. HEY, MISTER! IT'S OK. LOWER YOUR RIFLE. WE'RE HERE TO HELP," Frank hollered, mustering up as loud of a voice as he could.

Up on the hill to the right, a shiny glint caught Frank's attention. Raising his rifle and looking through the ten powered scope, Frank watched a man with an AK-47 heading to a stand of Palo Verde trees. He tracked him another twenty yards where he stopped, putting him in the line of sight of the man and the girl. The man raised his rifle up, cutting three rounds loose toward them. The rounds hit just to the right of the girl, kicking up dirt. Another shot and something the man was holding exploded out of his hand. Taking a deep breath and slowly letting it out, Frank squeezed off one round, hitting the man square in the chest, dropping him into a cholla cactus. Keeping his eye on him, Frank watched him convulse for a minute and then lay still. Seeing no more movement, he lowered his rifle. Turning his attention back to the boulder, the man with the little girl at his feet was no longer pointing his rifle in their direction. Two more men up on the hillside, one hundred yards behind the one Frank had shot, began making their way into a flanking position.

"I don't know what this is all about, but we've got to help those men and the little girl," Frank said, keeping his head down on the scope, watching the two men up on the hill.

"What are you thinking, boss?" Rick said, leaning against the rusty car, looking over at Frank, who still had his head down on the rifle.

"Run up to the corral and tell Pedro to grab the cutting torch and get that rig down here pronto. Load it onto the bucket of the loader and get down here with it. Did you get it running?"

"I've just got to connect a coil wire and it should fire right up," Rick said.

"Ok, good. And damn it, Rick, bring your rifle. I told you, down here, always have it with you. Now get moving," Frank said.

"Ok, boss. I would have had my rifle but Mary told me to run and catch up to you…"

"Stop talking—just get going. Hurry… I'll cover you. Get that loader and cutting torch down here," Frank said, taking his eye off the scope and looking at Rick, nodding his head in the corral's direction.

Rick nodded and took off running. Frank, turning his attention back to the scope, reacquired the two men on the hill, who'd moved another thirty yards further down the slope. *Go ahead, just a little closer… Keep coming.*

# Barrier

Carter lifted his head off the scope and rubbed his eyes, moving left to get his right leg off the rock that was pressing into it. He and Conway had run back, going prone on the ground, joining Doug and Rocco at the top of the rise. There were three trucks parked in the distance and men moving to the right, out of view. It made sense they'd make a flanking maneuver to gain higher ground on them.

"Three more trucks are joining them. Boss, Conway and I should get the M60 up to the ridge to the right. We'll keep them from getting a line of fire on us," Rocco said, pointing to the seventy-yard rise to their right.

"Do it. Carter, move down to where Mike and the girl are. Find us a way to get our trucks across. If you can't, then we'll leave them and cross on foot. I'm going to head over to the ridge, about fifty yards lower than Rocco and Conway. I don't know who those guys are on the other side of the fence, but it looks like they're friendlies. Let me know how Mike and the girl are doing. I radioed him, but got no response. We need to get her across at all costs," Doug said.

"I think Mike and the girl are pinned down. As soon as I reach them, I'll let you know their status," Carter said.

"Fuck. More trucks are coming up the road. You better get moving. On second thought, I'm going to stay put in case some make a move across the flat to the left," Doug said, looking to his right, seeing Rocco and Conway taking up positions on top of the ridge line. The two of them began firing up the slope, Rocco on the M60 and Conway with his rifle. Down below, on the other side of the line, shots rang out from the direction of the wrecked car. The distant report of an AK-47 ceased.

Carter turned, got up and jogged down the road to the right, stopping at the boulder giving cover to Mike and Kimyung.

"How are you two doing? You're bleeding like a stuck pig on the left side of your face," Carter said, looking at Mike and Kimyung, who was pressed tight up against the rock and Mike's feet.

"We're good except for my radio. We've got friendlies over there. Two of them. An old cowboy with a rifle and another guy. Two rounds hit the dirt in front of us and a third hit my microphone just as I was raising it up to talk. I'm good though. The old cowboy silenced the guy that was shooting at us. Any idea how we're going to get our trucks across? It doesn't look good. If I can, I'm going to get her onto the other side. Maybe those guys over there can get her up the road and out of harm's way. Problem is the open flat ground in front of us. We'll figure it out," Mike said, looking down at Kimyung.

"We will, one way or another. Hey, if it comes to it, I know where I can buy another truck," Carter said, grabbing his microphone and giving Doug a status report on Mike and the girl.

Looking across the fence, he studied the old car, the road leading north and the X-crossed steel girder vehicle barrier. A third of the barrier heading east was below the ridgeline and unless there was a shooter far up on the opposite slope, they would be out of the line of fire. The other two-thirds heading west were exposed.

"Stay put. I'm going down to the barrier. I'm going to see if I can find a weak spot. If I do, I've a tow strap in my truck. I'll wrap the strap on it, tie it to my truck and give it a tug. Who knows... maybe I can drag a section out of the way so we can get our trucks across and get the hell out of here. Cover me while I run down there," Carter said, looking at Mike.

"It's worth a try. I've got you covered... go for it," Mike said as Carter took off running.

Three rounds hit the ground in front of him. In three more strides, he slid down a shallow embankment to the barrier and out of sight of the shooters up on the hill. Dirt and rocks rained down on him with more rounds hitting the top of the embankment. One pinged off one of the steel girders. Staying low, he duckwalked ten yards to his left along the structure, looking for any sign of weakness. After five feet, there was a cross section that was partially cut away. He pushed on the crossmember, seeing and feeling it give a little at the spot where someone had cut into it. Looking further at the structure, there was another two cross-sections that, if removed, would allow the section to be pulled out of the way. If only he could pull it off. If he did, it'd give them enough room for their pickups to get through. He turned, looking up the road to his truck and then Doug's pickup. *Fuck... We're going to have to leave them... There's no way I'm going to move this thing.*

# ¿Comprende?

Frank turned to his right, hearing the old diesel engine rumbling down the road. With the bucket raised up and the acetylene rig tied down in it, Rick maneuvered the big Cat front end loader, with Pedro holding on to the left side of the one-person cab, up to Frank, leaning against the old car.

"You got the cutting torch attached to the welder?" Frank yelled to Pedro.

"Yes, sir. What do you want me to do with it?" Pedro asked as a round pinged off the loader bucket.

"Get down," Frank yelled at Pedro, pointing at the man and girl and another person in the trench near the barrier. Further up the hill, he pointed at the two men on the ridge and the one at the top of the road.

"We're going to help those people. I don't know what's going on or why, but it looks like they've got the cartel after them... They need our help. I remember seeing a place over there on the barrier that's been cut. Whoever did it must have gotten spooked and didn't finish. I want you to pull right up to the barrier and lower the bucket. We'll grab the acetylene rig out of it and move the loader forward. I want you to rest the bucket on top of the barrier so Pedro can work underneath it. Let's get moving, Pedro. You walk with me behind this thing," Frank said, stepping behind the loader with Pedro next to him.

"Ok, let's go. You're going to finish cutting what someone else started and then cut other points. I want you to cut a big enough section so they can get their trucks through. When you're done, we'll wrap some of that chain around the loose section and tie it to the bucket. Rick will pull that thing back and out of the way. Comprende?" Frank said, pointing to the twenty-foot section of heavy chain hanging on attachments at the back end of the loader.

"Sí, Señor Frank. I do," Pedro said as the two men walked behind the loader.

"And hurry. Rick and I will keep those guys up on the hill pinned down," Frank said, looking at Pedro.

Arriving feet short of the barrier, Frank and Pedro pulled the acetylene rig out of the lowered bucket. He then helped Pedro drag it into the trench, resting it against a crossmember.

"Thank you," a voice said.

Frank looked over to see a man with a rifle looking across to them.

"Don't thank us until we've got you and your trucks across in one piece. What the hell's going on here, anyway. You boys are in a bad spot. Who's the little girl?" Frank asked, looking at Carter six feet away from him on the other side of the barrier, down in a combat kneeling position, looking up the hill to his right.

"She was kidnapped in Tucson and taken to Hermosillo. We got the call and rescued her last night. I'll be honest with you. We left some cartel and Federales face down on our way out and… well… here we are," Carter said, shrugging his shoulders.

"Who are you boys? Military or some other branch of law enforcement?" Frank asked.

"I can explain later. No one knows we're here, and we need to keep it that way. All we want to do is get the girl back to her mother and then disappear," Carter said, looking at the rancher, hoping their activities wouldn't be compromised. *I wonder if...*

"Ok, we'll talk later. In the meantime, sit tight. As soon as Pedro here cuts this barrier, my foreman is going to yank onto this section to get it out of the way. You and your buddies get ready to drive your rigs across. Once across, a couple hundred yards up the road is a corral. Go there and we'll catch up to you," Frank said.

"Thank you, sir," Carter said, looking at the rancher then back up the slope. A smile went across Carters face hearing the pop of Pedro lighting the cutting torch followed by the steady hiss of the torch cutting into the steel. A torrent of sparks flew onto the ground and up into the air. Higher on the slope, Rocco and Conway exchanged a volley of rounds.

"Be ready to run to the trucks so we can get out of here. Got an old cowboy with two others helping us out," Carter said into his radio.

"Roger that," Doug said, laying down fire on two men he'd pinned down at the top of the hill.

"Hurry, Pedro. I don't want anyone getting hurt," Frank said, stepping back behind the right side of the loader. Raising his rifle, he looked through his scope. Five hundred yards up the hill, three men ran between some ironwood trees and boulders. He watched them stop behind the trees. Raising the crosshairs up to compensate for the distance and the slope, he took in a deep breath, slowly letting it out. Leaning up against the loader as a rest, his right index finger squeezed the trigger. Bringing the scope back into view from the recoil, Frank looked through it. One man slumped on a rock lay motionless as the other two ran back in the direction they'd come.

# Red and Wet

"Heads up, everybody. Won't be much longer," Carter said into his radio, looking up the hill, over to Mike and then back at Pedro. Pedro's cutting torch cascaded red glowing steel slag in all directions. Six feet in front of Carter, a flame ignited a patch of dry grass. In an instant he was there, stomping it out with his foot. He could see there was only a small section to go before the crossmembers were loose. Leaning forward, Carter gave a beam a shove... it rocked back and forth. *This is some heavy shit.*

Turning and looking up the hill, three shots, two seconds apart, rang out from behind the loader.

"Muy rápido, Pedro," the old cowboy hollered from behind the loader. Rick moved down to where Pedro was working just as he cut through the last six inches of rusted steel. Pedro backed up and the two of them grabbed hold of the cart, holding the acetylene and oxygen tank, pulling it back out of the ditch to the left side of the loader and maneuvering to put it back into the bucket.

"Leave it. Get the chains tied off on the crossmembers and the bucket and pull the section out. Come on, let's go," Frank hollered.

"Doug, you and everybody else get ready to get to the pickups. They've cut through the barrier. Should be any moment now," Carter said into the microphone.

"Roger that. Rocco and Conway, what's your status?" Doug said.

"We've six, maybe seven tangos down, but at the top of the draw, it looks like five or six are headed around the hill. Carter, keep an eye to the west at the bottom of the ridgeline. You might see some heads popping up," Rocco said.

"Roger that, got it covered," Carter said, leaning into the edge of the ditch, looking past the first ridgeline to the second one Rocco was talking about. To his right, the sound of the loader started up. Out of the corner of his eye, he watched Rick move the loader forward, putting the bucket even with the barrier. Pedro wrapped the chain around a center section and draped it through the teeth on the bucket.

Carter's left ear stung from rocks and debris as rounds hit into the bank. Bringing his attention to the far ridge at three hundred yards, three figures moved in his direction. Looking through his scope, he fired toward the three men. As much as he'd have liked to hit them at this point, he focused on laying down suppressive fire to protect the welder, driver and rancher as they retreated. Three reports echoed from the direction of the old cowboy firing rounds with his M1 Garand. Carter smiled, looking through his scope as another of the men folded. The sound of grating steel scraping on dirt and rocks reverberated in the trench. Carter looked over to his right as the front-end loader dragged the section of steel barrier back twenty feet, opening up a fifteen-foot-wide section.

"Get your guys and the girl and get over here. I'll keep those guys pinned down. When you cross, get up the road to the corral. My wife is there. She'll help you with the girl. We'll be right behind you," the old cowboy hollered.

"Doug, Rocco, Conway, let's go. I'll put Mike and the girl in my rig," Carter said, looking over at Mike waving him over.

"Roger that. We're on our way," Doug said.

Carter climbed out the ditch and ran the twenty yards to his truck. Getting in and turning the engine on, the sound of the back door opened with Mike and Kimyung jumping in.

"Stay down," Mike said, moving to the left side of the vehicle and putting the window down with his rifle up. At the moment, the hill they were close to was protecting them, but they'd be exposed as soon as Carter began crossing into and out of the ditch.

With the truck in four-wheel drive, Carter crawled forward, creeping down into the ditch and moving up the other side. The front of the pickup screeched, scraping the bottom of the bumper and then the skid plate coming out the other side. Rounds hitting the left side panel of the truck bed reverberated inside the cab. More shots rang out from the rancher and Rick, stopping the rounds from hitting his truck. Staring up at a forty-five-degree angle, he eased the pedal down, forcing the big Ford engine to pull them through to the other side. Once out, Carter sped up the road with rounds hitting the back end of the bed and the sound of shattering glass. In the rearview mirror, he watched Doug and the others doing the same thing. With the road curving to the right, he hit the brakes, skidding to a stop. An old woman was standing at the corral, looking at them. Mike opened the door, lifting Kimyung out.

"Give me the girl. She'll be safe with me. You two boys get back down there and help my husband and our two hands," the old cowboy's wife said hastily.

Turning around, Carter didn't need to say anything. Mike was already in the right front seat.

"Let's go," Mike said.

With the door slamming Carter did a hard-fishtailing U-turn flooring it, heading to the sound of gunfire. Ahead, the driver of the loader limped into the cab after he and the welder unhooked the chain on the barrier. The driver raised the bucket up using it as protection and began backing up the loader. To the right of the road, Doug's truck sat at a forty-five-degree angle to the fence line. Doug, Conway and Rocco, using it for cover, were laying down a heavy amount of fire toward the right hillside. Carter stopped his truck to the right, just behind Doug's. The right door opened with Mike laying his rifle on the hood as the rest began firing. Rounds hit the driver's side of Carter's truck. A warm trickle of blood dripped down the left side of his face. A metallic and salty taste reached the corner of his mouth.

In his haste to open his door to get out, he didn't notice the driver's door window was shattered. Running to the back of the truck, he winced, feeling a sharp sting in the back of his leg. Limping around the tailgate, he brought his rifle up using the top of the bed as a rest as he looked for targets.

"Carter, I think you're hit," Mike said to his right.

"What? Where?"

"The side of you face is bleeding and the back of your right pant leg is red and wet," Mike said.

"I'm ok," Carter said. Reaching around, he put his right hand on the back of his leg and brought it up to his eyes. Looking at his bloody fingertips, he took a deep breath before putting his attention back across the line.

"Weird. I thought I'd gotten stung by a bee. It doesn't hurt... well, maybe a little," Carter said.

"Hold on," Mike said, squatting down behind and began tending to Carter's leg with a wrap from his first aid kit.

"Thanks, brother. It's ok... No big deal," Carter said.

"Trust me, it's going to hurt later."

The sound of gunfire subsided. Carter, favoring his right leg, turned, looking up the road and seeing the loader going backwards with the rancher and welder holding on to the side.

"Let's get out of here. Hey, where's the girl?" Doug said after three minutes of silence and not seeing anyone on the other side.

Mike explained their arrival at the corral, and the rancher's wife looking after Kimyung. Two minutes later found them pulling up to the corral and stopping. Getting out of the truck, Kimyung ran up to Mike, hugging him.

"We're good, honey. You're safe now. It won't be long until you're back with your mother," Mike said, wrapping his arms around Kimyung.

"Ok. So, you boys want to explain to me why the cartel is trying to kill you?" Frank Chance said.

"Thank you for helping us. You saved our lives," Carter said, looking at the old cowboy. *Could it be?*

Doug stepped forward, introducing himself and the others to the rancher, his wife and the other two men. He explained everything. Carter kept looking at Frank and then his wife.

"Excuse me. You're Frank Chance, aren't you?" Carter said.

"Yes, I am. Do we know each other?"

"I was friends with your son, Todd. Back in our college days, after getting into some trouble down in San Carlos, we ended up coming through here. The two of you put us up for the night," Carter said, smiling at both of them.

"Holy cow. Mary, it's one of Todd's friends. Yes, I remember. Seemed to me you boys were always getting into trouble," Frank Chance said, smiling, shaking his head.

"How is he? I haven't spoken to him in such a long time. We lost touch over the years. Great guy," Carter said. Frowning, Frank looked at Mary and then back at Carter.

"He's gone. We lost him twenty years ago."

"I'm sorry. I didn't know," Carter said, placing his right hand gently on Frank's left shoulder, thinking of times past with their son and feeling a wave of compassion for the couple.

"Thank you. Listen, you boys should get moving. We're going to be doing the same. I don't think we'll get any more trouble out of those guys. They don't like bringing attention to themselves. In fact, I've witnessed nothing like this before. Glad you're all safe. Time to get this little girl back to her mother," Frank said, looking at Carter and Doug and then glancing at Kimyung.

"Sounds good. We can't thank you enough," Carter said to Frank and Mary.

"No, the pleasure is ours. Glad we were here to help. Hey, just get her home safe and sound to her mother. We're happy you boys were able to rescue her. You did the right thing. As far as we're concerned, you were never here. Right, boys?" Frank said, putting his arm around Mary, looking at Rick and Pedro.

"Thank you, sir. Let's roll, boys," Doug said.

# 10:48 AM
# FBI Field Office
# Tucson, Arizona

"I spoke with Agent Young in Hermosillo a little while ago to find out if he could get anybody down there to do anything," Ben Nottingham said.

Worrying a nail, Rebecca leaned back in her chair. She would not give any hint she knew they'd rescued her daughter.

"He said he contacted a Commander Yeppes yesterday. He's in charge of the Federales in the state of Sonora. The commander told him he'd 'look into the matter.' Agent Young said Yeppes reported to him this morning that he'd sent men to the house but found nothing. I have to be honest with you, Rebecca. Young wasn't very optimistic that anything will come of it. The Federales are on the payroll with the cartels in Mexico. We don't even know what the motive was in the first place for taking your daughter. I'm sorry, Rebecca. We're doing our best. I know I've already asked you this, but have you thought of anyone who might want to harm you or your daughter?" Ben Nottingham said.

"No, I don't," Rebecca said, wiping a tear from her eye, wanting to tell him about Congressman Granada and his effort to silence her. At this point, it didn't matter, all she knew was Kimyung had a shot of coming home. She'd deal with the congressman later... on her own terms.

"Ok, I'll keep you posted and we'll be praying for a good outcome. We'll find her," Nottingham said.

Rebecca looked down at her file drawer on the right side of her desk and opened the drawer. Reaching in, she pulled out the yellow legal pad, flipping to the page on Congressman Granada with her notes on his involvement with the Stinger missiles. *Maybe it's time I ask her about her uncle and what she might know. Maybe it's time to ask if she rifled through my desk. Fuck this shit.* Taking a deep breath, she knew this was not the time to confront Agent Sylvia Granada. Grabbing the cigarettes from the drawer, she got up, making her way outside. Halfway through the doorway leading to the designated smoking area, her phone lit up.

"They're crossed over and Kimyung's…" Dax started in a breaking voice.

"Oh… thank God. When… Where is she? Oh my God, Dax, thank you. Is she in Tucson? Where is she?" Rebecca said with tears of joy running down her face.

"She's in Arivaca. Look, I'm in Tucson right now. I'm going to meet the guys in Green Valley and pick up Kimyung… I'll bring her to you," Dax said.

"I want to go with you, please."

"No, too much potential trouble for you and the guys. As soon as I've got her, I'll call you. Go home. We'll meet you there in an hour and a half," Dax said.

"Ok, I understand. Thank you, Dax, and please tell them the same for me. I owe them big time," Rebecca said, putting her face in her hands and then looking up. "Thank you, God."

"Listen, you're even. You saved Carter and Doug's lives in Nogales. They're good with it... Nobody's keeping score, anyway. It's better we keep you from meeting them... Never know if they'll need your help sometime again. I'll call you in about an hour."

Rebecca hit the end button, lit a cigarette and took a long draw on it. She sat down on a chair nearby with her face in her hands and looked up.

"Thank you, God," she said again. *Damn right I'll help them... whatever they need.*

# 12:18 PM
# Back of the Safeway Parking Lot
# Green Valley, Arizona

"Dax, you're a sight for sore eyes. We've got a little girl wanting to see her mother," Doug said, looking back as Mike opened the right rear door of Carter's pickup and stepped out, holding Kimyung's hand. Carter, limping, made his way around from the driver's side of the pickup. He was relieved that Rocco drove from the Chance Ranch to Green Valley.

"You boys look a little worse for wear. Good job. Thank you for rescuing Kimyung. She's like a granddaughter to me," Dax said, looking at her. She ran up to him, giving him a tight hug.

"Uncle Dax, where's my mom?" she said.

"I'm going to take you to her... She's at home waiting for you. Why don't you get in my car? I'll be right there and I'll take you to Rebecca. I've got to talk with these men for just a minute," Dax said as Kimyung turned and climbed through the open right front door of Dax's car. Two feet short, she stopped, turned and ran back to Mike, wrapping her arms around his waist, holding on to him.

"Hey, kiddo. I'm so glad we got you back safe and sound," Mike said, picking her up and hugging her. "You're the bravest and smartest little girl we've ever known. Maybe we'll see each other again sometime," Mike said, putting her back down and watching her go to Carter, Doug, Conway and Rocco, hugging each one. Turning, she ran to Dax's car, got in and pulled the door shut behind her.

"We need to get Carter some medical attention. Mike could use some, too. Carter took a round in the back of his left leg… Don't want to take him to a hospital. You got a doc you could call for us that could patch these guys up?" Doug said, looking at Dax and then at Carter and Mike.

"I do. Give me a second here," Dax said, scrolling through his phone.

"Hey, doc. Dax here. I've got two guys for you to look at. Are you still at the same place?"

After confirming with the doctor, Dax went to his car and came back with a small spiralbound notepad, wrote the information down and handed it to Carter.

"He's a good man. He'll get you both fixed up, prescriptions… whatever you need. Good job, gentlemen. You should be proud of yourselves; I know I am. I'll be in touch," Dax said, scanning the eyes of each man.

"That's what we're afraid of," Rocco said with the group breaking out in laughter.

"Hey, Rocco, what do you say you get Carter and Mike to the doc to get patched up?"

"Already on our way," Rocco said.

# Carter's and Kim's House
# 1 Day Later

He'd been a surgeon with the Army prior to retiring after thirty years of service and had patched Carter up as well as any local ER unit could've... maybe even better. Carter, limping into the family room, plopped down on the sofa in front of the big screen TV and grabbed the remote.

"I can't believe all the cuts on your face. When you were sleeping, I counted thirty-four little nicks. It looks like you cut yourself shaving while you were drunk. How's the leg doing?" Kim asked, sitting down next to him.

"It's ok. When I got hit with shrapnel from that grenade going off at the mall, it was worse. It only hurts if something presses up against the spot where I took the round. My face doesn't hurt at all, but I'm not shaving for a while," Carter said, touching his left hand to his face.

"Are you hungry? I can fix you a sandwich and some chips," Kim asked.

"That would be great, honey. Thank you. I love you," Carter said, pulling her close and kissing her.

"I love you, too," Kim said, getting up and moving towards the kitchen.

Carter watched her as she walked away to the kitchen. He'd hit the mute button when Kim had joined him and now turned the volume back on to listen to Fox News.

"The looting and burning of businesses in both downtowns of Seattle and Portland during the last three days seems to have the support of the mayors and city councils in each city. Six people have been shot and killed, and another twenty-five injured. A group calling themselves Antifa and another one called Black Lives Matter took over six square blocks of Seattle today and is setting up barriers. The mayor of Seattle said the group has a lawful right to protest. She's ordered the police department not to harass the rioters and to abandon their police station at 8th and Vine. Later today, in both cities, the city councils are having an emergency meeting to discuss defunding the police department. In Chicago over the weekend, there were sixty-six people shot, fifteen of which died. Five were children. In New York City, violent crime is up 141 percent over this time last year with twenty-six people shot over the weekend, six of those killed. In Atlanta..." Carter muted the TV, seeing Kim approaching. *What the fuck?*

"Kim, have you been following what's been happening around the country the last few days? What the fuck is going on? I don't understand it." Carter said as Kim walked back into the family room his sandwich and chips.

"I have. It's terrible. It makes no sense to me either. The entire country seems to be coming apart and law enforcement isn't doing anything to protect the citizens," Kim said.

"This is surreal. We've just been gone for three of days and it's like I've come back to a different planet. This is un-fucking-believable. Thanks, honey," Carter said, taking the plate from her hands. Placing it on the table at the end of the sofa, he reached for his phone and hit the call button.

"Hey, Doug, have you been following what's been happening since we left? I don't understand it and the police aren't doing anything to stop it. Something's not right here."

"Your ears must have been burning. I just got a call from Dax. We need to meet…"

**Make an Author Happy:** If you haven't already, when you get a moment, please write a review on Amazon. Thank you.

https://www.amazon.com/gp/product/B07N6RMCLL/ref=series_dp_rw_ca_2#customerReviews

**Contact the Author** contact@jthomasrompel.com.

http://www.amazon.com/author/jthomasrompel

You're Invited to Join the *Citizen Warrior Series* eMail List and Receive a Free eBook, *Citizen Warrior – Origins.*

GET MY FREE BOOK

*http://www.jthomasrompel.com*

# Keep Up the Good Fight!

# CITIZEN WARRIOR SERIES

## Read Now

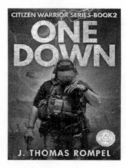

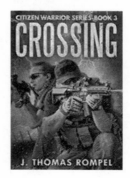

## Author Bio

J Thomas Rompel has lived in Tucson, Arizona since high school and understands the threats and dangers in having a porous border. He attended the University of Arizona majoring in Speech and Communication in the College of Fine Arts.

J Thomas Rompel has owned and operated a number of different companies since the mid 1970's.

In addition to this he's been a guest on numerous talk shows.

After the events of 9/11 he was involved in a business that dealt with U.S. military and law enforcement both at the local and federal level. This also included Border Patrol agents in the Tucson Sector. As a direct result of regular contact with the above over time he observed a growing trend of the United States government failing in their duty to protect the citizens against enemies both foreign and domestic.

Made in the USA
Las Vegas, NV
02 January 2022

40119537R00208